I0700357

THE CHILD OF VENLET

A warning is included to allow those who do not wish to read a book with such subject matter the choice to go no further. This book contains dark elements not suitable for small children, including or by mention alone: child abuse, sexual assault, and murder.

Book Cover Design by Fantastical Ink

© 2022, K.C. Nuzum / Prieto Publishing LLC

ISBN: 979-8-218-02306-5 [print]

All rights reserved.

No part of this book may be reproduced in any form or by any electronic or mechanical means, including information storage and retrieval systems, without written permission from the author, except for the use of brief quotations in a book review. For more information, please contact prietopublishingllc@gmail.com.

TABLE OF CONTENT

ZEL
Mountains of the Predicated
Holfenya
Valley of Venoxem
Venlet
Gilton City
Allsingdale
Glenloch
Red Sea

Central Zel

1

IT WAS MID-DAY IN THE VILLAGE OF VENLET AND SUMMER WAS well upon the valley. Nowhere else in Zel did the Sun relish as much. At its center came a crowd brimming full of lively, hungry people who stole away their time on the fields or wherever else to watch the Lordteller—a master in the art of myth and legend who traveled abroad to tell the tales no one else could. He was a tall man who grew ever taller the more he danced. He was graceful and hypnotizing, swaying rhythmically around the full plaza as he told the oldest of all tales.

"In the beginning of everything, well before us, there was only one who created all things after. It first made time with one flick of its finger and appointed it Judge to all things that die. It then bore two globes of light from within its endless folds and gave them to the sky, making one the Sun and the other the Moon. After, it formed Zel and the other worlds out of the falling crumbles of skin from its belly, and bade them good will as it set them among the stars to sit where they will remain forever..."

Those idle villagers, whose bodies were hard from work

but soft in their seats watched in awe as they always had when he performed his routine.

"For many thousands of years, it lived alone—high above where we cannot see! One night, while deep in slumber, seven gold teardrops fell from its eyes. When it awoke the next day, it sang a sweet song that still echoes between the stars, for there before it stood the Seven Golden Ones—it's sons and daughters!"

As he said his last words, he pulled out from his silky robe four gold puppets and the crowd went wild.

"Oh, how I love the puppet show!" said Tane jumping in her seat. She loved LordTeller's extravagant plays and never missed them. And she made sure her friends came along, whether they liked it or not.

She was an exceptional little girl with golden hair that glistened as bright as those suede puppets and a smile too sweet to ever say no to. She had been waiting to see him since last full moon and feared he left for the season already.

During that last performance, he kept the pretty puppets she loved so much locked away in his mysterious leather bag and it made her cry. The silver tassels that hung down its sides clinked when he showed it off around the plaza. At the top near the latch were jewels as bright as rubies that rested like those on a kingly crown. At every show, he would open it slowly so the audience could see the jewels sparkle but close it shut before they could sneak a peek inside.

She clicked her bare feet together before kneeing her friend, the Child, out of her daydream.

"Do you think he's got anything fun in there?" the Child asked as she rubbed her knee.

Tane turned to her and smiled, "You mean, like, more puppets kinda fun?"

The Child turned away to focus on the show. She had heard the same stories so many times, she could recite them word for word. As annoying as that was, she still enjoyed watching him. She liked the way he danced and knew all his moves by heart and would kick herself if the one time she didn't go, he told a new tale or showed off a fancy new dance. But she quickly realized this time was no different than the last.

She was an odd sort of child and was the only person she knew without a name. She spent most of her time with her friends observing people, especially outsiders who traveled the cobbled streets day and night. She saw so much of the world she may never have known just from them. Whether it was the clothes they wore, the way they walked and talked—all of it amazed her and her friends who were otherwise bored with their simple, day to day life.

The village was a fair distance from other parts of Zel and was further still from Gilton City, its capital. She often wondered what those far-off places looked like and hoped to see them someday when she was older, especially Gilton City. She had heard so much and wanted to prove more than anything if its buildings were tall enough to reach the clouds and if any of the Golden Gods lived in them. But that wasn't likely to happen—not for her at least.

Her life was not a good one. Some nights were harder than others. Sometimes, while everyone else was asleep, she walked along the one road that led out into the great beyond but stopped where the village ended and the dense forest began. She couldn't go on and leave, but she never wanted to go back. And she couldn't stay in that spot forever. Eventually, she would leave that road, just shy of the Sun, and make the long walk home with heavy feet and heart.

"I can only dream of knowing what's in there," she

muttered.

Tane, unaware of her friend's indifference chuckled at Lordteller who exaggerated his face in strange ways as he praised the Gods with each line he spoke—

"—and Siracon was the most beautiful and loving of all the Seven. However, the strongest, the biggest, the bravest...", the children upfront gasped as his expression turned from glee to grim. He flexed his long arms forward and paused before saying, "of them all..."

He paused again. He lurched closer to them and whispered, "was... Garaton."

Some children covered their eyes while others laughed and made jokes among themselves.

"Garaton is nothing more than a bad night sleep story!"

Both girls looked at their other friend whose foul words left a sour taste in their mouth.

"What in all Nine Planes are you talking about NOW Pul?" yelled Tane.

He laughed, "these so called 'Seven Golden Ones' never did anything for our people besides give us these stupid stories to laugh at and left-over crap lands they keep trying to steal back from us!"

Tane reached around the Child and hit Pul as hard as she could.

"Don't say words like that Pul. You could be punished for it," the Child said solemnly.

They were just a few of the many children in the village who were left out in the streets during the day to fend for themselves. They were too young to work but too old to be looked after by Sittermaids and thus were allowed to roam the streets free as a bird. It seemed customary for Venletian parents to force them out till dinner time with the expectation that they behave all the while, but they seldom did.

Kids weren't welcome anywhere adults liked to be. They were kicked out for one reason or another and spent a good deal of time jumping between them if nothing else. Eventually, they got bored of it and did something that was no doubt unlawful. Their favorite place to play was behind the many simple homes in the business district where they were safe from the rough punishments of those terrible adults who seemed to be waiting at every corner with fists wagging, looking for any reason to wallop them.

"—and with a righteous swing of his long and glorious broadsword, Garaton pushed back the consuming Darkness farther than anyone else has since. THIS is why he sits at the very top of Ozerith in the Realm of Light where he lives peacefully with his sister-wife Siracon who is our beautiful goddess of love and fertility. They are who we give all our praise to!" he ended the tale with a bow as the crowd stood and applauded.

"Ugh.... We've heard this story a hundred times... at least!" Pul whined.

He yanked at the bottom of his shirt that kept rising up his belly. He had asked his parents for new clothes but was given his older brothers instead. It only took a few moons for those to shrink as well.

"I think we should talk to him. What do you think Chil?" Tane asked the Child.

"I'm not sure."

Pul noticed the older villagers slowly leave the plaza and scoffed. "He's just a beggar. He'll never talk to us. And why would he? We have nothing to offer him!"

The three rapscallions—Tane, Pul, and the Child knew each other since before they could remember, and before that they were babies. They were closer to each other than to anyone else—even their families, and even though the

Child came from a different part of the village, they seldom spent a day apart. Tane and Pul, who came from the better part tried everything to bring the Child into it, even going against their parents' wishes a time or two. They didn't see what made her so different and it hurt their heart to see how openly she was disregarded. It seemed as though no matter how hard they tried, the rest of the village didn't—including her own mother.

The Child got up and walked over to Lordteller who was talking to a man asking for change.

"Excuse me?" she asked.

He turned around and looked down at the little girl with severely matted hair that was blacker than night. Her exposed arms and legs were covered in filth and her fingernails were chipped and stained. Her eyes were terribly deep, and he couldn't understand why. Their color was brown overall—like the earth beneath them, but deeper still were glittering swirls of gold and red that sprouted from their soil hue. He stood mouth open and speechless.

"Can we see what's in your bag?" she asked as he continued to stare.

He shook his head and grimaced. "Girl! Why would anyone want to see in a poor 'teller's bag?"

Tane ran up beside her friend and bounced in place. "I love your show!" she exclaimed, "Please can we see? Can we see?!"

"Children…" he stared off and sighed, "there is nothing for you in this bag and don't ask me why! You're too young and there is nothing I can do to make you understand. Now, be on your way and let me be on mine!" He spat out his words like fire and turned back to the bag. He then forced each puppet in one at a time before closing it.

"What if I tell you a story you haven't heard yet—can we see then?"

He paused and rubbed his chin, "Fine!" he yelled, "But I assure you, girl, I've heard 'em all!"

The Child stepped back and pushed Pul aside so that only she was standing in the heart of the plaza, "Let me tell you all a story that should never have happened, one that should never be forgotten, and, me prays, never happens again.

"Not long ago, there was a boy named Sarty who lived with his family on a farm not far from here. One day, a group of traveling soldiers from the Order of Garatos marched through their lands seeking shelter. The men were courteous, so they let them stay.

"For ten days and nights, the soldiers lived amongst them, helping around the house and tending to the livestock. They were respectful towards the mother and her five daughters who were all very beautiful. They told the family stories of far-off lands and tales they hadn't heard about the Gods. They were leaving the following day and the family were sad to see them go."

She paused and took a deep breath, waving her arms like a slow-moving bird. She looked over at Tane who knew the signal and covered her ears with her hands.

"On the eleventh day, at daybreak, however," she wiped her dirty face with her dirty hands and spoke, "the soldiers barged into their home and broke everything in sight. Sarty was the first to hear the commotion and hid but was caught soon after. Rather than hurt him, they made him watch as they killed his entire family, one by one."

Tane went to remove her hands but stopped when Pul silently shook his head. Lordteller's face had distorted into an expression of pain and discomfort. He looked around anxiously, hoping the story would soon end or someone would relieve him of this torture before it got any worse.

"They started with one sister, and then the next one and then the next one, and so on. He watched them all be destroyed by the men they spent time with, laughing and having fun. They treated them like family, and this was how they were repaid.

"After killing the mother and father, they slaughtered all the livestock and took whatever meat they wanted with them for their long journey back. They left Sarty alive. He begged to be killed, but they refused. When he asked why, they said their god Garaton despised the sacrifices that hid and ran but preferred the ones that fought and resisted.

"The Order of Garatos left after setting the farm on fire. The boy ran away and never looked back. And that is how it ends," she said wiping her face once more.

"Where in this world could a child hear such a heinous and ridiculous story?"

"It's true Lordteller, I promise! Can we see in your bag now?" she asked.

His face turned red as he acknowledged defeat. He twirled around and grabbed the bag. He carefully opened it then closed it again before the children could see. Without warning, he spun back and threw it on the ground.

"Fine! Just take it—take the whole damn thing you nasty buggers!" he screamed, walking away from the small crowd, swearing under his breath. The Child and Pul watched him confused, having heard far worse stories than that.

"Was it really, really bad?" Tane asked as her hands fell to her sides.

"Nothing you should ever hear," said the Child kicking dirt. She picked up the giant bag and wedged it under her small right wing.

"Alright, alright. Enough of that dark-story stuff girls. How about we take a little stroll down to the market and see what we can take?" asked Pul with a bright side smile. The other two agreed and they all skipped along the cobble road without a care in the world.

They moved around the village quickly like they always had. Most days, they were on the lookout for something fun to do and would have to resort to stealing, hazing, eavesdropping, or the like. But, with their new treasure and Pul's increasing and unending appetite to attend to, they had no time for anything else but finding a safe place to open the bag and some food to appease the grumpy boy.

When Tane was out of earshot, Pul nudged the Child and asked, "the story from earlier, was any of it true or were you pulling our legs?"

She looked at him wanting to be honest. She wanted to tell him that a few days before, she snuck through the back of the Inn to find some food. Standing in the entrance was a little boy covered in blood. She wanted to say that while she hid, the Innkeeper and his wife wiped him down and fed him. They tried talking with him, but he said nothing. She wanted to scream that after the boy rested, he spoke and told them the story and ran out the next day as they slept. She wished she could tell anyone she saw him see her and he still ran, so very fast down the road she walked every day at the point where the dense woods began, then disappeared.

"I made it all up. Gotcha didn't I?" she said as she poked her friend.

But somewhere deep inside, she wanted to cry out that no one noticed she had been missing and no matter how many times she tried, she could never walk into those dense woods.

2

———

"Oh, give it here—I want to see!" asked Tane, walking arms open towards the Child.

"Not yet. We have to find a safe place first," said Pul as he cautiously looked left and right.

"But why are we going to the church? Wont those creepy old men be there?" Tane asked with a frown. She dragged her feet against the ground as her friends watched indifferently. She kicked a patch of dirt, unaware its roots would hold her down. She flew forward, falling on her hands and knees. The pretty dress she wore had stained and ripped, and her legs were covered in rug burns. She pulled herself up, breathing in and out deeply without saying a word.

"You are such a clumsy girl Tanesy-lion!" Pul screamed as he held his belly and laughed.

Infuriated, she jumped to her feet like a wild animal and gave him a deathly glare.

"I think she's lost it. You better run, Pul," said the Child.

The two tussled down the busy street like mad Warlongs caught in their tusks, destroying everything in their path. The Child, who chose to meander behind followed their wrestling match to the only exit north. Along the way, the tike-sized wrestlers knocked down Band the Merchants' produce cart and ran away before he could grab them. Following far behind, the Child laughed as he cursed up a storm, unaware of the apple she took while his back was turned.

She loved when she could take her time and enjoy the loud and busy that plagued the streets and never got tired of watching her fellow neighbors live around her. She could see so clearly every freckle, wart, and blemish—most things people tried desperately to conceal. And when it came to their personal life, she saw all that too.

Moons previous, she watched a tall man outside of the Inn approach a young slender woman with flowers and gifts in both arms. They looked so happy together, but it was always like that in Venlet. Every day, women would hang on the many walls around the village, waiting for gifts and company, with just as many men running to meet them and their demands. They would enter the Inn together but leave separately. The women, who were slower to leave, would stand back by their wall and wait all over again, but not for long.

This date started no different than any other. The woman accepted the flowers with lots of adoring words and the pair took each other's hand. At the same time another woman came, bigger and older than the other. She stomped down the street, waving a giant stick, forcing her way through the Inn behind the two new lovers. Soon after, the Child heard the man's loud cries of pain and the distant sound of women bickering from somewhere inside that continued well into the night. They were talked about days after and were still mentioned when everyday conversation grew dull.

She stopped walking near the northern outskirts of the village where an established road leading north began. She turned her back to the forbidden woods. From where she stood, she could see down most streets, except those full of men gambling their dubels away.

She squinted and began her usual surveillance. She looked to the west where Pul and Tane lived, then to her east where the business district thrived. Her eyes rested on a small alleyway that separated Unta's home and Glat the Bakers' Bakery where she last saw the two lovers hold hands and embrace. The man had been beaten black and blue by what she later heard was his wife but appeared happier than he had ever been before.

But things had changed, and no one stood there anymore. Instead, the alleyway was left to ruin. The remnants of busted trash bins were scattered across its mucky cobble, and its only tenants, two bitter cats missing large patches of fur, hissed at each other as they sat in a pool of filth.

The sun beat down on her burning scalp she scratched to no end. She looked around and sighed, "I wonder if mother is wearing her hat today?"

Her eyes moved playfully, observing everyone gathered around food and trinket carts that appeared when the Sun was highest in the sky. They eventually stopped on Munta the Blacksmith—the largest man in the village. So much had been said about the great man, some true and some false. The adults whispered about his youth; how he once touched the top of one of the valleys' ancient fruit trees while on his tip toes. And they would argue and bet over whether he could bend a man in half with his bare hands or not. His strength was a subject of great debate that only he didn't partake in.

And with such a reputation, it was no wonder so few approached him and his forge. If it wasn't the growls he made as he hammered steel, it may have been the way he sat and peered out like a lion in a tree that kept passersby away.

He was a burly man that could hold an ingot or ten in one arm and did so regularly. His beard was a nasty red and brown that tangled when long, and his eyes were dark and hard to look in to. All the children were afraid of him except for the Child who knew better. She thought he was funny and told the best jokes, especially to the women who walked by his Smithing, making no attempt to hide their disgust for his manner and smell.

She closed her eyes and sighed. She knew everyone's business and everything they did—they gossiped, they lied, they cheated, and so on. And the more travelers and merchants that wandered through the streets looking to spend dubels on beds and ladies, the more corrupt the village became. And though it appeared that the outsiders were at the center of this degradation, it was the elders and Councilmen who begged for more to come, paying those leaving handsomely for their troubles, hoping they come back and bring friends, all while paying local johns far less to clean up the mess afterwards.

All of this bothered her. She worried needlessly, locking doors and windows left open and scaring drunk men away from women too drunk to stand, but no one gave her the same compassion in return. Every night, she would look up at the stars and wonder if this was all her life would ever be. She would then dream of her mother whom she wished was there, hoping one day it would be different.

She opened her eyes and looked through the busy streets for the one face she knew she'd never forget.

"Chil, are you there?" screamed Tane so close it made her jump.

"You nearly scared me to the Sixth world, you meanie!" she cried.

Tane wrapped her spotless arms around the Child's boney frame and squeezed in tight. She sighed. She never understood how her friend could stay so clean while her and Pul got so dirty.

They'd soak in mud all day and Tane would still leave as pretty as before, except for her dress which would be ruined. But she could care less. Her mother was an expert seamstress and made her new dresses constantly, so she never had to worry about it.

The Child pried herself from Tane's grip and turned her back to the village once more.

"Pul, are you ready to see what's in the bag now?" She asked.

He had lost the battle and was acting like a sore loser, taking handfuls of dirt and throwing them at Tane. He stopped when he saw her notice and hung his head. She then took some earth herself and rubbed it in his face. Infuriated, he ran after her as she screamed. The Child ran too and tackled him to the ground. Tane fell beside them and they all laughed under the warm sun for a while. They eventually got up and wandered back down the cobble road and took a small path east that led out of the village to a solitary road surrounded by ancient trees.

Between the great forests' cluttered edge and the village was a small growth of great oaks that kept hidden a white church. As the children walked the long narrow path through the growth, they felt up and down the greying oaks wrinkled bark, giggling as its rough skin forced their hands to dance.

"I wish I could be as big as this tree someday!" proclaimed Pul, hugging his arms around its massive trunk. He reached out one hand to the other and was surprised when they didn't meet. The Child rolled her eyes.

"Well, I want to be as beautiful as the leaves and buds that bloom from their arms. And not for a short while but for forever," Tane said seriously before smiling and tossing her hair, "What about you Chil?" she asked giggling.

The Child paused. She looked up at a large oak, admiring its stature and long arms. It was a unique tree among a sea of others, and she couldn't keep her eyes off it. She watched as small animals ran and played from one trunk to another, limb to limb, and wondered what secrets they kept. It moved slowly and only when the wind blew. No other tree could withstand any show of Zel's power, this she could tell. For the first time in a while, she felt safe.

"I think I am already like a tree," she said as she released Lordteller's bag from her sweaty arm and threw it to the ground. Her right wing had fallen asleep, and she was relieved to be rid of it. She then threw up both arms high into the air and jumped around with her friends joining in. They were making such a ruckus, it made them want to scream and jump even more.

Suddenly and without warning, the church door swung open, and out came an old man. He fell forward and caught himself on the handle, moaning and shaking as he brought himself up. Breathing hard, he looked around with eyes ablaze, searching for the cause of the commotion that disturbed him.

"In the name of— "

He stopped on the group of children dancing under the trees, "You... no good lousy children are not allowed around the most sacred Church of her Holiness Siracon without your parents! Go away or you will be punished!" he screamed.

He clumsily shut the door behind him before heading their way, limping and taking forever. He looked sickly, as if he hadn't seen the Sun in ages and hadn't eaten anything good for just as long. He came close enough for them to see his beautiful robe and sashes that glistened white, gold, and red, but stopped short of hitting range.

"Sorry sir, we'll leave now," said the Child. She picked up the bag and hung it under her right wing again, but this time tighter. They looked at one another disappointed but were not all that surprised. They sent their mournful eyes at the old man who stood unmoved and impatient, waiting for them to carry on. With Pul at the head, they traveled west on the road still fresh with their tracks.

"But I thought we were going to look inside the bag? What are we going to do now?" whispered Tane to the Child.

"Follow my lead" she said as they walked away. When they reached the end of the giant oaks where the old man could no longer see, they waited. Assuming he had gone back inside, they traveled along the trees where they were invisible to the outside world and emerged near the side of the church where an old brown door and a very small window too small to crawl through appeared.

"I've been through there before but didn't look around. Maybe we should come by at night and sneak in. Then we can see what those weirdos are up to," said the Child.

"But what about the bag?!" Tane asked red-faced.

Frustrated, the Child threw it down for the last time. She kneeled to examine it as her friends reluctantly followed. She brushed her filthy fingers over the jewels on the latch, and with a small gesture it collapsed wide open. She would have looked in if she hadn't been pushed aside. An eager Tane took her place and squawked with glee as her friends watched in disbelief. She then forced her head into the weathered bag. She looked in briefly before falling back on her bottom.

"Ew! It smells like rotting things in there!" She exclaimed as she retched.

"Be quiet Tane or they'll come out again," commanded Pul who was looking out for the group a few steps away.

"There's nothing in here, Chil. Just those four puppets and some old, moldy fruit. Why doesn't he have anything good in here? He said he had priceless artifacts like the ones in his stories. If he was lying about that, then what else? Did anything he say really happen? Are any of those stories real?!"

She became increasingly hysterical, sobbing so loud it echoed.

"Do the gods even exi—"

As she wailed, an abrupt cough came from behind them. Pul groaned. He had left his post after Tane got upset and joined them on the ground.

None of them noticed the man approach and neither could tell for how long he had been there. He stood tall with his back as straight as a statue. His robe was like the old mans from before, but his sash was covered in many more small jewels that sparkled endlessly.

Tane started to cower and Pul noticed. He turned to face him and became tense all over. The Child stood up but could not speak. As quiet as a mouse, he asked, "So, whose bag is it?"

Pul found his courage and stood up as well, "It belongs to the Lordteller. He gave it to us."

The man looked at each child and stopped on Tane

whose hands were still in the bag. Stale tears stuck to her cheeks and disappointment lingered in her eyes as she looked back at him like a wounded animal.

"Don't cry child," the man said gingerly, "Sometimes, Siracon and the other gods give us that which we don't ask for but have no choice but to endure. This is how we learn. They do this because they love us."

Tane rubbed her eyes and stood up as well. They bowed at the man and he bowed back.

"It's nice to see such young children who know how to honor their elders. My name is Plea Marcus Daniels, and I am the Grand Eunich of this church. Would you three like a look around?"

The Child stiffened.

"Don't worry, I won't hurt any of you. We are kind people, and our word is as sincere as our beliefs. Our matron, the Goddess Siracon loves children above all other creatures, and we follow her example," he said smiling.

She relaxed a little but couldn't shake the feeling that something bad was going to happen. But a part of her wanted to see what they hid behind that door, and she wasn't going to go home without having any fun first. She wanted to explore, and the church seemed like a good place to start. She would keep an eye on the Grand Eunich, knowing best of all in her group the deceits of adults.

She looked over at her friends who both shrugged, seemingly unsure of what to do. It was Pul who spoke up.

"If it's okay with my friends, we'll let you show us around," he said but not before flexing the few muscles he had. With one more bow, Plea Marcus motioned the children to follow, and so they did.

3

———————

The children stepped through the front doors, forgetting all about Lordteller's bag, leaving it on the ground for the squirrels to take. They had no idea what they were walking into and were shocked to find the church was much different than it appeared from the outside. The small and unassuming building had turned into an immeasurable castle right before their eyes. If it weren't for Plea Marcus' constant reminders to keep moving, they would have stayed in the doorway, too dazzled to carry on.

To their immediate left was a well-crafted, gold side table with one drawer that held high a floral centerpiece in a vase made of rainbow amethyst, where blanket flowers of bright red and yellow hugged pure white morning glory's that opened out to their new guests as they arrived. The children knew these flowers well and picked them while out in the valley whenever their usual crimes grew dull. They beamed.

"Every year my mom tries to plant these, but she can never get them to bloom!" said Tane, admiring their beauty.

"Welcome children. I have accepted you into this sacred

place. I have told you my name. Now, I would like to know yours before we go any further," Plea Marcus said as he hovered over them.

"Why do you need our names?" Pul asked exhausted from flexing his muscles for too long.

"Well, if for whatever reason you kids decide to, I don't know, defile this perfect and ancient place, I would need to tell your parent's what you did."

"You really think we'd do that?" asked Tane.

"Children—it is in your nature. You are meant to explore and ask questions, and sometimes destroy things. Everyone does this when they're younger. It's because you don't know any better. But you're not supposed to—not at your age at least, which is for your benefit. The more you know, the less you can enjoy. If I could live your simple life, not knowing what I do now, I would be in paradise," Plea Marcus explained.

The Child stood puzzled. She wished she didn't know either. Her life was no more a paradise than his, and yet he had more than she.

She shook her head, "Why is it so dark in here?"

"We Pleas find enlightenment in the light of our goddess alone—not in that bright ball in the sky. Now, names!"

"Well," yapped Tane, the blabber mouth, "My family name is Venal, and my name is Tane. My big friend here is from the Venam family, and his name is Pul. My other friend," she pointed at the Child, "well, her name is... uh..."

"I don't have one. I can give you my mother's if you want," the Child answered calmly.

"Impossible, every child in all the Nine Planes has one!"

She shrugged, "Well, my mother's family name is Hollon, and her name is Parity." It was something she said to anyone curious enough to ask, and their expression after said it all - especially at the mention of her mother.

Plea Marcus stared down at the little girl with the all too familiar look of befuddlement, like Lordteller earlier. His dull, dark-blue eyes had become acclimated to the lightless room and struggled to look into hers. He knew there was something different about her but couldn't pinpoint what.

The people from the Valley of Venoxm shared a similarity in their names—the Ven's lived in Venlet and Hol's in Holfenya. Their ancestors left their old names behind when they traveled east and chose new ones when they settled in the valley. They had high hopes of creating a life full and free, away from the gods, and they wanted their future generations to have it better than they ever had.

Aside from name, the people with the blood of Oxem looked alike. Because of his own travels throughout Zel and what he saw every week during service, he presumed most Venletians had blue or green eyes and light-colored hair, and the same for Holfenians though he only ever met a few.

The Child stuck out like a sore thumb. He had never seen anyone with eyes like hers—a brown that glowed a gold and ember flame that burned like distant stars on a winter's night. And more astonishing was how they changed shape and color the longer he looked.

He blinked a few times, then smiled, "You poor child, thank her magnanimousness, oh sweet Siracon for sending us this lost soul! I see it fit and my goddess agrees you need a name, and I would be happy to give you one. What do you say?"

She frowned. No one had ever asked her that before, and she didn't know what to say. Overwhelmed, she closed her eyes. That's when time froze. Like a cool breeze, she felt herself drift from the church to another place entirely of her own making. And she loved it there. It was her own special world, where great landscapes so vast unfolded endlessly past what eyes could see, and where bushes grew so fruitful, they could feed every starving child in Zel. And there were creatures, as small as a mouse and as big as a house that roamed freely and only existed inside her mind.

She walked barefoot over the lush grass that perked up at her touch and paced as she thought over Plea Marcus' question.

"Hm... Do I even need one? I haven't had it yet and I've gotten along okay. And what good is there in a name anyways? Tane calls us Chil, so—we could go with that, but it just seems, uh... Maybe we can pick something we like or, ugh—I don't know!"

"You don't even like the name Chil... at all!" said a voice hidden behind a bright bush filled with friendly birds. Ever since she could remember, this place existed with only one other she didn't create, who sounded just like her. After she found her, whom she called her Otherself, she searched far and wide through the vast plains of the Otherworld for an Other creation of her mother but never found her.

"Chil is not a good name for you," said her Otherself, "and what about me—I don't have one either!"

"How can I give you a name if I can't figure out one for myself! Ugh, maybe we should name ourselves after our favorite treats then!" the Child said laughing.

"I shall be Twirly Twists and you will be Bonts!" her Otherself cackled.

"No, not Bonts! I hate them!"

The two girls bickered and laughed back and forth until her Othersun came down. The Child tickled herself which made her Otherself laugh, who then did it back to her. After falling to the ground exhausted, her Otherself spoke,

"You need to go back now. It'll all work out someday, I promise."

"And I'll see you soon," said the Child patting herself on the shoulder. As night fell over the sky, she closed her eyes and fell back into the moving breeze from before. As she followed the wind, she could sense her world diminish back into her mind where it waited for her return. The dim glow of candlelight peered through the bottom of her eyelashes. She took a deep breath in and opened her eyes. Back in the darkly lit church, she giggled as her Otherself caught her in the ribs and tickled her one last time.

"What's so funny child? Would you like a name or not?" asked Plea Marcus sternly.

"Oh, I do but not right now, thank you. I'm sure Siracon, Goddess of Marvels will help me find one someday," she said.

Plea Marcus smiled and bowed at the little girl. He then turned and walked the children out of the foyer without saying a word. As they entered the nave, they gasped. Before them were dozens of pews, where many shuddering Pleas rocked back and forth, praying to their goddess as if their life depended on it. And they watched as slouching eunich's scurried to darkened passages, emerging on the other side of the enormous room like nothing had happened and all was how it appeared to be. Deeper in darkened corners were shrines to lost gods that barely showed through dying candlelight but could be felt from where they stood.

They didn't think it could get any stranger. And then they looked up. Well above them were buttresses of gold and silver, surrounding vibrant paintings of people and creatures, mountains and storms that moved as if real.

At the center of a giant wall in the altar was a beautiful portrait of a beautiful woman standing in gleaming robes, postured valiantly in the canvas' middle. She resembled what they had all been told was Siracon and her unbelievable beauty. Her hair was a bright gold that glittered subtle hints of pink. It fell down her shoulders and past her legs and didn't stop. It then cascaded down the sides of the portrait before merging into the many paths of the church where branches of it led down the aisles. It beamed a radiant magic into the world which they couldn't comprehend. They were utterly speechless.

"This, my children, is where all the eunichs come to praise and adore her most wonderful every day," Plea Marcus said with wonder in his eyes.

The group approached the center and most open part of the church where many eunichs gathered to exercise their extreme worship. The children watched concerned as grown men danced and convulsed over lines sung repeatedly. And the closer they got to the altar, the louder the entranced eunichs chants and songs became.

"What are they saying?" asked the Child.

"They are asking Siracon to continue to be beautiful and strong and to watch over all those who follow her. And some ask her to punish those who wish to do her harm," Plea Marcus said with a skip in his step.

"So, they're praying to the goddess for HER to continue to be amazing? Sounds a little strange to me..." whispered Pul to the Child who nodded.

She looked over at the Grand Eunich hoping he didn't hear him. She sighed, relieved he hadn't but stopped herself from mocking him further when his demeanor changed. The Grand Eunich had arched his back painfully backwards and his eyes had rolled to the back of his head. The children stood mortified as he left them in that state to join the other Pleas in their swelling chants. They waited cautiously to do anything and hardly blinked until the prayer had ended and Plea Marcus regained his composure.

"Praise to you children for being so patient. Let us continue to the library," he said breathlessly as he fixed his robe.

"You have a library?! How about a kitchen?" asked Pul.

Tane moved to hit Pul but stopped herself as she remembered where she was, "Pul, you bite your tongue!" she spat at him.

Plea Marcus watched and laughed freely at the bickering pair. They jumped when they heard it and stopped arguing instantly. They fell behind the Child and watched the Grand Eunich wearily. They had all assumed, like the rest of the village, that Pleas never laughed. And by the way it sounded, they were glad they normally didn't. The Child, suspicious of his odd behavior walked close behind as he rubbed his back and groaned.

"Ah... To be young again—whew!" he said as they pushed through a musty brown door that opened out into a long and dark hallway.

"This place is huge!" Tane exclaimed.

"Well, the more we worship the goddess, the more room she gives us."

Pul scoffed and the Child smiled. Only they knew what it was like to be on the outside looking in, where no one listened because of who they were. Not long before, Pul witnessed a traveler steal the coin purse of a woman in the village center. He screamed for help which scared the thief who in turn tried to kill him. The thief let him go, however, when no one believed him. Later that day, the woman went to Pul's home and accused him of the stealing. The village militia searched his home inside out and found nothing. By the time they listened to him, the thief was long gone. Ever since, anything suspicious that crossed their paths they kept to themselves.

The two stood with their innocent friend in the unending hallway in a place no one would ever believe they visited and laughed about it together.

"If Tane wasn't here, they'd probably have killed us by now," Pul whispered into the Child's ear. She tried her best to hold it in, but the laughter came spilling out of her mouth like a fissure and once it was out, there was no stopping it. What he had said was truer than either of them would have ever admitted seriously.

"Children! This is your first and only warning. No laughing here or anywhere in HER church! I will not allow you to make a mockery of her MOST HIGH!" Plea Marcus screamed before turning to Tane, "now, sweetie, what was I saying before the interruption?"

"Oh, um, you said that she," Tane said pointing up at the ceiling, "gave the world all its beauty after Garaton gave it strength, and their children were wonderful and right in every way." She was deliberate with what she said and careful not to miss a thing.

"Yes, very good Tane! And they only had sons because she was too beautiful. So beautiful in face that every little girl inside of her turned to a strong and perfect man," he said as he peered at the other two who looked on incredulously.

He glared at the Child then looked over at Tane and smiled, "through her blood came the children with gold hair like you and... Pal?"

"It's Pul, Grand Eunich, and I thank the goddess for such nice hair," he said sarcastically. The Child whipped her head at him, and he gave her a sly smile.

"Where did black hair come from?" asked Tane.

"Well, they say that when Siracon rejected the affections of the Dark One, he cursed a generation of her children's children with hair as dark as his despair and loneliness," Plea Marcus said, smiling at the Child shamelessly.

"Oh Chil, if I could give you some of my hair I would!" said Tane.

"Chil? I thought you didn't have a name?" asked Plea Marcus.

"I don't and only my friends can call me that."

"Oh, stop acting so old, little girl. You may not have a name, but you still have your youth. Do not squander it. Now, please," he said breathing in deeply, "take this time to educate yourselves. We will be in the library which cannot be filled with any sound but the turning of a page. If there is anything you can't read, ask and I will speak with you about it outside."

The children looked at one another and nodded in unison, agreeing to follow the Grand Eunich once more. Before opening the door, he turned and looked at them in the way parents did their children before entering a candy store. And they in turn looked away like children with sticky fingers would.

It took all his strength to open the door. It swung out into the room and echoed a slow creak that made those studying Pleas within turn and stare. The children squinted to return the gaze and could tell that the lack of light made their eyes off in some weird way. After the door was fully opened, Plea Marcus looked up at his lessers who fell back into their books. He looked down at the children and motioned for them to go inside.

4

THE CHILD WAS BEYOND GRATEFUL TO HAVE BEST FRIENDS AS wonderful as Tane and Pul. She knew that if it weren't for them, she would be lost, alone, or dead. They were there for her more than her own mother, which was her greatest shame.

For the longest time, her friends thought her mother was her only family, but that changed last year's sprouting months after she mentioned her grandmother casually, as if her existence wasn't a big deal. Of course, her friends felt differently.

After they prodded her for more information, she caved and told them as much about her as she knew which wasn't a lot, and they were shocked.

"Wait! So, why doesn't she stay here and take care of you?" Tane asked without hesitation.

The Child then explained how most of her family lived in Holfenya but only her grandmother came to visit. As much as she wanted to tell Tane all about the others, she didn't have anything to share, not even their names, but she did know they wanted her and her mother to live with them in Holfenya once they had enough dubels saved.

Tane and Pul didn't understand but accepted the truth all the same. They knew all their kin and grew up with them a stone's throw away and couldn't imagine family being anywhere else - no distance could sever the ancient bonds they shared. But for the Child, even her own mother, who could be sitting next to her, was no closer to her than her distant relatives.

Regardless, the three kids were a family of their own and suffered for each other, fair or unfair. Tane and Pul were not immune to the many pressures of having such a hated person around and were punished a time or two for the friendship. But that didn't bother them as much as having to play in secret or not at all.

This hurt the Child tremendously. It didn't help the many doubts she had already growing in her mind about their future but instead made them worse. Somewhere deep inside, she knew that someday they would leave her behind to pursue the simple village life their blood called them to, and she would have no one. She dreaded that day more than her own death. But they spat at the notion of ever leaving her side, even when they got older. They swore to never give up on her and tried with all their might to make her fit in so that her life and theirs would be easier. On occasion, Tane would give her a dress and shoes so she could wear something nice for once. But by days end, they were destroyed. Pul would tell her all the right things to say to the other kids, but it made no difference. And if it wasn't her friends encouraging her to change, it was her grandmother who was determined to make her like everyone else, whether she liked it or not.

The old, but energetic woman would come unannounced, barging into Parity's home, banging on every door until her perpetually hungover daughter got up. And she would ask her where her granddaughter was, knowing she had no idea but enjoyed how it irritated her, nonetheless.

But the Child was usually close, either sleeping in the barn next door or under a window near her mother's room. She knew her grandmother had arrived when her shrill voice rang through the house and the neglected kitchen was back in use.

She wanted to see her but not while smelling like cow manure and all covered in dirt. Those were the times she wished she hadn't ruined Tane's clothes. While the adults argued like they always did, she would take a short walk to the nearby creek and wash up, picking up fresh dandelions on the way back. She didn't expect to see her mother when she returned and was not surprised when she wasn't there. She liked to leave out the back while her own mother cooked and wouldn't return till nightfall—if at all.

When the Child finally came through the door with clumps of dandelions in both hands, she would drop them and jump into her grandmothers' loving arms. And though the greyed woman was tired and felt pains all over her arms and back, she would hold her granddaughter and squeeze her as tight as any bear could.

"What's her name?" Pul asked.

She only knew her as grandmother but heard her mother call her Agatha once during a fight moons before. She was a shapely woman who curled forward as she walked from years of farming in the harsh northern climate.

One of the Child's first memories was of Agatha coming to visit while the biggest rainstorm of the year was happening. Farms had flooded and the small rivers within the woods had filled over. Everyone stayed home, afraid that a giant wave of mountain water would drown them, especially those traveling north. But rather than a tempest, Agatha with a carriage full of goods came rolling through the pines into the drenched farmland where a toddling child played in the mud. Parity stood in her doorway, arms crossed. Agatha, unamused, dropped all the goods at her daughter's feet. Both cross, they fought over everything: how little she brought; how much her new, green-marbled rain jacket must have cost; and how Parity couldn't be trusted with money anymore because of what happened the last time. Eventually, Agatha gave up the fight and left in a huff as fast as thunder.

THE CHILD WENT OUT AT NIGHT WHEN SHE SHOULD HAVE BEEN sleeping. She would sneak around the village while the other children were tucked away in bed. She used to go to sleep hungry until she found tasty food in Glat's garbage years before. Since then, she became accustomed to eating other people's scraps. She knew when and where certain homes and businesses threw out their best leftovers and could sample many great foods by nights end. And she never stressed after making a mess. Most of her exploits were blamed on the infamous and elusive raccoons that miraculously showed up where she had been.

After eating, she would creep over to the Inn and watch her mother through the windows as she laughed, danced, and enjoyed life without her. Parity may have been cantankerous to those who wished to help her, but she was hardly intolerable to any man bidding for her affection and was sickeningly kind to those willing to pay her hefty tab.

The Child followed her in the shadows during the day and at night whenever she wasn't with her friends. She worried about her and needed to know she was safe before she could sleep soundly. A few times, she fell asleep in her little hideouts as she waited to see her mother again.

She remained in the shadows for other reasons and thrived for as long as she had because of it. Creepy old men would try and grab her, parents and village elders would beat her just to make an example, and so on. In her heart, she knew she could never have a life no matter how simple, like her friends were meant to, and she would always be on the outside looking in. But they didn't understand why, and she gave up trying to explain it to them. She never heard bad things about Pul or Tane's mother, and at least they had fathers; and brothers and sisters too. She wished her friends were her real family. What family she did have was already changing. Her grandmother visited less and less, and her mother was becoming more distant as the days passed.

She was going to miss seeing her grandmother whenever she stopped coming. For those few days or so, she was noticed and loved by one of her own. She always looked forward to sitting outside with her as she read one of her interesting books. She fell in love with each one she brought and would obsess over every page, observing the tiniest of details. She couldn't read but that didn't bother her. And no matter how hard her grandmother pushed her to, she wouldn't. She learned a few words here and there for fun but wasn't all that interested in going any further. Instead, she liked to stare at the pages which helped her zone out the rest of the world. All their monsters, animals, and everything in between were etched in her mind where she kept them, to look at whenever she was sad and alone.

She loved books like some children liked the box their

presents came in. She was amazed by how different they were and how they came in all shapes and colors. And each had their own scent which she took to memory as well.

When the visit was at its end, Agatha would pack them up to take back but not before letting her granddaughter look them over once more for as long as she liked.

THE CHILD SHOOK HER HEAD. SHE OPENED HER EYES TO A blurry world. She rubbed them until she could see a little better. She tried to peer through the dark, poorly lit library but struggled. She had become accustomed to gazing at the sun-drenched meadows in her Otherworld and didn't particularly like this place.

She winced as a headache came on. She looked over at a candle stick as its flame swayed from side to side. She felt a slight breeze go by and thought she saw a man. The candle's flame was the only way of knowing if anyone had been there. She rolled her eyes and walked towards the light.

Both Tane and Pul had already started looking through the shelves. They were careful and took their time picking their book.

Plea Marcus, like a wisp of smoke, put his hand on her shoulder and nudged her along. She tried to turn around, but his firm grip pointed her forward. Fully awake then, she embraced the dark and entered further into the library. She gasped at how many books she could see and guessed there were many more she couldn't. And the bookshelves were numerous and so tall that infinitely long ladders rested against them every fourth or fifth section.

There were many rows full of book sleeves all stained

with muted colors and made of the oldest fabrics. The writing on the binding, surely once gold and polished had become indentations only legible through touch.

Weary, the Child turned to leave but was stopped short of the judgmental eyes of the eunichs in grave study around her. And when she did move again, she knocked into a pale Plea who looked down at her in disgust.

She stopped again to orient herself. Across from her was a small staircase with dark-brown railings that led further into the library. She looked painstakingly for a sturdy spot to step on. Hesitantly, she put her bare foot on the first step nearest the middle and felt dust fly up her leg. It croaked a sound that lasted longer than all the doors in the church combined.

She froze.

Cough.

She turned and saw Plea Marcus, arms folded, shaking his head. At her wits end, she jumped over the last three steps and landed hard on the floor. A brief thud echoed, but she didn't bother to look back to see his reaction. Instead, she took to look for a book.

"THOUSANDS OF BOOKS AND YOU PICK THAT ONE?" PUL asked as the Child rubbed her backside outside the church. The natural light and cool wind were a memory to the kids having spent hours in there.

"It wasn't her fault Pul!" yelled Tane, "Plea Marcus said we could ask about any book. He didn't say, 'DON'T EVER TOUCHED THIS BOOK, YOU ARE BAD! BLAH BLAH BLAH!'"

"I didn't even get a chance to look at anything. Those

eunichs are a bunch of weirdo freaks!" said Pul motioning to the Child, hoping his words would help her throbbing backside.

The children weren't in the library long before they were forced out and reprimanded to near death by the Grand Eunich.

"Please, please, please, please, PLEASE tell us about it?" asked Tane.

"Yeah! We gotta know!" exclaimed Pul.

The Child agreed to tell them everything, but they'd have to wait till morning. Excited and no longer worried about their friend's discomfort, the two golden-haired kids ran up to their homes which were a few houses apart and turned to wave at each other and then back to their black-haired friend. She waved and watched as they gracefully entered their solid, warm, peaceful homes. She sighed and turned away from the best parts of her day. She forced her feet north of the village where her sad and cold home was. It was an uphill climb to the farmland and the road had worn down into a dirt path with a few muddied cobble stones left to walk on. She rubbed her head and behind as she walked, thinking back on what happened.

She had a hard time choosing the right book. Countless volumes that all looked the same looked back at her from the dark. Nothing jumped out and the harsh eyes on her told her she was already taking too long. After touching and pulling away from this book and that one, she knew she would have to choose by chance or else not at all. Her grandmother liked to play this one game when she came to visit. She would give her three choices, two were a gift and one was empty. She had to choose one with her eyes closed, and each time she chose empty.

She stopped at a random wall and planted her foot

firmly in place. She closed her eyes like she had with her grandmother and threw a loose and sweaty arm up in the air. Her hand landed on the spine of a bumpy book which was warm and felt like burlap. She brushed her hand across many more, waiting for the right one.

She paused suddenly deep within the dark with a knowing she didn't understand—that she had found the book and should look in it right then and there. She grasped it and tugged it out with little effort. Once freed, it collapsed onto her chest. A surge of cool air ran through her and she shivered. She turned it over in her arms and opened her eyes to gaze upon her gift.

With all her strength, she flipped it wide open. The first two pages were blank. But on the third was text. She tried her best to focus on it, squinting until her eyes shook. She could discern one word: The. She didn't recognize any of the others. She blinked away tears forming in her dry, weak eyes and continued to search for anything interesting. And it didn't take long.

She combed through the rest of it and found countless pages laced with symbols and abstract pictures surrounded by unknown words. Dogs, cats, and other animals danced from corner to corner the way they did in children's picture books. She grew increasingly hesitant as she memorized each page. It was rumored that only witches and Imagis spoke in symbols and scratchy writing like this. All magic and witchcraft were banned from the valley except when used for healing purposes.

She wanted to throw it away, far from her hands but for the life of her couldn't. And holding it felt like a million breaths on her all at once and nothing had ever felt as soothing. Unsure of what to do, she walked over to Plea Marcus who stood tall and proud at the center of the library.

He stared adoringly at the many pristine artworks of Siracon and felt his conviction return. He was determined to make a positive impact on the lively children by providing them with a once in a lifetime experience. He wished that more people would stop by and was desperate to try anything, including showing kids around to prove they were approachable and kind. Since he arrived in Venlet, the villagers showed little interest in the church and rarely stopped by.

The eunichs of the Church of Siracon were not Imagis, magicians, witches, or masters of illusions, and they refused to defile their goddess' image by performing petty magic tricks. Even so, the villager's gossiped about what they did at night with some saying they invoked their goddess with offerings of virgin blood and flesh. It took Plea Marcus most of his day just to clear up such rumors.

He was surprised to see the first of the three with a book was the child with no name. He pitied her, thinking she may not understand any of its knowledge and feared having to lie to her in the presence of his goddess. He led her out the door to avoid embarrassing her. Still in the doorway, he bent down to one knee, then two to be level with her.

"Now, child, let's see what fantastic work you've got there!" Plea Marcus said smiling, hand out, expecting she picked a Gospel or an Epic of Siracon. She reluctantly handed over the book, searching his face for any hints of its true nature. He turned it over in his hands and looked at the cover.

He froze. His face, which had been stuck in a grin, loosened and his eyes became vacant and large as he looked at the Child who also froze. He started to shake. His face changed into a red and angry mess—a face she knew all too well.

"What are you, a demon child?! Do you know what you've touched, what I'VE TOUCHED?!" Plea Marcus screamed as he violently stood up.

As fast as a jack rabbit, the Grand Eunich sprinted to the far end of the long hall where a grand fireplace displayed a small and humble fire. With all his might, he threw the book into the flames and watched as it burned to a crisp.

At that point, everyone in the library, including Tane and Pul crowded the hall, waiting to see what would happen next. Quickly then, Plea Marcus turned and jolted for the children. Frightened, the Child took Tane's hand knowing Pul would follow and ran at the big door separating them from a possible escape. When they reached it, they pushed as hard as they could and eventually made it through the threshold moments before the boney hands of the lesser eunichs could pull them back.

They made it past the followers chanting in the altar without them noticing. As they neared the front door, however, the Child felt a wild hand grab the thick of her black hair and pull her down.

She thought back to that moment while walking home, cringing at her pain and humiliation. She received beatings from adults all the time for things she did and didn't do, and even got one from Pul's dad for helping him lose one of his permanent teeth. She got used to it and knew that when it was over, it was over. All would go back to normal, and she'd be invisible once more. But even though Plea Marcus' beating wasn't the worst, it was certainly the most embarrassing. Her friends were forced to stand and watch as she got her hits. She didn't bother to look at them or say anything until they made it clear into the village.

She stopped shy of her front door, a light brown due to dust and dirt her mother never cleaned. The light in the sky was nearly taken by the dark. Her stomach rumbled and she sighed. She was exhausted but hungry too. But the day had gone on long enough and she wanted to rest badly. Undecided on whether to stay or go, she's walked in.

Her house was small and modest and was perfect for a family of two. Upon walking in, there wasn't much to look at or sit on. The great room where families were supposed to spend time together was empty. A small bale of hay laid next to the stairs that led to her and her mother's room. There were no lamps or candles lit but she knew her way around. It felt cold and unlived in.

She entered her room with no interest in staying. She made a small fire and lit one candle to see. Awhile back, her and her friends stole from the Blacksmith's forge while Munta chatted with some travelers about Veri Meak Powder. She found a piece of graphite and took what she thought he could do without. She was surprised the next day when she saw him see her, peaking at him through a merchant's cart and he winked. From then on, she kept away from the forge.

The walls in her room were empty and a dirty tan that matched her never-washed skin. She closed her eyes for a moment as she recalled the book from earlier and everything inside it.

Eyes squinting, she took the graphite and drew all its symbols from memory. A fun sense of power rushed over her as she realized she had knowledge that made those eunichs crazy. She had the feeling she was playing with fire —that the symbols were too dangerous to fool around with. But she didn't care. The air that came from its pages gave her a sense of peace she had never felt before and she wasn't going to let it go.

When she finished, she scribbled the first thing she saw on the third page. She had been familiar with "the" and what it meant but none of the other words. And it read:

The Words of Dreqtaton: Dark Is The Only Light We See.

5

———

LITTLE SHADOWS DANCED FREELY AROUND THE CHILD'S ROOM as she stood in the center of it. The walls were covered in dark graphite, overcoming the dull brown they once were. She had spent hours drawing pretty pictures of animals and other things she didn't understand, all from that terrible book. She stepped back to take it all in.

During her visits, her and her grandmother slept in this small room. They would cuddle on the small cot and tell bedtime stories until they both fell asleep. But when no one else was home, she avoided the cold room at all costs. She didn't like how it made her think and worry with no one else to talk to. Her bitter thoughts grew heavier the longer she stayed. And if she didn't leave in time, she would end her night ruminating over her fears and resentments until she passed out.

The poor girl hardly had a moment of peace. She incessantly believed so many bad things would happen to her. She feared she would someday die alone and hungry while she waited for her mother to come save her. She also feared she would spend the rest of her days taking care of her, dragging her home after long nights of heavy drinking with nothing else in her life that made it worth living. But no matter how dark her thoughts became, it was her friends and their memories together that calmed her down and stopped her from doing the unthinkable.

She shook her head, forcing out troubling notions so she could think. She stared quizzically at the images until she remembered something peculiar. After her punishment in the church, she overheard the other eunichs murmur the name Dreqtaton with fear in their voices. They were panicking, as if a beast had found its way in. She then remembered all the stories Lordteller told about the Dark God—he was a bringer of darkness; destroyer of all things created; and malevolent to all, including his followers. Though she heard the tales that no doubt made him into a monster, she looked at his pictures and saw no evil.

Dogs and cats—are they bad? She thought.

The many symbols that made up the interior of that infamous book came in diverse shapes with precise angles, like on the well-crafted reliefs in the Church of Siracon. They were arranged in a way that tricked the mind if one were to look for too long and could puzzle a person even if they understood its language.

There was one symbol she concluded was more significant than the others. It bordered most of the pages and grew with every turn until the very last where an ink-drawing of a man dressed in black armor stared back menacingly at the reader.

She stood across her best rendition of that repeated symbol that seemed linked to the dark figure. It was like a star, but rather than five arms it had many that overlapped one another in a terrible, messy way. But of all its arms, three were darkest, and inside them were tiny figures that posed like fluid dancers stuck in time.

She frowned. She wanted to know what it all meant and wouldn't rest till she did. While pacing, she thought of an elderly woman who lived south of the village. Everyone believed she was a witch. She never left her home and heckled at the kids who spat at her windows. And if what Lordteller said was true, most witches were followers of the Dark God and could interpret his arcane language without going mad. It was starting to make sense to the Child who had already talked herself into another sticky situation.

As she walked out of her bedroom, she turned to look at the symbol once more.

Should I get rid of it? If mother sees, she'll beat me for sure!

She smiled and left the room less afraid than she had ever been. She jumped over the stairs and grabbed an over-sized coat along the way to keep her warm and concealed in the dark. She hurled out the door and left it cracked before bolting into the night.

The dirt road she lived on was one of several that connected to the cobble one leading to the village. Only farmers and poorer families lived this far out—one out of many reasons why her friends didn't come over to play.

Outcasts seldom lived in the village. The woman thought to be a witch was an exception. Her home was a rock's throw away from the southern entrance and few ever trespassed there.

The Child had enough experience in the shadows to walk through them unnoticed. At sundown, torches around the plaza were lit to help wanderers make it home safely. In the thick of night, it was impossible to see anything outside of their glow unless the moon was showing off. This was her prime time. She was just small enough to hide in those black spaces and creep around undetected.

She entered the village swiftly and darted into the darkest alley nearest her. She surveyed the flames from the newly hung torches before leaping into a dark gap besides the Blacksmiths workshop where she stood and waited to make her next move. In the alley behind her, two men deep in conversation were headed straight for her. Startled and afraid, she braced to turn on her heels when she noticed the barrel. It had been left out by the Bakers to be picked up and refilled again by merchants at daybreak.

She opened the lid and crawled inside. Her small body allowed her to stand with bent knees. She peaked out of the lid to have a look. The men walked where she had stood before, stopping in front of the Bakers front steps. Closer now, she could pick up what they were saying.

"No, no, no Sten! It has only been nine days, not ten! The Order will pass by and not even hit us! We can thank Lady Siracon for that!" said one.

"Listen Murl, I'm taking my family after we're relieved, and I'm heading north. They are looking for people to hurt and they haven't gotten us in years!" said Sten.

"Plea Marcus Daniels says if we continue to give our praise and thanks to Siracon and hand over our—"

"Oh! Plea Marcus Daniels and his crazy, ball-less men are going to save us from young, murder-hungry ones using the love of Siracon?!" asked Sten, "Will they offer us sanctuary from their wrath, hm? When the Order came through the last time, the women and children that ran to the church and banged on its doors got turned away. You wouldn't know, you weren't even born yet and thank your lucky stars for that, my friend!"

Word had spread that the Order of Garatos were

creating havoc on their way back to Gilton City and Venlet was along the way, but few took the threat seriously. The young boy, Sarty from a few nights before was proof they had every reason to fear a visit. The Child trembled at the thought that his walk to the village could have taken him several days.

Could the Order be here so soon? What day is it…?

"You're right Sten—I wasn't. Plea Marcus Daniels said his predecessor didn't hear the women and children and they still pray about it daily. They even planted trees in honor of all those who died. They're not so bad I think."

"Murl, they killed everyone. I was just a boy then. My father hid me under our house which saved my life. The rest of my family wasn't so lucky and so was most of the village. They left bodies lying everywhere and what they did to them was unforgivable— " Suddenly, the Child heard a door open abruptly.

"Hey! Keep it down out there! We're trying to get some sleep!" said an angry woman close by.

"Sorry miss, we'll be on our way," said Murl, "Now Sten, how many dubels you got?" Their voices faded as they walked away from the bakery. When there was no one left in sight, she leapt out of the barrel and ran straight towards the darkened wall closest to her. To avoid any further run-ins with the guards, she sprinted south.

Outside the woman's withered house, she moved the weathered gate to the side and searched the dark for a way across the garden which was unkempt and in disarray. A cluster of broken stones popped out of the weeds and appeared to form a path. Barefoot, she stepped on one and then another.

The overgrowth of grass swayed and made weird, unnatural sounds. She thought she saw hundreds of little eyes stare back at her but when she closed hers, they disappeared. She shook her head in disbelief. Scared, she sprinted for the door but froze when she got there. She had been adamant about speaking to the woman all the way there but lost all her bravery then. She feared another beating and had no idea what she was capable of. Eventually, she found her strength and rapped on the door. She knocked four times, paused, and then loudly knocked a fifth —a Venoxem custom.

Tane laid in bed as she tried to calm down, but it was no use. She watched her mother glide across the room, like a swan in pristine waters and wondered how she could be so flawless.

"What's the matter Taney Tane?" her mother asked as the light from a nearby candle revealed her hair—a long and glossy silk of fine tendrils that gleamed of bright gold and strawberry.

Tane adored her mother like most daughters do and waited patiently for bedtime when they played and laughed together, just the two of them. When she was out with her friends, her mother, who went by Shane, was out strolling the market, showing off her beauty as if it was her job. Tane was told by everyone she knew that her mother had many suitors before she met her father, some even coming from far-off places just to seek her favor. She was giddy over the fact that someday she would be just as radiant. Hardly patient, she constantly watched her own reflection, anxious to become a woman, unaware of all that comes with it.

Because her father, Prus Venal, was a Councilman, her mother didn't work. Their wealth allowed them to hire help to cook and clean around the house. She grew up in one of the biggest homes in the village, away from the market district but closer to the Council Chambers where most of the Council members and their families lived. It made sense in their community for her and Pul to be friends—both their fathers served as Councilmen to the Lord of the Land, and they lived so close to one another. It didn't make sense, however, that they were friends with the Child.

Tane stared, hesitant to answer her mother. She was already banned from seeing her friend but that didn't stop them from playing when her parents weren't looking, which was often. And that was a lucky break even from the beginning.

"Mommy, why do people treat Chil—the Child I mean —so badly?" asked Tane.

Her mother moved gracefully to kneel by her bed. She put her soft, skinny hand atop her head and patted it tenderly.

"Taney, she is not like us. It isn't her fault. We stay within the village, with our blood. Maybe she'll outgrow her problems and become a great lady someday, but she cannot be your friend or your responsibility anymore. You know that. And what about your friend Rela, hm? Why not play with her?"

"But mommy, why does everyone hate her? I see it every day! I don't understand! They throw things at her and they call her names," Tane said and quickly caught herself, "Pul and I see her in the plaza sometimes - that's why I ask."

"I've heard differently little lady. I heard you, Pul, and that girl walked outside the village towards the church this afternoon. What on earth were you doing my sneaky child?" Shane asked, tickling her to tears. They laughed until Tane remembered what had been bothering her all that time.

"Do you hate her?" she asked softly.

Shane looked at her and smiled half-heartedly.

"No, but I pity her. Now it's time for bed. Close your eyes and count to ten or— "

"Dreqtaton will burn you dead! Night mommy!" said Tane. Her mother blew out her bedside candle and kissed her on the head. She rested on her fluffy pillow and closed her eyes before counting to ten.

THE CHILD STOOD SHAKING IN FRONT OF THE DOOR. THROUGH a dusty window she saw a person move quickly past.

"Hello, is there anyone there?" She pressed her soft face against the door to hear if there were any footsteps coming.

"Who but wanders upon my dirty home?" a voice deep and scratchy asked on the other side. She jumped back, alarmed by their approach.

"Uh... me, mam. I'm just a child."

"Why is just a child sneaking around my garden? Perhaps you are lost and know not what you have stumbled across? Are you here to mock me, child?" the lady asked with both sugar and spice in her voice.

"Listen, please! I need to see the witch of this village. I came across a book full of symbols. I think it has to do with Dreqtaton and it might be bad. Can you help me, please?"

The Child meant to speak confidently like an adult would, but her words instead came out sheepishly. For a moment, she heard nothing. She slouched and prepared to walk away without ever knowing the truth behind those symbols. But slowly, the door opened. An old, wrinkled face peered down at her. She averted her gaze from the old woman's judging eyes and instead stared at the floorboards. Usually, she could evade any danger by staring into her pursuer's eyes. For some reason she didn't understand, it stopped them long enough for her to get away. She could sense this woman was different and could not be easily manipulated. The woman reached out a small, curled hand and grabbed her gently, nudging her through the door.

Boxes and shelves full of knick-knacks, cloth, and jars took over the interior of the home which gave little space to move around. The Child had never seen so much of anything in one place before and started to feel closed in with each step. She walked in, amazed by the many towers of trinkets and ancient-looking tomes in their path and was sure she was the only other person to see them for a long time.

The older woman had shimmied to the far-right end of her home before the Child could notice. She coughed and then signaled for her to follow to the back. Unlike most homes in Venlet, this cottage was separated into two sections; the first being the general living area full of cluttered books and trash, a small cot, and hanging racks for things she didn't know what. She looked up and saw a giant arched and open doorway separating the two areas. Squinting, she could tell that the other side was bright and full of light and space as well. She walked cautiously through the threshold and saw what looked like a giant kitchen compared to the ones she had seen. Cabinets and hanging shelves took over the walls and were kept perfectly neat and tidy. At the center of the room was a giant table, the kind she imagined Lords of the Land ate on. And in the middle of it was a big, round hole.

To the far right of the room was the biggest sight of all. There reigned a mighty fireplace with hefty stones oddly shaped, pushed into one another around a crown of fire as wide as the open doorway.

The Child turned to the older woman who waved for her to sit down, and she reluctantly obeyed. She looked around and gasped. Birds and bats were stuck to walls by giant needles and above them were yellow paintings of doors and endless hallways that awkwardly hung close to the ceiling. Her stomach turned

They sat together in silence until the older woman spoke.

"My name is Shen'rai. What is yours?"

"I don't know. I guess I don't have one. It doesn't matter anyways."

"Oh child, there is so much power in a name. There are ancients of this world and the next that could rise again just at the mere thought of it!" Shen'rai said, patiently waiting for the Child to react and was disappointed when the girls solemn face didn't change, "There are thousands of villagers and travelers and city-dwellers whose terrible lives are made better when their name is on the lips of the ones they love. But you already know that, don't you child?"

Shen'rai's tone had changed from their initial encounter moments before. She was beginning to sound like any grandmother would. But the Child didn't have time to play pretend and was going to get some answers one way or another.

"Earlier today, my friends and I visited the church. The Grand Eunich let us look at the books in the library. I picked Dreqtaton's by accident, I really did. There were characters and letters and symbols that I've never seen in the village before but looked harmless... He beat me because of it. I don't know what it said, and I'm worried I might have cursed me and my friends. That's why I'm here," The Child confessed.

Shen'rai squinted, perturbed by her words.

"Do you remember any of the symbols?"

The Child nodded.

Shen'rai staggered up from her seat to a rough looking bookshelf where she grabbed a scrap of parchment and a pen. She approached the girl who winced in anticipation of pain at her touch. She smiled and petted her as she laid the materials in front of her.

The Child looked down at the empty page, waiting for the ink, a cool black, to fall out like rain. Deep in thought, she drew what her mind threw up. Ink smeared in some places but most of the symbols remained blemish free. She turned the page in a circle as she drew the large sigil that was all over her room.

The woman's eyes glossed over, and her face was emotionless—like Plea Marcus' right before his rampage. When the girl finished drawing, Shen'rai hesitantly picked up the page and walked away, staring daggers into it. A few moments passed before she spoke.

"My child, the book you chose was the one and only copy of *The Words of Dreqtaton*. The symbols you drew were made to invoke many things, good and bad," Shen'rai said slowly.

"Am I cursed?" asked the Child.

"Your attention to detail is astounding, little girl. You are not cursed—you've just invoked the spirit of a view animal deities that guard the forest which isn't too terrible. They'll go away when they realize you're just a child. They're harmless. Oh! Another thing—you can't see them, you haven't the power or ability to! Not yet, at least. So don't try looking for them!" Shen'rai said, wagging her finger her.

"Can you see into the future, Shen'rai?"

She winced. She hated doing the ritual; so much work and sacrifice for something the gods didn't always provide.

And then there was the consequences. She couldn't witness another soul fall apart over their horrible demise.

"Sometimes I can. The Golden Ones will show it to me but only in parts. And that can't always be trusted. What would you like to know?"

"Will the Order of Garatos come through our village soon?"

The witch laughed loudly, bending backwards which frightened the Child.

"What does it matter to you, child? I haven't seen you before but by the state of you one can assume you are not treated fairly by the others, so why care? If the Order comes through, they will kill whoever they wish, and the village will have to start all over again. Just like before. It's the natural way of things in Zel. It's been this way since Garaton made it so," Shen'rai said, too bitter to admit how much she enjoyed watching the sadness she caused run down the Child's face.

"The others... my grandmother says they're afraid of me, just as much as I am of them. I don't know about that, but even though they hurt me, I don't want them to die."

Shen'rai was taken aback. Being an outcast herself she knew how mean and unforgivable people could be and without reason. But she was just a little girl. In her first years of life, she had already been taken through the wringer. And yet, she didn't want to see those who did her harm be harmed in return. It was astounding.

"You should join a church or something—you are too forgiving! Have you been so conditioned in your little life to accept such horrid conditions, that you would accept that you deserve it, and furthermore that they deserve to treat you as such and not be held accountable?! You need to be a child, not a thief or a beggar. Leave town, leave tonight so that you may survive, not just the Order of Garatos but the villagers who would throw you to the worst of men if it would save them the rats in their basements."

Shen'rai spat out a crusty, black something with disgust.

The Child began to cry.

"I am sorry. I shouldn't have said those things. You poor thing! May the Golden Ones and their offspring shine their rays of glory upon you and those you love forever and for always!" she said sweetly to the Child. She crouched down to kiss her head and held her as she cried.

6

———

THE CHILD SLEPT IN AN OLD BED, NESTLED IN THE SHADOWS just outside the candle's clandestine circle. Shen'rai hovered over her, worried and dismayed. The more she looked her over, the more her anger bubbled inside. The little girl was neglected, and the signs were all there. She had scars up and down her arms and her hair had dried blood in some places. She was a scared girl who should have told someone else of their upcoming doom, yet here she was, passing all others to ask the witch for help, knowing all too well the others would turn her away.

Shen'rai cooled her bubbling rage and gently laughed out what little frustration was left. She hated loneliness just as much as anyone but wouldn't break her silence for any of the cold-shoulders out there. But the girl was different and could endure their rough rejections without breaking.

The Child turned over as she snored, facing away from the light's protection.

"What do you want with this one, Dreqtaton?" Shen'rai whispered to herself.

Very slowly, she slithered around her giant book-stacks,

careful not to knock them over. In the middle of one tower was a bundle of books made of burlap. She pawed at each one as the tower heaved left and right. She flew through their pages before chucking them over her shoulder. She was on the lookout for a special book she kept hidden but forgot where. It was never meant to be used again, but the occasion called for it.

She glanced over at the girl frequently, afraid she would leave when she awoke. She would rather keep her close and would do anything to make that happen. She understood her well in the hours since she arrived. She was not only courageous, but compassionate and honest as well—all honorable traits Shen'rai once had but lost eons before.

She pulled out more books as her thoughts simmered away. Eventually, she felt a buzz in her wrinkled hand. Looking down, she held tight a small journal. Turning the cover she read, *Incantations and Restorations*, and knew it was the book. She searched it wildly before stopping on, "The Invocation of a Long-Lost Friend," spell.

She set it down gently, leaving the page open and exposed to the light. She ran to her closet and grabbed a small cauldron. She placed it in the hole in the table, filled it with lavender water, and set a fire beneath it. Next, she gathered all the ingredients the ritual called for: a bluebird's feather, a rabbit's nail, a dried sunflower, and a personal effect of the invoked.

She walked away once the water started to boil, stopping a few feet from the great fireplace. She fell to her knees hard, sighing as a familiar pain rushed up her back. She set her right ear to the floor and knocked it several times before yanking a loose board out from the others. She picked up the small wooden box hidden there and hugged it close to her chest. She then left lily petals where it had rested for years, closing the wooden tomb once more.

In the box was a dragon tooth, her most prized possession. It was given to her by the one she was wished to invoke as a token of his gratitude. For many years, she thought the prize was worth the hell she went through to get it but eventually realized it wasn't.

She threw the bird's feather, rabbit's nail, dried sunflower, and reluctantly the dragon tooth into the cauldron and began to chant. The words she spoke would have disappointed the children who constantly harassed her with gibberish, thinking that kind of hysterical acting was how spells were cast.

"Golden Ones, if you hear me, please fulfill my request: I am in desperate need of a long-lost friend who I knew best. Accept this offering, so sweet and kind that my friend and I can share more time," she chanted, sighing after her last words.

Moments later, she felt a new presence enter her home. It stood over the Child as she slept.

"Why waste such a useful gift, Shen'rai?" asked a sly, low voice from the dark.

"I have something interesting to discuss with you, Dark Golden One."

The figure leaned against the wall, too tall for the hut's high ceilings. His armor was black and as sheen as glass. It shimmered slightly in the light like an untouched lake in the dead of night. His black helmet had horns that pointed downwards into a spiral of two colors, obsidian and gold that radiated a silver hue.

"I am already aware of this child, Shen'rai. She is more valuable than I am certain you realize."

"I've been made perfectly aware of that, Dreqtaton," the

witch snapped, only stopping to lower her voice, "she found your book at the Church of Siracon—the same one that has been missing since before I was a fledgling. She remembered all the pictures, all of them! She is a special girl that could be of service to you if—"

"If what, witch? I never give a human more than one bargain and you've made yours. What are you willing to give that you haven't given already?" Dreqtaton spoke forcefully but somehow it didn't wake the girl.

Shen'rai collapsed as memories of the horrible deed she did in the name of the gods came to her. She was offered everlasting life if she could stop one of their offspring—an ill-bred half-man, half-animal who used his powers to harm others. What he did to her forever changed her.

For centuries after, she tried to sleep her eternal years away, hoping the dreams of her youth could replace those of torment and endless remembrance, but it didn't. Eventually, she stopped sleeping and instead focused on her craft. The outside world wasn't worth her time after that.

"Your bargains are never fair, I would know. I fulfilled my task and even gave you and the other gods more than you asked for and deserved. I would give back my eternal life for that of a human one if you, please, take this girl and protect her from the Order of Garatos," her intention was evident on her face where gestures could no longer be discerned under folding skin.

She looked at the girl, her arms wrapped around her legs, sleeping a way a comfortable child wouldn't. She could feel her pain—the abandonment, neglect, abuse, and hunger. She had provided the same horrific life for her own children whom she never got to know. Shame plagued her every moment—she left them behind to fend for themselves and never looked back. They didn't ask to be born and it didn't matter whether she wanted them there or not, whether she consented to carry them or not—they still existed. The Child's unexpected visit was a gift to her. It was her chance to save a life from a fate worse than her sons.

"Hahaha! What makes you think I won't just take her, witch? Her small toe is worth millions of dubels more than your entire being. Regardless... I accept the offer, but I can't take her now. I will be back for her in a fortnight, and I will find her wherever she is—whether you're there or not!" he said laughing as he disappeared into a plume of smoke that lingered over the bed. Despising the shadow, she grabbed her broom and brushed it out the door.

"What in the Ninth Realm did he mean by wherever she is?"

She sniffed the air and figured she had a few hours left till sunrise. She ran to her other closet, blocked by dozens of moldy boxes, and fetched two leathers bags. In a haze, she threw knick-knacks like dried parts of archaic animals and books as rare as the one the Child found into one. In the other, the bigger of the two, she shoved in enough clothing and plenty of food and water for a day's travel. She looked over at the girl, then at the clothes, then back at the girl, hoping the shaggy wears would fit her emaciated frame.

Two hours had passed, and the Child was still fast asleep. Frustrated, Shen'rai shook her awake. Confused and scared, the Child scurried to the other end of the bed. She stopped when she saw two bulky bags next to the door. Her stomach turned. From the look on Shen'rai's face, she knew the bags were for them and that they'd be leaving Venlet forever—without her ever saying goodbye to her friends or her mother. Though she yearned for this before, she didn't want to go just yet and was willing to fight her way back to her friends if she had to.

Shen'rai noticed her fear and spoke softly, "Child, I'm here for you... We need to—"

Without saying a word, the Child jumped off the bed and sprinted for the door. She pushed the bags out of her way and nearly ripped the door off its hinges. She galloped out towards the steps but froze—she was stuck in mid-air! She couldn't move any part of herself, not even her eyes. She had never felt so out of control.

"You have no choice but to come with me, child. We will walk through the forest towards Holfenya and search for a place to rest until our aid arrives in a fortnight. "

She pulled her in from the doorway without ever touching her, a grand show of her magic. With her other hand, she closed the door the same way. She moved her back to the bed. With a subtle flick of the hand, the Child fell onto the mattress. She sobbed until Shen'rai went in for an embrace. She glared at the witch before looking up at the ceiling. For the first time in her young life, she prayed to the Gods.

"I don't like doing this to you, son, but you give me no choice."

Pul's father held his son's shoes in his hands and weighed them thoughtfully, not bothering to look at him as he spoke. He had been a difficult child and was nearly impossible to discipline. No amount of scolding, beating, or starving stopped him from getting into trouble, and as such they had to resort to other ways to punish him.

He was one of eight in his family and the middle child, and they all looked alike. Their ancient home was plenty big for them, but even in a home with two floors and a basement, they spent their time in the living room together, day and night, sharing blankets and telling stories and would have it no other way.

Puls brother, Pelt, was near his eighteen years and the oldest. He was round and moved slowly, spending most of his free time eating out their mother's cupboard or harassing the young, pretty maidens near the Inn. The second and third oldest, Pan and Pen, who turned thirteen years last moon were twins who hated their names. They weren't good at cooking nor writing but were exceptional thieves. Then there was Pat at four years. He had enough energy to pull a wagon. He'd take the shoes from their father's workshop and bang them throughout the home until he was forced to bed. And the youngest was Perrin. She was the only girl and the most spoiled baby he had ever seen.

His mother Darrin didn't work which made her as round as Pelt. She had always been a bigger woman but grew larger after Perrin. She stopped being a doting mother then and made her older children do most of the household chores. With her new free time and baby girl in her arms, she frolicked around the plaza, gossiping with her friends until Purn was expected to be done with work. Since his older brothers didn't want to cook, Pul was stuck making dinner most nights. Unless, of course, he was out late with his friends.

"I need to get out. I can't take it here! I need to see my friends!"

Purn's eyes widened, "You cannot keep seeing that... thing, Pul! She doesn't belong here. She has outside blood.

It is completely out of the question! Have you forgotten your studies? Don't you remember what those people outside of the valley did to us? Or were you not paying attention again?!" Purn screamed which startled the baby into a fit.

Pul sighed, walking away from his reddened father. He sincerely cared for his friends like they were his own sisters and couldn't imagine them not being there. He knew the Child was different but accepted her, and she accepted him in the way his family refused to. The name Venam didn't matter to her like it did most Venletians and that meant a lot to him.

He stopped himself from opening the front door, resting his limp hand on the knob. Whether he left or not, he was in trouble. Eventually he'd have to come home, and he knew the punishment would be worse if he ran now. But he wanted to see his friends before they locked him away for a few days like last time. He sighed out in defeat.

Purn put a warm hand on his shoulder.

"I'm sorry my son. Now, it's time to be a man. Let's go,"

Purn led him downstairs into the crudely built basement. At the bottom step, Pul looked up at his father. The light from the lantern was strong and steady and Purn's expression was solemn and regretful. Pul bit his lip and held back the tears. He didn't want his father seeing him scared. Men didn't cry.

He took the lantern as he stepped onto the cold, dirty ground leaving a creek on the old crusty staircase he left. The light from the doorway illuminated the first set of stairs like they were heaven sent. But past that point, there was nothing. He focused on the black smoke ebbing from the wick of the lantern's candle to steady his breath.

"You know your way around. Don't bother opening the door, it'll be locked," said Purn.

Pul nodded. His father had taken his shoes and gave him slippers for the basement's harsh, icy floors.

Though he knew his intentions were pure, Pul hated the way his father controlled his life. He couldn't go or do anything without his approval and nothing he did was ever right. He had tried shoemaking and didn't like it. And he even tried playing with his neighbors but didn't like that either. They were totally different, but his father refused to believe it.

A few steps into the blackened ground, Pul heard the creaky sound of the door shutting behind him. The halo of light caved in like the nearing of a new moon. He didn't bother turning around. No amount of pleading or begging could get him out of there—it hadn't worked before.

He stepped forward, holding the lantern out to see better. In what seemed like the halfway point of the basement, he could make out hard rocks protruding from the earth, dusty and ill-colored. A coldness emanated from invisible walls all around him. As he grew closer to them, he saw more rocks with the addition of wooden beams hugged in each corner. As he came upon the farthest wall, he began to shake. An old, wooden work bench sat there untouched by time. It belonged to his ancestors, and would no doubt belong to him and his brothers someday which he dreaded.

He knew this would happen. Bad luck followed him wherever he went. He feared this fate since he came home to an angry mother and father. His fear only grew when his mother expressed her distaste with how he spent his day with his friends at the church and how embarrassed she was that all her friends knew. She accused him of purposely trying to destroy the family name and suggested the worst punishment and his father agreed to it with remorse. He preferred the beatings over the basement.

He could feel his feet begin to freeze but didn't bother walking back to the staircase. Eventually, the steps would turn to ice and there would be no warm place to stand. He sat on the ground and waited.

He hated being alone. As much as he disliked living with all the noise of his rowdy family, he preferred their company over silence. He also hated his thoughts. They liked to point the finger of blame at him for everything wrong in his life so far. Nothing was ever good enough for them. He wasn't good enough either, or so he thought.

After some time in the dark, he would start to see and hear things that made it difficult to sleep. Figures danced around him, and odd voices tried to whisper strange things in his ears. He knew they weren't real, but it still terrified him. And when the lantern went out, his only comfort was knowing, eventually, his father would allow him back upstairs.

7

————

Purn Venam took a seat at the center of the stage and got comfortable. He sighed before telling his tale:

"Their feet ached for rest the further they traveled west. The rough brush of the wild and strange lands they explored scratched away their old scars and made new ones —a small price to pay for their life and their freedom.

"They were the sons and daughters who spent their entire lives walking and were nearing the end of their journey. They were all that remained of the first slaves who left. The children who survived the harsh journey grew up to be hardy men and strong women. And the mothers whose children grew up running and hiding alongside them, and the fathers who outran wild, unbelievable beasts, to feed and protect them down the untraveled roads, whose weakest looked to them for comfort and protection, aged with nature and were ready to enter the realm of everlasting life, some before ever stepping foot onto their people's new homeland.

"Their leader died long before the eldest elder was born. Stories about him were told a million times over. He did not travel with his people. He stayed behind in that great city and gave up his life to our ancient oppressors as payment for all of us to be free.

"One day, along the journey, a tired young man named Po asked an elder this question: 'If Oxem, our leader, could see what we would go through to find our free land, how we curse his name under our breath out of fear and frustration of never reaching the end, do you think he would still make the sacrifice?'

"The elder said nothing. Rather, he took a small branch from a weeping tree and with both hands forced each end to face one another. Po waited and embraced himself for the break. But it didn't happen, no matter how much the elder tried. He smiled at Po and gently laid the branch against the trees trunk before sprinting to catch up with the rest of his group. And Po followed.

"By his fourteenth year, he had a wife and baby to care for. Like the others, he was born facing east and had cuts on his feet before he spoke his first words.

"He feared his family's future would be like so many before his, and they too would die before finding their place in the world. Out of the hundreds of thousands of slaves that left the city, just a few thousand remained to see their dreams to fruition. Many had given up years before, settling in the neighboring cities and villages along the range. Others had filled the bellies of many horrible beasts that still roam these forests today.

"Those still on course reached the mountains many times over with no luck of finding a way around. They eventually came across a large hole on the side nearest a riverbed. A brave group went in but never returned. The rest carried on and grieved the loss. They didn't notice the area around them change until it was too late. Gradually, their path became unrecognizable, and it led them to an area they hadn't explored.

"They wandered carefully through more brush and more harmful forests for many days and nights. They could only go forward, the path they knew before was no more. It was a cool day when it happened. A young girl snuck away from her family to follow a rabbit. You may have heard in other tales she chased a fawn or a pup or a cub—all of which could be true. We'll never know! Anyways, she ran after the small animal through the thickest part of the forest where no one else had gone. She screamed out for the others and boy—were they surprised!

"Somehow, by luck or divine guidance, she found a hidden way, untouched by Man. It took them a full moon cycle to reach this sacred land—our home, the Valley of Venoxem. Ever since, that same passage has been the only way outsiders can come and enjoy our beautiful homeland, from Venlet to Holfenya. From the highest hills one can see her beautiful long river systems that follow the Mountains of the Predicated for miles, the infinite rows of trees, some of the tallest in this world, and the abundance of green and gold colors that shine from our lush grass to our Venletian rooftops and are brightest during these warmer months.

"Naturally, they took their time getting to know the area and slowly built every stoned home from here to the end of the cobble road. They wanted their family to have better than they had ever known.

"Luckily, while on their travels, the slaves taught their expertise and ancient customs to their oldest of great grand-children who did the same to theirs. These are the same customs we practice to this very day, that we'll pass down to the next generation!

"As Venlet was coming to be, a large portion of the

people ventured north, curious to know what could be past our looming forests. Years passed without a word of what happened to them. Then, on a cold snowy day, a young man from the north on a giant sled brought many gifts, claiming to come from the new city of Holfenya. There, they had found strong metals that could be used to strengthen their buildings and equipment. They also discovered alien creatures that were delicious but dangerous, that carry in their blood fantastical magic powers.

"Po was an elder near death by the time the Inn was built. He spent most of his adult life building and gathering resources and made his sons do the same. He was one of our first leaders and was a great friend of the people of Holfenya. On his deathbed, he instructed his sons to erect a statue of Oxem to celebrate his martyrdom and additionally a church and statue for the Goddess Siracon as part of their agreement with the Gods.

"He was my great, great ancestor and my family reside in the same ancestorial home he built. We are a strong and hardy people. We can endure anything…"

He sighed again as he reached the end of his story. He sat cross-legged in front of a mass of his own countrymen. He watched the children in the front row with ants in their pants while the adults sat in the back taking turns napping. He smiled.

He enjoyed the many familiar faces that stared back at him. The Bakers and their beautiful young daughter. And Shane Venal. She sat like a regal swan in a sparkly new robe with Tane, his son's closest friend. Her beauty stole all his attention and he blushed. He had fancied her when they were young, but unfortunately for him, her father didn't think he was good enough. His shoemaking business, passed down to him, wasn't as alluring as her husband Prus' properties in the farmlands and couldn't provide the luxurious life she was accustomed to.

Purn cleared his throat and spoke once more:

"Let me end with this. My friends, let's be kind to outsiders. In our valley, we shouldn't judge others harshly, and we should never tolerate oppression in any way. We should be hospitable whenever possible. Everyone is welcome to live here, with the approval of the Council, of course," he paused and bowed his head, "And, to the valley and even to the Church of Siracon, I pray that Oxem protect us all in this life and the next, from those who would do us harm. Thank you!"

Purn had memorized his family's story like all his siblings since a young age. He carried on the tradition, retelling it whenever he had the chance. He had hoped Pul and his brothers would follow in those footsteps, but that seemed unlikely.

He left the stage and found his wife and children in the crowd. Only Pul was missing. His sense of worth fell at the thought of his son sitting alone in the darkened basement all night long. He spent his night questioning his decision as a father and whether it would bring Pul closer to the family or push him farther away. He knew from the bottom of his soul that once the meetup was over, he would release his son and never do it again.

He sat next to his wife as the audience moved around in their seats, talking to one another before the next speaker was up. He turned to his daughter who was jovial in a baby sort of way. Content, he closed his eyes.

Then, suddenly, he heard a scream come from outside.

. . .

SINCE ENTERING THE THICK WOODS HOURS BEFORE, SHEN'RAI tried talking to the Child with not much luck. She understood why she felt the way she did but hoped she'd have forgiven her by now.

"What do you get when a Warlong and a Cloncluck have a baby?" Shen'rai asked with a playful tone in her voice, "Well, Hm? Don't know what you'll get when a Warlong and a Cloncluck have a baby? How about... a ham hock!" the witch screamed as she laughed. She looked at the Child and searched for a smile but found none. The little girl's head hung low and had been that way since they left the village.

Even though she forcefully changed her and the Child's life forever, she didn't regret what she did. They were better off dying in the woods than with the others in the village, she knew that better than anyone else. She knew of the horrible atrocities the men of the Order of Garatos committed on the Eleventh Day, and she didn't want that for the girl. She witnessed children be taken from their homes by the Order and later sold to labor camps and underground cities, forced to work themselves to death as slaves. The worst of fates were for those children who were selected by men, for a fee, to enter a dark and perverse place where their innocence and light were taken away forever.

The Child had been staring at the ground for too long and needed to look somewhere else, anywhere but at that witch. Because of her, she would never see her family and friends again. She looked up and out, focusing on a distant tree whose trunks and limbs twisted in odd, unnatural ways. Behind it stood a mature stag; its two antlers turned downward like no other deer before. She lost herself and began to feel sleepy then.

"Why didn't we warn the village?" she asked as she shook off her dreariness.

To her surprise, Shen'rai looked at her once more but with tears in her eyes, "I have told so many people for so long of the eventual end of peace and tranquility, that chaos and devastation can happen at any time, but they only hear what they want to and believe what they think is true, whether it is or isn't. I am sorry, little sprite. Your village would have never listened."

"But they will die! That's not fair!" the Child screamed, wanting to pull her hair out, "I want to go home. I would rather die with them than stay with you!" her cry echoed through the trees and caused a murder of crows to fly away.

Shen'rais' eyes changed from grey to black as she walked with arms raised towards the Child who closed hers. She imagined she was hard, like stone—like a cocoon readying to be smashed. She waited to feel something but didn't. She instead heard a light thud on the ground nearby.

When she opened her eyes, she saw Shen'rai in the grass writhing. Her hands, like claws, grabbed and scratched at her chest as if she were trying to rip it open and reach inside. She struggled to speak even with her mouth wide open. The terror in her eyes was like that of a pig the Child saw slaughtered in the village plaza a year before. Its screams were maddening and intensified as it was gutted, slowly, from its crotch to its nostrils.

Shocked and confused, she fell to her knees and held Shen'rais's hand while the other grabbed at the earth. The witches breathing seemed too heavy for her small frame. Unbelievably, her chest blew out and didn't fall back inwards. Her bones bent in an inhuman way that made the Child shake; she could tell her agony was beyond words and she too could not speak.

A small voice came from inside Shen'rai's mouth that wasn't hers. The Child leaned in closer. Deep down her throat came muffled, joyous laughter. She sat back and help-lessly stared at the dying woman.

When Shen'rai finally drew her last breath, her enlarged chest caved in. From her open mouth came a wisp of smoke. Her eyes darted crudely to the little girls and stayed there as their light diminished.

The Child had never seen a dead person before. She had no idea what happened when someone died and didn't know what to expect. She knew her people performed cere-monies that joined their ancestors after their death, but didn't know how to do it herself. Shen'rai's body just laid there, her arms as hard as petrified wood and her face akin to bark off dead trees.

The Child waited next to the body, expecting something to happen.

Maybe she will get up. She has to get up. What am I supposed to do now?!

She dropped the dead witch's hand and looked at hers bewildered.

Am I going to die now? I don't want to die alone!

She jumped from the body and ran to the bags, her saving grace. She reached in and grabbed a comfy blanket. She intended to keep it for herself but felt Shen'rai needed it more. She draped it over her body, tucking the blanket's ends under her arms and legs. The sun shone down on her white hair that peaked from beneath the covers, looking a lot like wavy snow.

The quiet of the woods had grown after the witch's death. The Child knew she needed to get back to the village and warn everyone of the coming danger. She took the smaller of the two bags and removed what she didn't need and added what she thought she might. But, after trying to carry it, she couldn't. Reluctantly, she removed most of what she thought was essential and began to fear the worst.

She took one last look at Shen'rai and said a prayer:

"Please, if you can hear me, great Golden Ones, please forgive Shen'rai for all the mean stuff she did to me and the village. I don't understand why, but—I forgive her and I want her to rest in peace."

She looked down at the ground and saw one of her foot marks. She remembered pounding her feet into the path in anger all the way from the witch's cottage. Her spirits lifted —now, she had a way back. She forgot all about her situation and instead focused on her path home.

Behind her in the distance stood the stag with the warped antlers, watching her carefully. It knew what waited for her ahead and was ready to play his part in the shadows.

"Let's see how this one makes it..." said Dreqtaton, hiding inside the mouth of the buck.

8

____

THE CHILD RAN QUICKLY THROUGH THE GIANT BUSHES AND jumped wearily over exposed roots that zig-zagged down her path. She wouldn't have been in the woods if it weren't for Shen'rai, and now she was lost and alone.

All children were forbidden to enter the thick forests that surrounded the valley. This was an ancient decision made by the villagers earliest Councilmen. They swore an oath, as every Councilmen has since, to do whatever they could to protect their people, at whatever the cost. Unspeakable creatures were rumored to have lurked these woods, especially those closest to the mountains. They were believed to be as dangerous as any ravenous bear and as bloodthirsty as a Warlong, and not a soul could survive their attack. It was also said that a feral, incestuous people, also descendants of Oxem, lived deep in the forests east of Holfenya, who butchered and ate that which they caught, beast or Man.

She hurried through trees, keeping her head down to stay invisible. She ran and ran until her body could run no more. Slowing down, she heard a nearby bush rustle. She stopped to gather her thoughts. She opened her nostrils to hopefully catch wind of a familiar scent from the village. In that moment, she would have done anything to smell Glat's sweet honey-crest rolls, or even the Venam's pungent shoe glue that stained the air for hours even after the shop closed.

She shut her eyes and took a moment to steady her breath. Her head was hot, like a marble left out in the sun for too long. She stood in the shade and allowed the brisk, morning wind to hit her. She felt her feet cool down in the dewy grass, but her shins ached. She needed to rest.

Somewhere close she could smell something sweet. The maple syrup leaking from the trees gave off a welcoming aroma, but she knew she wasn't any closer to the village. She opened her eyes to watch it ooze down. She had heard these same trees witnessed thousands of winters and summers, but she couldn't tell them apart from any of the younger ones nearest the village. She grimaced

She looked intently at another tree, smiling this time. She remembered then, in one of her grandmother's books a great, big oak with small animals living in it. Squirrels and owls had little homes with little beds and bookshelves of their own. For a moment, she forgot where she was.

She fell out of her trance suddenly when another sound came from the bushes. She had spent a lot of time with the livestock in the farms near her home and knew most of them were heavy footed and loud, even as they breathed. The thing in the bushes was none of those things.

She had heard horrible stories about wolves and bears eating children who wandered into the forbidden forest alone. She also heard they liked to creep into homes with unlocked doors and steal the children from their beds.

Luckily for her, those tales weren't true. Otherwise, she would have been taken a long time ago.

She heard a twig snap nearby and, without thinking, ran opposite the way she intended, where her staggered tracks disappeared. She no longer wanted to be in the woods. Her sense of smell was compromised as her breathing worsened and became painful and her vision blurred into near blindness. She looked back whenever she felt its presence closing in on her. At times, she thought she saw an old man, out of shape pursuing her. Other times, the figure was unrecognizable.

She ran some more until she caught a faint sound in the distance. She had forgotten how good she was at picking up noises, loud or soft, close by or far away. A year before, while playing a hide-and-go-find game with the other kids, she heard a boy very carefully sneak up behind her. He wasn't the go-finder but thought he had a better chance of winning if he had her hiding spot. She could hear his wheezy breathing awhile before he approached her. They fought at first, hitting and kicking each other, but eventually stopped and came to a truce. They both waited there till the game was over.

Lost in her thoughts, she blocked out the ongoing pain in her legs and ran closer to the faint sound. She couldn't tell what it was then, whether it was good or bad. She ran faster. And faster. She ran so fast, she thought she was flying.

An eerie wail from a woman suffering close by stopped her dead in her tracks. She had never heard anything like it, not even from livestock being slaughtered, and those were the cries that kept her up at night. Her mother would scream when she cried sometimes, but never like this.

Too scared to move, she shook, even in her bones.

Another scream from the same woman arrowed through the trees, this time her words were clear. She was begging something unseen for mercy.

The present sounds of pain reminded her of her first beating. A Councilman had taken her feet and repeatedly struck them with a stick. It hurt tremendously and stopped her from ever running through Glat's bakery barefoot again. Even though it happened when she was three, she felt ages had passed since then. Her youth, her entire six years of life flashed before her eyes and what she endured so far was sad and unforgettable.

Having stopped for too long, the pain returned to her shins and had worked its way up to her hips, causing them to go up in flames. Her neck creaked as she tried desperately to turn her head to the left but stopped before she caused herself any more discomfort. Her body had become too tense to move.

That woman in agonizing pain seemed so close. The Child tried desperately not to think of what she could be going through, whatever could possibly make a person scream like that, but the thoughts found a way in. Though the village was close, nothing seemed farther than the home she left that morning.

Urine trickled down her legs and stung against her wounds. The smell alone woke her, but she still couldn't move. Her body, as hard as stone, fell forward with her arms too stuck to her sides to catch her fall.

The woman screamed again but sounded weaker. The Child rolled onto her side. She closed her eyes wishing she heard the familiar song of birds instead.

"I...need...to...get...up."

She was terrified beyond belief but knew she had to make it home, no matter how long it took. She felt a sour pain stretch from between her eyes to the back of her throat. She shook her head where she laid and squeezed her face in tightly.

"I don't want to cry! I need to get up!"

Somehow, out of the still and hot air and without a hint from the rustling of trees, a gust of soft, cool wind rushed over her. Eyes closed, she lost feeling over her body but didn't panic. She was traveling to that place in her mind where her Otherself lived—the only place she could truly escape to. When she emerged on the other side, it looked the same as before. The land was still vast and green. Pure water poured out from rocks and landslides endlessly for all the creatures that always lived there but nowhere else.

"I can't stay here! I need to go back! I need to get up and I need to go back!" she screamed, standing alone in a long, endless meadow. From all around her came a chorus of loud childlike voices that grew louder with every passing moment.

"Your pain is our pain. Open your eyes, and walk, we are always with you!" said one voice, the loudest of them all.

She closed her eyes again, feeling the breeze cover her once more. Out of all the times she went into her mind, that was the first time she felt it all over. It stayed with her, inside of her, attaching itself to every inch of her body. What had ached before now hummed like struck ice and turned numb.

When she opened her eyes, her legs were moving, like a dog's running in their sleep. The Sun had moved across the sky. So many hours had passed since she was last awake. She got back on her feet and again sprinted.

I hope everyone's ok!

Smoke came at her like a hoard of locusts as she got closer to the origin of the screams. Through the smoke's thickness she could make out familiar buildings. A surreal amount of relief washed over her. She would have jumped for joy if she wasn't so exhausted.

She was nearing the smaller homes of the day laborers and farmers in the north part of the village. They took a long walk to work every day while their wives stayed home and tended to things. Some were Sittermaids and would watch children for a small fee. She had Sittermaids but stopped seeing them when she turned five.

Mother's not far.

She anxiously looked through the dense trees for a way out but couldn't see much through the clusters of branches. She could barely make out the outline of homes that were too alike to discern apart. Her legs had not stopped moving since the unknown breeze picked her out of her head and was pacing out of fear of stopping for good. Frustrated, she walked over to a proud-looking oak. She pressed her face against its cool, jagged skin. It soothed her reddened face exposed to the Sun for too long. She gave in and allowed her body to collapse onto it, enjoying another moment of rest that seldom came to her. Not knowing what was waiting for her opposite the oak, she whispered to the gods and begged for her friends to be okay.

THE FIRST HOMES SHE SAW WERE INTACT, BUT THEIR WINDOWS and doors were destroyed. Standing north on the outside of the village, she saw little of the devastation. Her home, in the distance far behind her, was on fire, and so were all her neighbors'. The trees near it caught fire but thankfully didn't spread very far.

Tears fell down her face. She imagined her mother,

alone and drunk in her room, burning to death. It was then she felt the reason for running home was already gone. All she had left was her curiosity, and so she started down the cobble road once more.

She heard whimpering over the crackling fire but couldn't care. She wandered lifelessly, marching slowly towards the heart of the village, down where the cobble road used to be. The once ancient road that held millions of travelers in its time was no more, ripped out from the ground by hooves of steel and malice for no reason she could understand.

She kept onward but did so without purpose. Out of the corner of her eye were people crouched low by the sides of buildings. They all appeared to have gone to war. Their clothes were ripped, and their demeanor appeared to be permanently darkened. One elderly woman held a battered man drenched in red breathlessly, shaking his limp body, begging to die.

The streets were covered in bile and blood that touched every surface like freshly spattered rain. Countless pale naked bodies were dragged off the road and onto the sides like shoveled snow in winter and were left there to rot. They left lines in the ground they traveled, making roads of their own; hundreds of smaller, blotchy brown ones that always led to death.

All she could do was look and carry on—her mind not registering what really happened. She couldn't see their dead faces, and she didn't want to. They weren't human to her anymore. She couldn't face the fact that she knew another dead person and instead wandered elsewhere.

Not far from the village plaza, she heard a rumble of voices come towards her and realized there was nowhere left to run. She hung her head as the same villagers who thew rocks and called her horrible names ran to her.

To her surprise, Munta, the silent, red-haired giant embraced her, and his brother, Unta, patted her tenderly on the back. Besides them came many others, cooing and pawing at her as if she were their own. They ran their hands through her hair and held her face for a moment with tears in their eyes. She had never received that sort of attention from them before, and she wasn't sure what to do with it.

Munta who held her close let her down carefully as if she were made of glass. She noticed he had red stains on his arms and legs like the limp man by the road. So much was in his eyes—a thousand leagues of ocean blue that didn't move; stuck in a moment forever.

The stink of sweat and fear was permanent on the surviving villagers and not one inch of them was free of sot. But another stink came barreling through the air and hit her the hardest. A strong reek, heavy and sour from the bloated carcasses laid out everywhere caused her to gag and gag again. It was the smell of death.

She tried to look through Munta's legs that were as big as two pale pillars with zero success. She heard metal clamor coming from the plaza, louder than his hammer on the forge. She tried to focus on it, but her attention could not rest on one thing. A storm of unpleasant sounds – weeping and begging and scrapping and grinding twirled around in her head and into her ears, no matter how hard she tried to keep it out. The sound of suffering plagued every square inch of her life and she saw no end to it.

She looked up at Munta, "Where's my mother?"

He shrugged.

"Where are my friends?"

Her voice broke and she cried.

"We need to hide you. If they knew we had another child in the village…" As Unta whispered this to her, the loud clamor from the plaza rung its loudest. He turned around to face it this time. The rest of the villagers hid the girl behind them as he approached a shape she could not discern.

"We want all the women and children here, now, fat boy. Don't make me wait!" said an angry voice.

"You have all of them, you monsters! Our lives are ruined now. There is nothing left. Now, leave!" screamed Unta with the fury of a demon.

"What's behind that soft-headed pepperman, ginger boy? What ya' all hidin' there?" said the angry foreign man. He had a thick accent, muddier than the villagers but could be understood clearly.

As the men spoke, the Child noticed all those who greeted her aside from a few elderly women, were men.

Where was Tane's mother? And Pul's?

Suddenly, a scream echoed everywhere and stopped the bickering men for a moment. It belonged to another child who begged for their mother.

"Tane? Is that you Tane?" she screamed, dodging the arms of the weak villagers who tried their best to keep her hidden. She ran faster than she had in the forest.

She ran past a mound full of dead, naked women. She had never seen anyone naked before. From what she could see, some were whole while others had been cut up. Random hands, heads, and torsos poked out from every inch of the mounds.

She tried to ignore the soldiers working on the outside of the plaza, dressed in dark and light gold armor, cutting away at more people who looked very dead.

All the heathen soldiers stood by and watched her, amused. She hit the giant cage at the heart of the plaza with all her might, hugging it with all the strength she had left. Inside the small prison were most of the children she had grown up with, crammed and stacked together in a most despicable way.

She screamed out for Tane whom she couldn't see right away. A small hand aggressively waved at her over a sea of small, barely clothed children and she knew it was her.

The cage was the size of two caravans but not nearly big enough for all the children in the village. She screamed for Pul. She screamed and screamed but saw no hand waving back.

"We will take the girl and make our leave. I don't care who you leave alive—I'm done with this place!" said a man whose posture and demeanor stood out above the rest. Animals and symbols were carved into his armor and wardrobe unlike any other soldiers there.

Two men took the Child by the arms, twisting them painfully before throwing her on top of the other children through the hole above the cage. She screamed for Tane and found the eager hand once again. The many children beneath held her up, surely thankful she was so small.

She took the tiny hand into hers and held it tight. An old man with a long white beard took one end of the cage and hooked it to four horses. With two clicks of his foot into the horse's side, the affluent soldier put on his helm, more ornate than his chest plate, and led the convoy of his soldiers and the horrific display of scared children south of the village—leaving the same way all other travelers did.

9

———————

Parity sat in front of the church's large fireplace with no desire to move, hypnotized by its jumping cinders that lightened her heavy mind.

It was early in the morning when she was forced underground, into the catacombs with the other survivors who made it to the church before the attack. They waited for hours in those dark, mirky tombs before stumbling out when all became silent, scared and confused, except for her who alone stopped to sit by the fire.

Her body trembled uncontrollably when she didn't drink and would tremble worse around loud noises. When her child was just a baby, she lost her temper too easily. She would slap her and pinch her sides, thinking it would stop her crying, but it only made it worse.

Somehow, the dancing flames softened her trembling, and the thought of ale was clear from her mind. For a quiet moment, she could think.

Why?

She asked herself so many times, her voice had grown

weak from it. She knew the answer was deep within, but she couldn't reach it.

Plea Marcus watched the disheveled woman stiffen in her chair and approached her gently. The night before, he sent a Plea to the homes of the children he met earlier to inform their parents of their disrespect and ignorance while in the church.

The ex-slaves made an oath to the gods that protected them and their future generations from their wrath, so long as they fulfilled their end of the bargain. Some didn't like the giant statue of Siracon tucked away in the thick forest and refused to be members of the church but went along with festivities for fear of punishment. And there were those who hated sacrificing Warlongs and other animals to Garaton but did so because his presence, felt most infrequently of the gods, brought with it an insurmountable fear they could not ignore.

Plea Marcus Daniels wished the Child understood those traditions. Had he known what was to come, he would have helped her and her friends before they were stolen. He spent hours praying for them while the Order defiled the village, and for the first time in his life, not one was answered.

He could not believe they were out of Siracon's reach of love, but he knew they wouldn't receive her protection, especially the Child. Somehow, she brought Dreqtaton's book into existence, into Siracon's home where it is forbidden. It had not been there before her. That made her dark and unholy in the eyes of the church and, though his heart protested, he couldn't help but feel the same way.

He forced the Pleas to join him in rummaging through every bookshelf, looking for any reason why it or any book like it would be there. When the Order of Garatos approached, they were still in the library, unaware of the many frightened villagers climbing over pews and person to save themselves.

The only books permitted in the library were the ones Siracon approved. Some focused on her beauty and splendor while others retold tales of the vital role she played in her brother-husband's wars. The number of books about her were endless with many more being written as she continued to interact with Man. The books retelling her adventures with the first people and her relationships with the other gods were the stories most written and most sought out. These included her relationship with Garaton, and her mysterious encounters with Dreqtaton kept hidden in the Mountains of the Predicated by request…and force.

The Child's clothes were too thin - there was no way she could have snuck the book in, you fool!

Plea Marcus spent hours repeating those thoughts, praying to Siracon for relief with not a sign from her well after the madness ended.

In a mad haze, he returned to the library and ransacked the entire collection without care and consideration. On the cold ground were messy piles of books and tomes with their binding and threading exposed. Pages ripped and those most brittle and ancient turned to dust. The Pleas cleaned up after him as his back was turned, afraid of receiving the brunt of his topless temper.

He sat down heavily in the chair next to Parity, like a bag full of dirt. The enormous heat from the fire stuck to his face like a metal mask left on the forge for too long. The light from the fire showed the depth of his age and discomfort. Guilt was yet to wash over him as he sat in a malaise soon to be revealed.

"Parity, will you come help us? We could use the hand."

He put his on her shoulder and rubbed his thumb over the bone. She took his in hers and squeezed. She turned to him, her eyes wrought and red, no longer giant marbles of blue and green. Her upper lip had swollen and was growing larger.

"Oh, sweet Siracon, have mercy..." he said.

He then took a clean part of his robe and extended it to her. She turned away. He caressed the back of her head with one hand and, without warning, wiped her face vigorously with the other—like a mother would her baby. She winced at the rash that formed above her lip that screamed at the touch.

He grimaced. There were many things said about her, most of which were distasteful and said behind her back. She had come to Venlet with a swollen belly and was incredibly thin. She was near death and a few days shy of having her baby. She came alone with few possessions and lesser dubels. The villagers welcomed her with open arms and offered their home to her. Her beauty helped her gain even more support and trust which she squandered away. Even with her swollen features and negative disposition, against the flames her sublime visage could have been compared to that of Siracon if it wasn't a crime.

He had heard about the birth a few years back. Most Grand Eunichs were invited to visit the baby during its first days, to bless it and offer their good graces, but that did not happen for the Child. Rather, he heard what happened through rumors. It was said that the baby's hair was full and black as night, and its eyes were multi-colored unlike anyone else in the village.

No one knew the father, and no one got close enough to the family to find out. And even though Parity had friends in Venlet, she kept them at arms-length. No one dared approach the old-abandoned home given to her by the Councilmen because of her erratic behavior. She told everyone she met she didn't trust them and ran away whenever asked about the baby. Over time, those that tried to help stopped.

He wished he had met the girl before yesterday. The rumors he heard were true: her hair was as black as night and her eyes were unlike any other. Because she didn't have a name and behaved much like a boy, he assumed she was one which made what he did all the more heartbreaking. He felt her absence the most, like an anvil in the chest, and hoped her death was a quick and painless one.

Parity pulled away from him and sat back on the comfy chair. She peered again at the flames. Her hair, made up into a clean and even bun the night before had fallen around her face. He could see the distance in her eyes as he left the chair and knelt to meet her gaze. He noticed her lips moving, slightly parted, releasing a voice too soft to understand. He shook her shoulder reluctantly, careful not to injure an already broken woman.

Those who made it safely to the church had injuries both seen and unseen, slight and fatal. He remembered she arrived early for service and was forced to stay. She kicked, screamed, and begged to be let out, even if it led to a horrific fate. Her wounds could not be seen.

"Why what?" he asked, finally hearing her. She stopped and closed her eyes, keeping them closed as she spoke.

"Holy man. Grand Eunich. Can you answer my question?"

"Are you, child, prepared to hear it?" He faced her with his eyes wide open, ready to embrace hers. And she did stare back, with such resentment. He saw the Child in her then—the strength, intensity, and hate. It was stronger than any force he had ever experienced, even from the goddess. The red within her eyes pushed the light green to crash into the dark blue, forcing cold and warm water to be as one.

He looked away from a sad glare for the second time in two days. She took his chin, as he had taken her child's and pulled his face up to hers, eyes still mad.

"Do we deserve what happens to us in life?"

He looked at her sheepishly. He had been asked this question too many times during his reign and seldom gave the answer they were looking for. He knew better than to give false hope in the absence of truth, especially to a woman he had little sympathy for. But he saw something else inside her, under the surface that affected her enough to push her child away when she needed her most.

He looked away again, defeated with no answers to give.

"Don't you speak with them?" she asked, pointing up towards the ceiling, "Don't you know what they do? Does your goddess speak to you, oh Grand Eunich and tell you all she knows? What of her plans—do you have a say? Or do you sit with your ears to the sky and wait like the rest of us? They do whatever they want. There is no justice, no punishments. And we wait. And cower."

Before Plea Marcus could respond, she continued, "I used to wait and listen. Everyday. We would pray to all of them, those monsters in the clouds—"

He winced.

"We gave them our best tributes and prayed for everything: food, prosperity, protection, fertility..."

She trailed off, lowering back into the chair as if she said nothing. She looked away from Plea Marcus and again focused on the flames.

"Life is a gift, girl," he said, "If we can't control our circumstance, we can control how we live with..."

He stopped as she jumped up and walked to the far side of the hall. She rested her arms heavily against the wall, palms flat and shoulders hunched. Her breath quickened.

"Maybe we should talk again later, Parity. Right now, we need to be of use to others - let us help those who need it!"

She turned around violently and screamed, "But what about me?! Do I get a helping hand to mend my inner wounds?! Do I?!" She paused, turning back to the wall to assume her position. It was cool there—the fire had become too intense.

In a soft voice, she repeated as she had before. Plea Marcus got up to stand beside her.

"I... begged him to stop."

She expected him to pull away like the others she tried to tell. Instead, he put his thin arm around her shoulders, and she removed herself from the wall, embracing him. She let out a deep breath, feeling a relief she had never felt before.

TANE STOOD IN A CORNER OF THE CAGE WITH THE CHILD BY her side, sneering at the other children as they sneered back.

"Where's Pul? Wh-where is he?" She couldn't help but ask, whether her friend knew or not.

The Child looked down at her bare feet, unable to respond. She zoned out. Her last moments back home filled her mind already foggy with negative thoughts. She had never received such a warm welcome or been embraced so honestly until that day.

She felt like running, more than she ever wanted in the forest. She wanted to feel that love again—it didn't last long enough, and she needed more. But her mind played tricks, bringing up all the horrible things they did to her, and she couldn't enjoy it anymore. Her heart sank.

She wiped her tears and turned to peek through the bars for something new to stare at—an odd-looking tree or some foreign animal. The expressionless faces of the kids she once knew disturbed her and she would have closed her eyes if she wasn't afraid to.

The stolen children who gave up ever seeing their homeland again traveled without care. They didn't bathe and seldom ate. The roads they traveled were riddled with exposed roots and rocks that made the cage rock. Every bump and rattle hurt them, sometimes breaking their bones, but they wouldn't dare ask for help from those monsters who stole them.

The children had all stopped crying and screaming for their families many trees before. Those in the beginning who tried to escape were taken out of the cage and beaten to death. One by one, disorderly boys and girls were removed and never seen again. Only one feisty boy came back with a face red and swollen that grew bigger as the days passed. His eyes were closed shut for a while, but at least he lived.

Tane and the Child had to mourn the loss of their old lives in silence or face death. Unfortunately for Tane, she couldn't help but wail sometimes when the grief became too much.

When the Child turned away from her, Tane couldn't keep it in anymore and sobbed loud enough for the soldiers to hear, "I'm never going to see mommy and daddy again! I want to see them again, Chil!"

The Child felt a sour knot twist between her eyes and a wail form in her throat.

Don't show her—stay strong! You must stay strong!

She swallowed her spit and calmed down. She smiled at Tane, and her sobbing lessened.

"Do you remember when Jessen left her door open, and we snuck out to go to your house?" she asked with excitement in her eyes. Tane nodded but looked confused.

"Was Jessen the Sittermaid that screamed at us and called us evil snakes or was that a different lady?" asked Tane. The two looked at one another before laughing weakly.

"No, that was Mare. She's the one who put us out in the garden for being bad."

"Yeah, Jessen was younger, like mother, and her house was the one closest to the village," Tane smiled.

"We were four years, I think. We went through a couple of 'em, somehow ending up back together after they kicked us out—you, me, and Pul."

The Child stopped briefly, needing all her energy to bring back her bright demeanor, "She left the house to speak to a neighbor outside. We ran out the back and went to your house. Your mom wasn't home." Tane rolled her eyes and laughed. Her mother was never home.

"We knew your mom had a lot of stuff. We played dress up, danced, and sang and Pul ate all your family's treats!" They both laughed louder than they should have. They stopped and looked around frantically. A soldier watched them disapprovingly. Tane dropped her head, her mouth turned back into a frown.

"We got in so much trouble, Chil. We couldn't see each other anymore. I was so mad at mommy and daddy. I can remember why I was so mad, but I can't feel it, you know? I just want them here now, I would never get mad at them again." Tane brushed a tear from her eye and kept her head low. The Child watched her brilliant friends' light diminish.

"Jessen got so mad, she ran after us with a broom handle, tripped, and fell backwards. Right on her bum," she said, smiling which grew when she noticed Tane's slight one.

She sighed. There was still some hope left in them.

10

THE ENSLAVED CHILDREN TRAVELLED FOR WEEKS AND HAD NO clue where they were headed. Their journey was not a good one and the first few days were the worst. The children stuck at the bottom of the rigid cage were over-burdened by those on top. They suffered tremendously and because their broken bodies couldn't heal, they stayed disfigured. They cried out above the rest until they eventually died. And their bodies remained there, to bloat and combust until soldiers, tired of the smell took them away.

The rest of the children caught on quickly to their unfortunate situation and did whatever they could to survive. Through whispers, they announced the incoming of soldiers and other dangers to one another. Those who hung off bars would whisper to the person closest to them, and that person would whisper to the person next to them nearest the middle, and so on. After twenty or so were murdered, the children tightened their allegiances and remained as quiet and still as possible, hiding those they suspected would be next until their foe found a new target.

One of the last children to die was a boy by the name of

Dade, whom they called Big Dade on account of his size. He took up a lot of space in the cage but kept the cold winds from burning the others' skins for which they were grateful. But as the miniature herd got smaller, he stood out to the thinning soldiers desperate for a decent meal.

The children watched anxiously as the monsters ran out of food, eating whatever scraps was left from their village. The strange men who once walked confidently along the cage, banging the metal bars, and scaring the children, who galloped proudly on their wide horses were dragging their feet, using the cage for support. Desperate, they ate a few of their own horses which angered the bald man in charge. Those with enough energy to hunt rode ahead of the party but came back empty-handed if at all.

If there were any villages or cities along their treacherous journey, the children did not see them. They had hoped to be saved, somehow, before they reached their end but gave up that dream after Big Dade. They prayed and prayed to the gods for help until they had no strength left.

Even though they lost more children than they anticipated, the soldiers had no idea the journey would take as long nor that they'd run out of food so quickly. For many of them, this was their first time in the Valley of Venoxem and the past odd weeks were spent mostly with the people, not the terrain. When they tried hunting the oversized Warlongs, they lost a few of their own and only gods' knows how. And if there were lakes to fish in, they were too far into the hostile woods to ever want to trespass.

When the Eleventh Day came again, the whole precession stopped and the brakes were locked. Dozens of soldiers surrounded the cage, laughing and poking the children with their swords and sticks. Two soldiers, indistinguishable from one another, grabbed Big Dade. The Child told Tane not to look. A soldier with a long knife slit his throat and they all sobbed as their life passed before their eyes.

The soldiers took their time cutting him up, using his body parts as puppets, making fun of how Venletians speak. They threw his innards and waste at the cage as if he was nothing.

The children cried so hard they gagged. And those that didn't cry stared lifeless into the woods. Tane sobbed and the Child wept silently to herself, wiping away tears before her friend could see.

The soldiers set up a fire before they murdered Big Dade. The children hoped it was for them—to warm their bodies during the icy nights. Instead, they used it to roast him in parts; cooking the biggest piece, his torso to his upper thighs, in a big cauldron, to simmer and build flavor. After they had their share, they gave his scraps to the children who took it reluctantly, too famished to say no. Tane and the Child tried to resist but couldn't.

IT WAS THE MIDDLE OF THE NIGHT ALONG THEIR DESPAIRING journey when the girls first met the Venpas. Those still living were barely getting by and spent this time planning, talking, and sometimes fighting over the best spots to sleep in. As the Child slept, a little boy skinnier than her approached.

"Hey, hey, hey—you! Hey, wake up! Wake up!" he said gently before taking her arm and pinching it. She awoke and nearly screamed.

"We should all be sleeping. If they catch us—we're dead meat!" she said with anger in her eyes.

"We want to know what to do! I want to go home! I

WANT TO GO HOME!" cried the little boy. Another child approached, an older girl who put her hand over his mouth. He turned and sobbed into her shoulder. She looked up at the Child with eyes as empty as the night sky.

"My name is Cara Venpa, and this is my brother Care. Our parents..." She trailed off and looked away, "we know you—you're the one who lives with the cats, right? You're used to going without food. We're so hungry. Please help us!"

Some children close by overheard the conversation and began whispering amongst themselves.

"She can help us!" said one.

"But she's not like us!" said another.

All of them spoke at once which overwhelmed the Child. She wanted to help but also wanted to run away, and Tane who claimed the only corner the soldiers couldn't see came first in her eyes. Confused, she took a step back to take everything in.

From inside, like a hot tidal wave came all the memories of her being bullied, abused, and neglected, that bubbled up from the most protected parts of herself. She felt as though she would burst. Memories she wished to forget flashed through her mind, constantly triggered by her reflection in the children around her. They looked like she always had, and in their eyes, she could see a familiar fear and sense of abandonment that could only be shared amongst survivors.

She searched for Care's eyes while he hid in his sister's shoulder. When he finally unraveled, he looked at her unblinking with tear stains down his face. His eyes were almond shaped and a simple blue. Through them she felt his yearning for his mother and home life and knew it would never go away, and she could see he was a kind boy that lost everything he had ever known. He didn't want to live anymore, and she understood that all too well.

She sighed.

"I don't think we can escape," she said to Cara. A unanimous groan came from the unruly crowd forming, "It would be too hard to break out and not get caught. And even if we made it, they would still find us."

Their murmurs, much like the song of crickets ceased as they waited for her to speak again. She hated the hope in their eyes. She saw no way to escape.

"We'll have to wait," she said as the ones facing her stared like angered Warlongs, "We need to behave and not make a fuss. Some of us have been standing in the corners for a while, so we'll need to change spots every day without them knowing. I think they killed Big Dade because of the Eleventh Day, so we'll have to hold tight for a few days at least!" she said.

"And what should we do if we're still here next Eleventh Day?" asked a voice in the bundled crowd.

Her eyes darkened. A cool wind brushed against her neck, "Then we'll try to escape and die if we must. I will die for all of you—will you die for us too? Together till the end?"

Since their capture, the children grew closer in every way. Their skins always touched, and they had no choice but to care for one another. When night was at its coldest, they huddled up together like they never would have back home.

Like the first people of Venlet, the children of the great Oxem, they would persevere together and look out for one another no matter the obstacle before them. Their slave blood had generations of courage that could never be contained nor diminished. Like their ancestors—they would rather die than be slaves again.

In unison, the children softly chanted, "Together," and did so till they fell asleep.

Tane turned to her friend, "I want to be strong like you. Am I Chil?" she asked, holding her tight to keep warm.

"Yes, you are. We can make it through this. Together."

They fell asleep and had good dreams that night.

11

THE CHILD, ONCE ISOLATED FROM THE OTHER KIDS, WAS AT
the center of everything they did. Not a single child slept,
ate, or relieved themselves without her knowing. Their presence both soothed and hurt her. Even as their eyes became
puffy and hair matted, they still perfectly resembled the
people of her village she had already begun to miss.

Their clothes had been left to ruin, much like the village.
Torn flaps and pockets were used to cover their feet and
hands. Those with longer sleeves ripped those off as well to
give warmth to the kids without.

The warm green tones of their shirts stained into brown
and black. She could recall in great detail the vibrant colors
of Venletian garments most Sittermaids like Jessen made for
extra dubels. There was a high demand for Cloncluck
feathers which often adorned the tunics of powerful people
but could only be found in Holfenya, much to the dismay of
many. The giant bird was taller than most men and could
grow to be as big as a house. Their feathers were so rare that
many roughed the dangerous routes through the valley just
to see them, let alone buy them.

When the ex-slaves entered the valley, Clonclucks were one of the first vicious creatures they encountered, but over time, they shrunk in size and adapted to domestic life on farms near the Mountains of the Predicated where they couldn't escape.

In one of Lordteller's stories, a single Cloncluck feather could give anyone holding it the ability to fly. The magic, unlike any other in Zel, came from the creature's blood but was released through its feathers, where its color showed the power of its magic as well as what it could do. Most of their feathers were green and gave their holder incredible speed, while fewer were red and yellow which allowed their holder to fly like a bird and shout like a lion. The rarest were purple, and no one knew what they did.

The Child saw Cloncluck feathers all throughout the village, but particularly on the Councilmen who all wore plain, creaseless tunics, grey and dark green with one feather to show off. The most prominent Councilmen wore their big feathers on their collar and on their shoulder where everyone could see. It was also stylish to wear the feather at the center of the chest where both sides of the tunic met. The Lord of the Land appointed to the Valley of Venoxem, whom the Child never saw lived privately south of Venlet where it was believed he owned a tunic made entirely of green ones.

She remembered Tane's father, Prus, having a feather of his very own and it was the biggest in the village. Its elegant design worked well with his features which likewise would have his lovely daughter. The feather glowed with a splash of bright green that traced the outside fluff that fell into the hidden purple swirling into the quill. She also remembered how often he walked past her and never looked her way - even while in Tane's company.

She opened her eyes and looked over at her friend who had moved to a different corner in the cage. Since their midnight meeting, the children had found a way to work together. They were determined to keep it going for as long as they could and be side by side till the end.

She looked over at Care and Cara who were cleaning the wounds on the heads of two smaller kids who had been crying all night. The brother and sister used whatever saliva they had left as well as their own small and brittle fingers to comb through the girls' matted hair, giving her temporary relief.

Cara, a smart girl of eight years was not the oldest in the cage but knew better than most her age. Her mother worked for the Councilmen as a secretary and was determined to give her children an education. She wasn't pleased with the lack of schooling in the village and wanted better for her own. Back home, she owned a Bookhouse that many considered to be a place of higher learning. She was from a city far away but moved to Venlet after she fell in love with a local she met while visiting.

She spent several years asking for permission from the Councilmen to open a Bookhouse, the first the village would have ever had. They declined her offer, however, and told her they couldn't afford the potential loss of business and tourism as well as how unnecessary it was for the village. She decided to take a job working for them instead to provide for her growing family. Her husband, whom she loved dearly, had worked on the fields until an accident bound him to a chair.

She tried to get her daughter into reading, but the more books she brought home, the more Cara fought back and instead played outside. Care tried to read but had a hard time, just like his father.

The Child watched as Cara pulled on the balls of dirty, matted blonde hair on the smaller girl's head who held her mouth to muffle her screams. She could tell by the young girl's clothes, a brown dress with not a hint of green that she was of lower class, or her parents worked out in the fields. The social structure of the village was evident on the everyday wears of its people. The cleaner they were, the better the family lived in the community. Tane always wore green but wasn't particularly fond of the color. She much preferred red which her mother never let her wear. Pul's family tried to stay within the social structure but fell short, wearing clothes more brown than green and not entirely new or least worn in. But he didn't care as much as his family and just wore whatever they gave him.

Pul never cared about anything, that stupid oaf!

She shook her head, angry that her other best friend wasn't there. It was always the three of them, ever since she could remember.

"You need to accept he's gone," said a soft voice deep in her mind. She shook her head again and stared onward.

"It's not your fault, it's not his fault—so stop it!" her Otherself insisted, crawling around her inner skull, making her ears itch.

She turned to focus on the soldiers who in their dozens formed formations as if they were preparing for some grand performance. She pressed firmly against the cage, its rough, jagged bars spread oddly across her back as she observed the way they walked. They stood tall, with their toes and noses pointed forward like that of a child called for a beating.

"Please—talk to me!" her Otherself pleaded.

She noticed the soldiers lift both knees, one and then

the other after a certain number of steps. She squinted her eyes and began to count.

"Eleven steps," whispered a low voice unlike any other. She froze. "Eleven steps... For eleven miles... For eleven days," said the voice again, belonging to a man she didn't want to meet. She kept her back to the voice but trembled as her skin moved against the rough metal with the jolting of the cage. The man put a hand on the small part of hers exposed through the bars which she quickly pulled away.

"I can help you get out of here," he said with the same low voice as before.

Her eyes widened.

Could this be our chance for freedom?

She knew they were going someplace terrible, and they may not survive it, so what did she have to lose?

She used all her remaining strength for the day to turn and see the man. And when she did, she no longer felt the bars around her as her soul soared out from her chest and into the clear sky above—the endless blue with only the Sun to keep her company. She had never felt so weightless and free. The closest she ever came to flying was when Purn Venam threw her out of his home the one and only time she visited.

She looked down at the brown earth beneath the soldier's feet and found herself back in the cage, cold and tired. The clouds were gone. The smell of urine and feces overtook her sense of smell. She wanted to cry.

"Oh, sweet soul, it'll be okay. I will save you—don't you worry!"

The Child looked up again—this time, holding on tight to the bars. She took a moment to look over the man's face. She had seen so many new ones that they were all starting to blend together. Her mind, though strong, wanted to remember his but seemed to forget it whenever she looked away.

She went over his words carefully in her mind and was reluctant to believe him. She narrowed her eyes.

"I can't trust you. You might hurt me like the rest of them," she said with a feral voice. She noticed then how malleable his face muscles were when he shifted from shock to amusement in a flash. He had both soft and strong features unlike anyone she had ever seen. His chin and jaw were strong and angled like the crest of a mountain. His eyes were big and bright, and his nose was neither slender nor wide. If one feature was different in any way, he would have looked totally strange.

In his moment of shock, he showed her his many lines of aging that curled around his mouth and eyes. She knew those belonged to happy men who lived long lives. She had never seen a man look so young and old at the same time.

He didn't resemble the other soldiers either whose faces were scruffy and dirty, and not as handsome.

"I won't harm you. I promise—you have my word. I can help you, but you must help me in return," he said with a condescending look.

Before she could ask about her friend's safety or anything else for that matter, she noticed something peeking out of his gold and black armor. It looked like hair but couldn't have been—it was green. She reached for the feather like an animal, her arm scrapping at air halfway out of the cage. He leaned back, grinning at her attempt.

"It isn't polite to take what isn't yours, girl. Now, tell me —will you help me when I call upon you?"

The Child noticed then that the man had been walking sideways and was out of sync with the rest of the Order.

"Why aren't you doing the eleven steps?" she asked.

"Oh, psh... I don't have to. I can make them see whatever I want them to. I have powers, you know. And if you serve me, just this once, I will give you powers too and maybe you and your friends will survive," he said as smooth as a snake.

"Well... I don't know. How can I trust someone I don't know?" she asked.

"Hm. Well, I would tell you my name, but I don't like it—never fit me! I would rather be called something else. Hows about... Strongman or Incredible Guy—does that work for you girl?"

She laughed. "At least you have a name. My mother never gave me mine. And I'm not calling you Strongman or anything silly like that. I much prefer Jester."

"I'm tired of that one! Okay, fine. You can call me... Tom! Now, stop joking around and tell me yours."

"I meant what I said—I don't have one. Everyone calls me the Child. Well, except for my friend Tane who calls me Chil," she was surprised by how much she told this stranger. She felt comfortable with him but didn't understand why.

"Nonsense! I have the perfect name for you. How about I call you Doe—like the deer that runs through the forest. You are a lot like them too, you know. You've been caught by things that should never have been in your world. And they hunt you, hurt you because of your nature for which they don't understand but wish to control. You will be saved, Doe, but only if you help me."

His words echoed like a shepherd's distant call to his flock. She had seen deer frolicking in the forbidden forest and wondered where they frolicked to. She loved their elegance and their lightness—they were so free! She wouldn't admit it, but she liked this name better than the others.

"What do I have to do?"

Tom shook his head and replied, "No, no Doe, not today —some other day. Now, let's do this right: will you accept my offer and serve me when I call upon you if I help return you to safety?"

"But what about my friends and the other kids?"

Guilt overcame her. She forgot all about them and it was all because of this weird man.

He rolled his eyes and looked away.

"You are difficult to bargain with and ask too much. I will do my best to help the others, but I can't make the same promise for them. Keep those you want saved closest to you. So, do we have a deal?"

He moved closer to the cage but was still walking sideways. She noticed his unnatural gate and how he had kept up with the speeding cage but said nothing. After heavy thought, she leveled her head with his and nodded.

12

———

DAYS HAD PASSED SINCE THE CHILD MET THE ODD MAN NAMED Tom and many more since they were taken. She did her best to keep track of the journey and was adamant it had only been sixteen days since their capture, but when she told the others, their counts were different than hers. Anxiety reigned over them as another infamous Eleventh Day was approaching.

They continued to meet each night to discuss their escape. She wanted to tell them about Tom but wasn't sure he would follow through on their deal. She noticed a few of the others with shifty eyes who also talked to soldiers. Trust was in short supply.

"I can't believe it," she said to Tane who didn't respond. She stood still in her usual corner, looking down at her bare feet and hands. She was stuck where she was, replaying the memories, good and bad. She remembered how her Sitter-maids used to scrub her hands so hard they burned. And after, how her mother would coo over her cleanliness and show her off like a little doll.

The Child elbowed her side. She lurched over before hitting her back.

"Ow! What was that about?" the Child snapped back, rubbing her tender side. The skin was tighter there with not much flesh or muscle left to guard her guts.

She scoffed and then laughed, "Look over there! They want to be friends with those bad men, but they will turn on them—I'm sure of it," she said smugly.

Tane turned to face her. She had always known Chil to be kind and understanding and never as hurtful as those who hurt her. She didn't like this other side of her. In the past, she would have put her in her place, but she was reluctant to do or say anything that might upset her. She was all she had left, and she wasn't going to lose her too.

Her confidence fell to the floor where her eyes remained, "But what about your new friend, Chil? Are you not doing the same?" she asked timidly, unsure what to expect anymore.

The Child grabbed her by the arms and squeezed. She forced her eyes to meet hers.

"I told you Tane, he's different. He's going to get us out of here. He's already brought us food. I'm almost sure we can trust him," she said before loosening her grip.

As the Child talked with Tom, Tane watched from her favorite corner disapprovingly. She didn't like him very much. He didn't look like a kind and trustworthy man. She could see a deviance in his eyes and knew from some eerie, far-off feeling that he would lead them farther away from Venlet than anyone else.

When the Child returned to her eager to talk about what he said, she refused to listen and wanted no part in his plan.

Back home, she never had to worry about that kind of stuff. Everything important was handled through her parents. The most Tane ever had to do was bring it to her mother's attention. But that was all over. Her mother was gone and so were the safe shutters that kept the dark truths of the world away from her. She was now exposed to everything and was ever weary of it.

As she slept, she thought about Chil and what she went through back home. She used to pity her. She would give her gifts and her left over clothes to keep her warm. She wanted them to be the same, at least in that way, but she realized then, sleeping out in the cold, abandoned and parentless, just how silly she had been. Not even the prettiest of dresses could ever make her the kind of happy she used to be.

She sometimes had nightmares about the unfair torments her friend had to endure every day and she hated them. She would reach for her, wanting to help as she scavenged for food, looked for her mother, and endured the humiliation of being born unwanted, but wake before they could embrace.

She didn't need a mirror to know how differently she looked from before. Her golden hair had darkened and the bright redness in her cheeks had disappeared. Her face had turned charcoal brown from the dirt and dust off the traveling parade and her eyes felt pink and dry all the time. She didn't want anyone to see her like this—like Chil, so she hid her face. Only Chil could see her.

Although she disliked Tom from the beginning, she became a little less paranoid when he brought them all food and water. But while the others danced and enjoyed his company, she watched his every move.

They were hardly ever given anything bigger than scraps

to eat. But water was a different story. The soldiers liked to throw water jugs through the top door, sometimes half empty, and too often the jugs would explode all over the cage. Those desperate enough would lick it off the nasty floors.

If the soldiers had no scraps, they would gather berries and low-hanging fruits—whatever they could get their hands on, and throw it at them through the bars. Frankly, that was what they ate most. Every few days or so the soldiers would hunt down a deer or rabbit but not much would be left for them. The last source of meat the children had was Big Dade. The thought of him made Tane's jaw tense and sour as she watched her friend relax with the enemy.

THE CHILD HELD HER CLOSE, TRYING TO KEEP HER FROM hurting herself. She had fallen asleep and was having a nightmare, she was sure of it. She shook. Her legs kicked out violently, almost hurting everyone around her. The Child did all she could to keep her contained but it was no use. All the hushing and rocking back and forth could not stop those episodes from happening at night. She would ask Tane about it in the morning but was sure to be ignored again.

She had changed so much since they left. She used to be fiery and free, like new metal fresh from the fire—fierce and flexible but difficult to hold. She was the fastest runner in their group and caught Pul many times.

The Child smiled to herself.

"What ails your friend, Doe?" asked Tom quietly as the cage sat still in the dead of night.

"Nightmares, I think. Could be from the day we were

taken," she leaned her head against Tane's, like real sisters would.

"I can fix that. You can fix that too. There is so much I must teach you," he said nicely. He didn't make her feel uncomfortable and his words didn't bother her. They spoke like old friends. At least, that's how she saw it.

"I don't know about that. I just want out of here. My arms, my legs—I can barely stand up and I don't know how many more days I can take this."

Tom shifted his position, tilting his head to the side. She could see the wheels in his head turning.

Her eyes suddenly became heavy. She turned her head back to Tane who had stopped moving and was snoring loudly. Through all the terrors they had endured so far, she was happy her friend—her sister was there and slept soundly for once. She closed her eyes and fell asleep.

She awoke to screaming outside the cage. It came from a young soldier running away from the woods. His arms swung wildly around him as he screamed for his brothers in arms to wake up. The rest of the children awoke too—startled, shaking, and scared. They asked each other if it was in fact the Eleventh Day—if it was their day to die.

The Child caught Tom walking slowly around the cage, acting as if nothing was happening. Men half naked ran out of their tents and grabbed whatever they could carry before bolting for the forest.

What monster scared THESE monsters?

As all the children moved to one side of the cage, she noticed Tane standing by herself at the farthest corner away from the madness unfolding. She was staring Tom down. The Child rushed over, pushing her way through the crying crowd slowing her down.

Tane whispered under her breath as she looked unblinking at him.

"Tane, what are you doing?"

She tried blocking her vision, but Tane forced her out of the way. He was walking away from the cage and straight into the chaotic campsite up ahead when she finally spoke.

The Child leaned in to hear her words.

"Siracon, hear my plea, take this man away from thee..."

Shocked, she pulled on Tane's arms to snap her out of it, "Tane, stop it! We need his help!"

"Siracon, hear my plea, take this man away from me..."

"Tane, please!"

"Siracon, hear me wild, take this man away from the Child!"

After her last words, Tane collapsed onto two children besides her before hitting the hard floor. The Child stared in horror as her friend lied lifeless.

What have I done? This is all my fault!

She let staggered tears fall down her face before she got the nerve to help her friend. She wasn't there like she said she would and Tane was now in danger of being taken. In that moment, The Child felt hopeless.

As if on cue, Tom spoke, "It isn't your fault, Doe—she'll be fine. I'll remove all of that... messiness from her mind and she'll be back to normal when she wakes. Tomorrow, we'll be in Glenloch. Hold on tight my brave little friend, the journey isn't over—not even close to it."

She gazed at him perplexed by his cavalier words. There was no way what he said could be true. There had been no signs of any upcoming cities or villages and no change of scenery since Big Dade. And she overheard a soldier mention to another a few mornings back they were still weeks away as well as how long the journey took them the last time they were east of the glen. He also mentioned a small farm they visited just before Venlet; one they had their favorite Eleventh Day yet. She felt the hair on her back and arms stand at attention as her piercing anger grew.

She didn't like being angry. When she blew up, she hurt people and sometimes herself even when she didn't mean to. But she couldn't control the fire this time. She hadn't thought about Sarty since her story to Lordteller and could only imagine what horror found him. His name was just another on their long list of ghosts she kept close that never stopped growing.

How many more people in my life will the Order of Garatos destroy? She thought through gritted teeth.

TANE AWOKE LATER THAT EVENING. MOST OF THE SOLDIERS had gathered up their tents and started the parade to continue onward. Word had spread that a wild mountain bear attacked the site and killed four soldiers, wounding ten before escaping back into the woods. The Child knew Tom had something to do with it but wasn't sure how he pulled it off. She asked Tane if she remembered anything before passing out, but she didn't, at least not right away. Gradually, she recalled the Eleventh Day, the murders, the hunger and thirst, the children's late-night meetings...

When the Child asked if she remembered a man by the cage walking weird alongside it, she looked at her dumbfounded.

"Tane, you don't remember a man talking to us these past few days?"

Tane turned her head confused and thought about it for a moment as if she did remember something, but it was out of reach. She smiled.

"Nope, sorry. At least I remember everything else and you're here with me!"

The Child hugged her as hard as she could. She was happy her friend was somewhat her old self again—bubbly and hopeful. She didn't bother asking about the strange prayer from the night before, but she wouldn't ever forget it.

As Tane talked to Cara and Care, the Child turned away to look out into the distance. Near a small clearing stood Tom. He waved before walking into the woods, removing his armor piece by piece until he was completely taken in by the forest.

13

The Order of Garatos with their party entered Glenloch twenty days after leaving Venlet in ruin. They stole all its children from their dying parents and held them in an iron cage meant for prisoners and blasphemers of Garaton. The travel-weary troop were relieved to be home and cared very little for the lost children after they arrived.

As the parade of soldiers entered the city, they were greeted by beggars on their knees and kids in adult clothing asking to shine their shoes for a dubel. In the homes above were women and children waving their handkerchiefs at them. The city had been waiting patiently for their return, expecting them days before. They were hungry to hear about the Valley of Venoxem and presumably their simple people.

Glenloch's Lord of the Land allowed his people to exercise their beliefs freely if they acknowledged him as the closest thing to the gods in Zel. The city had some of the deepest roots in the ancient customs and beliefs surrounding Garaton that they continued to practice millenniums after his first meeting with their people. For just as long, they boarded up their homes and held their arms close to their chest, waiting for the inevitable onslaught on the Eleventh Day. But that was a normal part of their life—some weeks were easier than others, but they prepared for the worst, nonetheless.

The children were in awe of the city. The many buildings that rested closest to the main road were plenty big from a distance, but up close seemed as big as the mountains.

As the cage creaked along, they were greeted in such abhorrent ways. They were insulted, hit with fists and weapons through the bars, and were heckled from every direction. But what bothered them most was the loud screaming and hustle that was nonstop around them. Child after child begged everyone they saw for help, pleading to go home. Sadly, those free people mocked them, pretending to cry and beg for their parents too. There were also those who threw whatever they could get their hands on at the cage – glass, metal pieces, rocks, and rotten food that slashed away at their skin.

The Child did her best to protect Tane from the pelts, but they came from everywhere. She wrenched in pain with every blow that hit her head and sides. But she did not cry. This was something she felt she had to endure. Even in the village, now miles away, her and Pul tried their best to keep Tane's sensitive soul from breaking, not sure what would happen if it did.

They both missed him a lot. So many unfortunate and unforgettable thoughts crept into the Child's mind, just imagining the horror he may have gone through and if he had tried to find a way to them was enough to keep her awake at night. But she felt she didn't deserve to sleep for what she thought she had done, and when her thoughts of him subsided, she would think on the many people she killed—not by her hands, but just for existing. She couldn't reach them in time to warn of what was to come; so many lives could have been saved, or so she thought. The vision of all those naked, blank people in piles were always present in her mind. At least the physical pain distracted her for a little while.

The witch who stole her first was dead, her mother may also be dead, and those that survived, who embraced her for the first time in her life, were left in pieces as she ran away from them and into the clutches of the murderous fiends that destroyed everything. She could still hear their solemn cries as the cage entered the dense forest, forever echoing their regrets and prayers unanswered. She would never be the same.

The children watched in horror as the noisy cage no longer covered by grabby peasants aimed for a giant pavilion ahead. At the sight of it, the Child's stomach turned. She looked to the soldiers who seemed relieved but anxious about something she couldn't understand. She fell back against the bars and thought hard about it. Ever since the animal attack, they marched faster than they ever had and didn't stop once—but why?

That incident didn't make much sense to her and neither did Tom. The only things in Zel that could do what he possibly did were the Imagi's or the Illustros who were part of the many tales that weren't supposed to be true.

She relaxed for a moment. She was happy to be thinking of anything else but the present. In the middle of all this chaos—from the cold rotten floor under her to the strong foreign herbs in the air around her, she could still find an escape through her thoughts.

No one knew why they were taken, and they'd dare not

ask a soldier for obvious reasons. She did ask some of the others if they had an idea since they were taken before her, but none could say, or would say for that matter. But she knew, like her, they'd prefer to never think of it again.

Growing up, the children in Venlet were told many ancient stories, passed down from generation to generation. Some were about animals and monsters that ended with a child, sometimes bad, being taken and never seen again. Other stories outside of their realm were told by Lordtellers and merchants who didn't believe in them themselves, but that didn't change how the people of the Valley felt about them. They were always superstitious and adamant about their practices, following them regardless of what the rest of Zel said. Their biggest beliefs rested in their faith in the Golden Ones no matter what terrible or unjust thing they did. An essential part of the practice was to honor them without ever questioning what was asked. But even a Venletian can break tradition. While in their last moments of life, those plagued by that Eleventh Day begged the Golden Gods to tell them why they allowed this to happen. And it was in their moment of death when they knew who the real goblins and monsters were, and they were worse than they could have ever imagined.

The Child wanted to remember the faces of the men who took them and wouldn't rest till she did. She stared at them closely and made sure to catch their every color and wrinkle. If she were to return home, she would be sure to hold them accountable for their crimes.

"These little monsters are bad for Glenloch! They're cursed! They should be thrown to the wolves or given to the dogs to snack on!" said an old, limping soldier, tall and skinny, with yellow and black teeth nearest the pavilion. He spoke to a man who didn't look like one of them. He wore a long, white robe that exposed his naked ribs on the left side. The armor over his chest was shiny and flawless. It wasn't like the ones Munta used to make.

Back at my old village, but not anymore.

She sunk knowing that another thing in her life was gone for good, like the books her grandmother brought to her but took when she left.

The book!

Her mind raced like a galloping horse as dozens of white knights surrounded the cage. The children were in an uproar, but she was paralyzed and lost in thought.

If I had never found that book, none of this would have happened.

She could not shake the feeling she was responsible for the Order of Garatos and their ruining of the village. All those dreams of running away seemed so silly now. She would have rather died in her homeland as she was before than suffer in this strange and foreign place without ever seeing her family and the many people she was accustomed to again.

One at a time, soldiers in white took the children out of the cage, their approach gentler than the gold and red ones who threw them in. The children didn't have the energy to resist so they went willing and fell into their arms. When they were set down on the glistening road, a wave of relief washed over them, and they were happy to be on solid ground again with a fresh whiff of air in their lungs. They had difficulty walking and standing up straight at first and kept their arms close to their bodies, having acclimated to being as small as possible to fit and be as comfortable as one could be in a cage.

Their stomachs screamed for weeks, and they barely made it with the little food they got. And the thought of never going home hurt more. They didn't think it could get any worse. Truthfully, they were done thinking and were happy enough with the rickety cage being gone. Unfortunately for them, they had no idea what they were walking into.

THE CITY OF GLENLOCH WAS A POPULAR PLACE, ESPECIALLY for sailors and merchants traveling from far off lands. It gave easy access to the rest of the region east of Gilton City. This robust and busy place was the first to have new spices, metals, fabrics, and foods that sold for higher nowhere else. It was expensive to live there. Many ex-Lords of the Land and famous warriors called it home. Like Gilton City, it was praised and blessed by the gods, but most importantly Garaton whose personal practices and expectations of Man they took the most serious, no matter how archaic they seemed to the rest of the world.

Extreme depictions of his body and his exploits were idolized onto each building in one way or another. All day long people prayed to his likeness, leaving food and dubel offerings, and every night, workers would clean it all away. They left no trace of the many prayers which made those who left them believe they were received and would be honored.

It was tedious work keeping the beautiful city pristine. Every white surface outside, no matter how dirty, was scrubbed down. To say the bright from the white marble was blinding would be an understatement. The streets were always busy with travelers and merchants nonstop from the sea. And if they didn't come through the port, they would enter from the north where a road led west through many small towns, eventually leading the way to Gilton City. And when that road ventured east, it turned to dirt and was surrounded by thick forest. This one led to the Valley of Venoxem and to another port city farther east.

Upon entering either by sea or by road, one would be bombarded by droves of seller carts and loose women anxious to sell any product or irresistible service for a hefty price. Most that chose to vacation in Glenloch were aware of this and the many diverse luxuries that weren't available anywhere else. They were willing to pay bucketfuls for the experience.

"Anything your heart desires!" they would say, or, "my son can be your slave for a dubel a day!"

On the outside, it seemed like the perfect place to live, especially during the warmer months. Unfortunately, like a giant Tentactacon who appears above water as a beautiful woman, beneath the surface it is a smelly, evil creature that enjoys the suffering of its victim caught in its claws. And everyone who lived there knew it and were desperate to leave. They worked all day and night for a few dubels. It was slave-work that cost them more than what they were owed. Most of their homes were on lien by their employers too. To leave was an impossibility. And to complain led to a punishment worse than death.

Hundreds of years before in Gilton City, the great and lovely Gilton, son of Garaton and Siracon, heard about the people of Oxem who were oppressed and enslaved, who left free to start a new life on their own. He was unaware of how many people in what was then called Golden City were still being treated. Millions of slaves and paid workers spent their entire lives building gold, elaborate buildings for the gods to call home, however, when it was close to being done, they'd change their minds and want to live somewhere else, and the work would have to start all over again. This was the breaking point for Oxem and his people. Revolts and protests stopped this new production from ever happening. Desperate, the gods agreed to release thousands of slaves and pay more to those who stayed.

Gilton was appalled that there had been no change since Oxem's people left. With his gift of persuasion and thoughtfulness, he convinced his father to abolish slavery throughout Zel and give dubels to those who needed it most. But all those changes didn't prevent previous slave owners from keeping their businesses and employing their ex-slaves to work for slightly more than a slave's wage. Most of them had no choice but to take those difficult jobs. The cunning business owners still had all the power and used it to build immense empires both under the watch of the gods and behind the scenes. These were the empires that stole children from their families knowing no one would do anything about it.

WHILE THE CHILDREN WERE REMOVED, THE CHILD AND TANE were separated. Both reached out for the other but were led through different archways on the pavilion into a mass of red and white.

The Child was thoughtfully set down. The soldier nudged her forward and the other children crowding around her were made to do the same. Dozens of small heads moved from side to side. The children were baffled—they had never seen anything like it before. Large columns held up the huge pavilion and its halls were long and open, much like the hallway in the Church of Siracon. They were put in the atrium where more archways laid before them, as well as more people they didn't know.

There were many women and men with long white

tunics and robes walking around anxiously attending to one child and then to another. Some of the women reminded her of the wives in her village—the ones who would gather to help a young wife give birth or offer support to a helpless wife whose child was ill.

For a moment, she was warm but that changed as she locked eyes with one of the other soldiers in gold and red. He watched her and the rest of the kids with sinister eyes that made her turn cold.

She looked around frantic. She traced the many faces before finding Tanes. They weren't far from each other and when their eyes met, they smiled. Another warm feeling filled her, but it would be the last.

She noticed there were more children in that giant space than she had ever known. There were hundreds of them standing around waiting just like her. Big lines began to form that led to women and men at desks waiting for them with tongs and hammers where they did even more examining. There were lots of different children, some with black hair like hers but with hints of blue and purple, and some had shorter legs while others had bigger feet. She couldn't tell any of their ages, but she knew they couldn't be old enough to work or have children of their own.

She also witnessed, for the first time, a young child with hair the color of fire. Striking he or she was even with what looked like dirt speckled all over their face. And there were others with hair orange and yellow like the setting sun. All of them, though different, were similar in how dirty, thin, and scared they were.

She looked back at Tane who was busy talking to some kids behind her. She seemed to be enjoying herself.

At least she looks to be feeling better.

"I don't like the way I feel about this. Let's change

places!" said her Otherself, scratching the inside of her left ear. She shook her head and moved forward as a child up ahead was taken by the hand and led inside the building. That seemed to be where most of the children went.

Young boys and some girls who looked strong for their age were led to the entrance on the far westside of the building. The one on the far east side was where all the sickly-looking children went. A child whose right hand looked wrought with infection was taken there by a woman who refused to touch him.

The middle entrance was where most of the girls stood and was the slowest to move. She had seen a child, she thought was a boy, be taken there as well as the few bright-haired kids. When her group had neared its turn to enter a line, the boys were all sent to the far west entrance and the girls were sent straight down the middle, including Tane and the Child.

The middle line then turned into two. On the outside were desks with men sitting on them. They were a mix of the gold and red soldiers and the gold and white ones, both transfixed, amused, and somewhat bored.

She witnessed a man take a girl from the line and look at her. One of them asked her to lift her arms and turn around. She seemed confused and tried her best to do what they asked. She remembered then how in the village only mothers and Sittermaids were allowed to touch girls or see their bare legs. She looked down. She didn't want to see them do anything else. She heard murmurs and whispers from scared voices around her. Suddenly from the desk came a loud laugh before an even louder scream. The Child looked up and saw the first girl, the one several girls ahead, kicking and screaming. She was taken away by a giant man into a room opposite them. Her screams continued as more little girls and boys were examined and taken to that room as well. Some wet themselves. A girl behind her did this as well, "...so they won't touch me!" she said.

The Child didn't know what to think and she didn't know what to do. Before long, Tane would be next. They looked again at each other and held their breaths.

"My, my—what a pretty little girl," said a gold and red soldier standing at the edge of the desk. He walked over to the girl and took a small piece of her hair, curling it like her mother used to.

"What is your name, precious?" asked another in all white behind the desk, pen in hand and emotionless. Tane paused before shaking. She didn't look up or down, just forward and couldn't see or think of anything. She clenched her teeth. Her shoulders tightened up excruciatingly. Her body used the small amount of energy she had left to react to the threat around her and she was mortified.

"Alright then, little sweet. You ain't got no name. We'll just call you... Pup. How does that sound?" said the gold and red soldier lifting her eye lids up and looking into her ears.

"N-n-n, no... My name is t-t-t-Tane!" she said through a tight jaw she painfully forced open.

"*N-n-n, no! M-m-my name is t-t-t-t...*" teased a different soldier which caused the others to laugh.

The Child knew they were in worse hands than before.

"Screw that, dog—you are a pup and that's your name, you understand?" screamed the man at the edge of the table as he tried to move her dress around her.

Tane felt trapped, crammed in this open space. She could see in the eyes of the men behind the desk that they didn't see a little girl, helpless and afraid. What they saw was flesh and bone, like a dog or a pig. She was not getting out of this—she would be stuck in this moment forever.

The men continued to laugh as the man grabbing at her successfully caught her and pulled her into his arms - a different sort of embrace than that of the gold and white soldiers early.

She screamed and screamed for the Child.

"Chil!"

"CHIL!"

"MOMMA!" Tane sobbed loudly and continued.

"PLEASE, SOMEONE HELP ME!"

The Child who had been watching breathlessly saw the world around her melt into black as her legs buckled. She was gone from that cruel world—the one that took the village, her mother, and Pul from her.

And now, Tane.

All that was good was now gone, so—she escaped.

14

———

THE CHILD LAID PEACEFULLY IN A BED OF PINK PEONIES AND roses as spray from the waterfall nearby kept her refreshed. Little fireflies bounced around her, leaving a little buzz on her cheek as they fluttered by. She was their only guest, and they made her feel right at home.

Tane would love this! She shook her head at the thought.

Days passed without the sun ever setting. She took to swim in the newly formed lakes without a care in the world. So much had changed since she was a baby. What was once a pond became an ocean, and her small sprouts had become giant oak trees. Nothing stayed the same, not even in her mind.

A solitary house sat quiet in the fields beyond the great lakes. It was just like hers back home. She imagined herself there, and so there she was, just outside the doorway as if she were free from time and space.

The sun began to set then, and she saw candlelight flicker where her mother's bedroom would be. She ran through the black door, entering as night flew across the sky. Inside, everything was clean and polished. The ceiling was jeweled, and the floors were marbled—like in a Lord of the Land's home, or so she thought. The fireplace back home was a hole in the wall, covered in sot and charred flesh. Here, it was big enough to walk through, and like the buildings in Glenloch, it was covered in expert paintings.

Glenloch, that sounds familiar?

She walked through the kitchen and smiled from ear to ear. The smell of maple and honeydew filled the room through an open window where a pie sat, baked and ready to eat. She yawned and rubbed her eyes. She looked out the window and marveled at the bright stars above.

Her eyes became heavy, and she knew it was time for bed. She ran to her mother's room—up the stairs and to the right. Before opening the door, she tried as hard as she could to picture her mother's long brown hair, big blue-green eyes, and pretty face. She could see her wearing a long blue dress with white images sewn in. Some were of horses and cows while others were dancing bears and sleeping Clonclucks. Although she never saw her mother like this, it was how she wanted to remember her forever.

She wasn't surprised when Parity wasn't there—she had never been. She could imagine anything else but her. And so many times she looked for her regardless and went to the house, cold and alone. What kept her coming back was the small chance she would be waiting for her, baking pies in the kitchen, anxious for her to return.

She took her time walking over to the vanity in the corner of the room, the same one her mother used to have, but white instead of a dusted brown. Inside was the dress, blue with the white embroidery of shapes that moved as if alive. Each story it told was close to what she had envisioned and some she had never seen before. These were the stories her mother was supposed to tell her whenever she appeared.

She laid on the ornate bed that had never been used and closed her eyes. She curled her knees to her chest and tucked her head between her arms. As she fell asleep, she heard a loud bang come from somewhere in the room. When she opened her eyes, she was somewhere else. The walls around her were a blinding white and there were giant blankets that blocked her from seeing anything outside her room. At the end of her bed sat a woman in a white tunic. She recognized the clothes immediately. She realized then she was back in that horrible city. A thousand thoughts ran through her head at once. She hoped Tane was still alive but couldn't imagine either of them staying that way for long. She started to cry.

"Oh, you're awake! Are you feeling better?" the woman asked like a mother would. The Child furrowed her brow and crossed her arms. She didn't want to speak or do anything for that matter. As far as she knew, life was at its end, and she wasn't going to cooperate with any monster—not even those who wore a nice lady's skin.

"You gave the Order a right ol' fright, didn't' ya? That's okay—don't worry! It looks as though you have an infection and will need to be evaluated later. Sorry love! Are you ready to join the others—do you feel light-headed?"

She put her hands to the Child's throbbing head after she refused to answer her. She gave her some medicine, helped her down, and walked her out of the clothed cubicle all in one quick motion. As they were leaving, the Child could see they were in an immense space with other little cubicles like hers scattered throughout, and she heard coughing and crying in the distance and figured they were in an area near the far east entrance where all the sickly children had gone.

The woman pulled at her arm and dragged her through as she resisted. She didn't want to go back where she could be examined and feared that the worst was still to come, but she figured Tane would be where she was headed if she was still alive. Biting her tongue, she resigned to walking with the woman, but made her life miserable all the way there.

THE ROOM WAS DARK, AND THE ATMOSPHERE WAS SOLEMN. A few windows high on the wall let some natural light in but were permanently shut to stop any child from escaping. Because of this, the stench of waste and sweat was excruciating. And there was only one door, bolted shut that no child dare come close to.

For those poor children assigned to this room, their life was a madhouse. There were more children than cots or cement to stand on. So many slept a few to a bed or had to lay in filth on the floor, but that was the favorable option for cooling off in a room with no air and it was the best place to hide when the women came to take them to work.

They were left there for hours on end. Throughout the day, the women in white would come in and examine whatever child they could grab. They would pick a few and with great effort leave with them. A few hours would pass before they were brought back, clean and with a belly full of food. But when they returned, they were not alright. They would stare off into the walls until sleep got them. Eventually, they would return to filth with the rest of them until it was time to work again.

The Child's head was covered in bandages. The women and men in white had tried cutting out a severe infection from her head unsuccessfully. She laid unconscious with the other sick and dying before awakening unexpectedly a few hours later.

Her head ached but her heart ached more. She had searched for Tane first thing when she finally got to the room and found her on the ground, face and body covered in feces. Her old dress was gone and instead she wore what looked like a burlap sack. She didn't bother to move or say anything when the Child held her close.

She rocked her for hours, telling her stories from not long ago. They were still children after all and should have had a life full of promise ahead of them. In that moment, however, they were terrified they would remain slaves in that mirky, grotesque room and be forced to do horrible things forever.

Cara's brother Care found the pair amongst the many bodies on the floor.

"You guys are still alive?!" he asked surprised and relieved.

"I'm so glad to see you Care. Where's your sister?" the Child asked. Care sat down next to her and looked out into the dark around them.

"The things we've had to do since we've been here..." he said trailing off, "my father never talked about these things in the scary stories he told us. Men can look like men but act like..."

"Monsters..." Tane said under her breath. The Child closed her eyes, heartbroken by the pain in her voice.

"We can't die like this," she said with tears in her eyes.

Care continued, "We were in line together. She took my spot ahead and I watched them look at her, all over, you know. I didn't want them to do that to me. I wanted to fight but she told me to calm down. She... told me to calm down," he repeated himself again and again until he couldn't speak.

All three children cried together then. Tane's tears fell down her impassive face and she didn't make a sound. Care tried to explain what happened next but couldn't. Children were not meant to process such horrors.

The Child felt relief she had not been through what they had, but felt bad afterwards. She almost puked from the guilt she felt but held it back, like everything else.

"They killed her. They killed her and threw her out the window, like leftover meat for the dogs!"

When he said dog, Tane shook. The Child knew right then and there she had to get them out of this. She was not going to let them be hurt again. Enough was enough.

She had lived a terrible life back home but could endure it as long as her dear friends were by her side. She loved that they lived better than her and it gave her great comfort knowing they were safe and sound in their homes even if she wasn't. Their happiness gave her hope that one day she could have some semblance of it in her life. She would have done anything just to see them thrive and be happy forever, but that dream was gone, and their old lives were over. She had a small chance of saving those closest to her now and she was going to take it if she could have nothing else. One way or another, they were going to escape.

It was late and the bar was at its peak as an endless flow of customers came barreling in like every night before. Women and ale were everywhere as well as children rushing to do their job. Aside from those entertaining the men at the bar, some children were told to clean up and deliver food to customers only. Her head was still aching and bandaged but the Child was expected to work regardless of the fact. No one lived in Glenloch for free.

She was in a constant panic. She was forced to leave Tane with Care, where both could be grabbed at any time for any reason. And what was worst—tomorrow was the Eleventh Day. It was hard to believe they had only been there for four days; it felt like much longer. They thought they had escaped the Order of Garatos but soon realized they were at the center of their terrible practices that occurred without the need of a special day.

It was her job to hand out the ale and bring the empty mugs to the back to be cleaned. She tried to do the job right despite her aching head and worrying. It didn't help that many of the customers she served were hostile, rude, and needlessly impatient, and they had no problem scolding a little girl for any small thing, even if it wasn't her fault and laughed at her discomfort.

At a table in the corner of the bar sat a man who didn't blend in with the rest of the patrons. She noticed him right away and was immediately shocked by appearance. His hair was near white and was long and straight, falling well past his shoulders, and his eyes were a bright blue that flashed around the room as he watched them all like a looming hawk. He was impossible to ignore.

Wow, there are so many interesting people here.

Lost in her train of thought, she tripped and fell over another patron's boot, spilling ale all over him. He screamed. The whole bar turned to look as he slapped her across the face. The drunks moaned and sighed. They all laughed before moving along with their conversations. But unlike everyone else, the blonde man in the corner noticed her bleeding nose and froze, shocked and horrified.

He watched the girl pick herself up from the crummy

floor and wipe the blood from her face before walking into the backroom. An angry man stormed in right behind her.

"It can't be true—it can't be. It must be me," he said out loud, shaking his head in disbelief. He quickly gathered his things, ready to leave. Another patron pushed the front door open, forcing a small wind to whirl around the bar. It found the man in the corner and brought back the smell of the little girl's blood. It was unmistakable then—there was no denying it.

"In the name of Garaton, this cannot be true!" he said louder, banging his left hand on the table. His servant rose, "M-master Ganguen, what is it? What's the matter?"

Ganguen looked up at a man dressed in white and gold armor and beckoned him over. His shoulders were broad and the exposed skin on his hands and face were heavily scarred.

"Barry—go to the barkeeper and tell him to send me the girl that just fell. Do you understand me?" The tall soldier nodded before walking towards the bar, pushing everyone out of his way.

"WHAT DO YOU THINK YOU ARE DOING?!" SCREAMED THE barman at the frightened girl shrinking in front of him, "Ale is worth more than you, girl! You best remember tha!"

From out of nowhere came a giant hand, taking the barman by the shoulder. It pulled him back, twisting him like a tornado. The Child looked up through her black hair to see who saved her and why and was surprised by what she saw. He was taller than most men and bigger too. His face was full of scars, and his dark hair was oily and course. After battering the barman, he picked him up and told him his lord demanded the little girl's presence, and she wouldn't be returning that evening to finish her job.

The Child felt dread flush all over. Somehow, by the grace of the Golden Ones, she escaped the tortures her friends endured, but in that moment, she feared her time had come and there was no way out of it. Her life was in his hands, and it was nearing its end.

Heavy thoughts not meant for a child flooded her mind.

What about Tane? What would happen to her if something bad happens to me?

Her friends would be left unprotected and exposed to those monsters. Care wouldn't be able to protect them. They needed her more than ever.

What if they take them again? Her mind raced.

Both her and Care came up with a system that helped them evade the adult's grabby hands and it worked most of the time. The others that were taken were the ones out of their minds, or the ones so used to those horrific visits they stopped hiding and went along willingly.

Because Tane found her peace in the muck on the floor, the Child had to move her around whenever she could. And if she wasn't watching, Tane would put whatever was around her into her mouth which was a pain to try and take out. She also had to watch Care who would daze off from time to time as he looked out for the door. It was his duty to alert them of any oncoming hands but nearly got them plucked twice while dazed.

They were careful and kept their heads low, beneath the cots where the women never looked. They knew they could walk in and look around, but it was unlikely. And when they did come snooping around, they stepped like long-legged herons in the mud and grabbed the closest child with the least amount of muck on them.

It was later in the day when the Child got nabbed by the barman and a frazzled woman as she tried to steal a blanket from a recently taken child. They took her to the bar's kitchen as she tried her best to fight them off. She was smacked a few times before the barman gave her instructions on how to serve the ale to the patrons and warned her to never waste any of it.

The big, scary man grabbed her by the arm and dragged her through the kitchen door and back out into the main room of the bar. The blonde man watched her struggle as she tried to break free, kicking everything in her way. As he reached the table, the big man pulled out a chair and sat her down as she kicked him hard and scornfully bit into his tattooed arm.

"Barry—she's just a child!" said the blonde man, unamused by the brute who in response shrugged and stepped away. "I'm sorry little lady. My friend is not good with children," he said smiling.

"Don't touch me!" she screamed, exposing her teeth like a Warlong ready for battle. He laughed as she continued to hiss.

"You are feral, poor thing! Let's get you cleaned up," he said snapping his fingers.

Out of the corner of her eye came a gaunt man peeling out from the shadows, stopping short of their table. She heard him call the blonde man Ganguen as they spoke nicely to one another.

Sounds familiar.

She didn't notice Ganguen's servant take her arm and pull her off the chair until her feet hit the ground.

She breathed out, frustrated and exhausted.

Why does everyone pull my arm? Just ask me and I'll move!

The Child, again kicking, biting, and spitting, was taken through the building and escorted to an elegant suite where she was to wait for Ganguen. The servant bowed to her before leaving. She sneered at the gesture and turned her back to the door as he closed it shut.

At the center of the room was a mammoth bed leveled a step higher than everything else. Its wooden frame was finely whittled down and depicted gods fighting gods; the kind of art most travelers would love to see in a city like Glenloch, but the Child was uninterested.

Cascading gold curtains surrounded the bed like

whipped icing on a lovely cake. It exuded elegance and prestige. It was a luxurious dream come true for her. She wanted to run up and touch every frill but stopped before she could get into any more trouble. She gushed over everything beautiful until she remembered that Ganguen would be there soon. So, she panicked.

She searched for windows and secret openings, desperate to escape. Tired and scared, she ran dizzily to the ornate nightstand by the bed and emptied its drawers, hoping to find something sharp.

She knew what a weapon was and grew up with a myriad of them hanging all over the village. She thought they were for decorations or used for tribute when sacrificing animals until her long trip taught her otherwise. A year before, she watched a Warlong be sacrificed with a lance that always hung above the Innkeepers desk. The act was scary, but it didn't disgust her. She watched intently as its body reacted to the sensuous cut made across its throat. It convulsed so badly it nearly broke its binds. Eventually, its jerky movements slowed to a stop. She looked into its eyes which were wildly reaching for life—grasping at any chance to run and be free again. They finally settled down in its last moments alive, and a veneer of dull contentment was all that remained. She despised the villagers who cheered and laughed as it passed on. It would seem she alone cared for the creature. Afterwards, she waited patiently to see if its spirit would rise or fall to another world like the old tales said. She waited well after they took the body, but nothing happened. Just like Shen'rai, there was no smoke or cloud that rose out from its bodies. Just silence.

She rummaged through the closets, the cabinets, and chests looking for anything to protect herself with. When she thought she found something shiny under a side table, the front door opened. In came Ganguen, tired and disoriented. His hand remained on the door handle as his body swayed from side to side. Releasing the door, he staggered away, dragging his boots to meet the short steps. She trembled and her stomach ached. She felt the same fear she had while waiting in the pavilion. She noticed Ganguen had two daggers fastened to his waist. If he got too close to her, she could go for one and hope for the best.

He tripped over the last step with his right boot and swore at it as he caught himself. He then put up his other leg and fell face first on the bed.

He laughed and the Child softened. She heard a lightness in his voice, much lighter than Toms and it bounced like a child's. He seemed younger then, like her and her friends. Even so, she sneered and squinted at him as he rolled around the bed.

"Oh, whatever you bastard! I'm not going to rape you!" Ganguen said loud, laughing at his own drunkenness. She had heard that word before among the older women in the village, but they would hush up or push her out before speaking on it.

She felt as though she should fear whatever it meant and was somewhat relieved he wouldn't do it to her—if she could trust what he said.

Ganguen, still laughing, made mocking noises before talking to himself. His slurring made him difficult to understand so she crept closer but never let the daggers out of her sight.

"Mahaha... 'it's not possible' they'll say! 'You're just looking for attention!'" he said, mocking someone she couldn't place in the room.

"Ah! Why me? Grandfather, why is it always me?!"

When she reached the giant last step, she flew up and landed on the bed still acres away from the drunken man. He sat up and stared at her.

"I thought I told them to give you a bath," he scoffed before attempting to snap his fingers at some imaginary force. She tried to get his attention, but his focus was elsewhere. He closed his eyes. He tried and tried to snap but nothing happened. She was besides herself. She had never known a man act like such a child. She didn't know whether to help him snap or scold him. She felt the corners of her mouth rise and she tried not to laugh but couldn't help it—he was acting so silly.

He took a deep breath in and let it all out. A grimace formed on his face before he opened his eyes. They were full of sheer golden tears.

He's not human, she thought as she moved farther away. He followed her with his gold-speckled eyes. There was something about his face that seemed so familiar but she couldn't place it.

"Do you know who I am child?" he asked.

She shook her head.

"I am Ganguen—son of Gilton and grandson of Garaton who is the greatest of all the Golden Ones."

Suddenly, the room started to spin. She fell back on the bed to rest her eyes and mind. She cried. Of all the godly spawn to meet, it had to be Garatons. She had tried praying to him but she didn't think he listened. The first time ever was the night before the Eleventh Day in Venlet. She prayed as the witch spoke in riddles to herself and fell asleep while doing it. When he didn't respond, she gave up on him. She knew then, more than anything, that Ganguen would let her down too—it was in his blood.

He put his hand on her forehead and her dizziness

instantly went away. She looked up at him and he smiled, like how she imagined a father would.

"I hope that's better. There is so much you need to know but... You are too young yet. And I still don't know what all is going on myself. We'll need to head north to the Mountains as soon as possible," he said removing his hand from her head.

She shot up and turned to him, "I won't go without my friends!" she screamed. Fear fell across his eyes as she stared back befuddled.

She didn't like being fatherless, but it was who she was. But in that moment, she realized she didn't have to be —not anymore. A flurry of butterflies flew around her tummy as she thought about her father—who he was and what he might look like.

A father? For me?

She grinned wildly, *Like Tane and Pul?*

Then reality struck again. She couldn't leave without Tane like she had Pul. And Care had no one either. It would be all of them or none of them.

"How many friends are we talking here?" he asked, turning up his brow.

"Just Tane and Care—they're from my village," she blurted out. She stopped to think back at her words to be sure she said them correctly. No one was going to be left behind this time.

"And what of your village, where are you from?" he asked. She didn't respond and instead thought of all the other children.

What about the others in the room? What'll happen to them? Can they come too?

She realized then she couldn't leave with just Tane and Care alone. All the enslaved children would have to come too. She figured Ganguen wouldn't go for it, and he probably wouldn't let her go that easily either. She had something he wanted but she had no idea what that was.

"... and your mother, who is she?.. Have you talked to any other adults about your situation, about your father?"

As he asked more questions, a great idea came to her. She would need Tom, wherever he was, and she didn't care about the cost. This time, they would all be free for good.

16

———

THE CHILD SPENT THE REST OF THE NIGHT WATCHING Ganguen as he slept, gripping his daggers. He had fallen asleep after she told him a story about her mother and father which wasn't true. He didn't seem pleased and at one point called her a fibber. Whatever he wanted from her would not come easy. The more questions he asked, the more she resisted. Him saving her from the barman showed her that she was at least valuable to him, but she wasn't sure for how long. She was willing to go along with his plan if it meant her and her friends might survive.

She was eager to leave and be with Tane who might have assumed the worst had happened. She felt bad enough leaving her before, and she didn't want to let her down like that again.

As Ganguen snored and slept like a baby, the Child crept to the door and tapped at it ever so slightly. She waited but nothing happened. She then banged on it furiously until it opened forcefully from the opposite side. She fell on her behind and winced. The gaunt servant from before looked down at her and sighed. He laughed before closing the door and locking her in.

She got up and stomped back to the bed defeated.

"You cannot leave, they'll do bad things to you," said Ganguen with a lazy and soft voice, "we don't condone these things, you know? Our line helped create this... Barbarianism when the first of Man was made from Zel. But the times have changed. My grandfather doesn't participate in any of it—he never did," he chuckled, "if they only knew how much he didn't care."

After some more small talk, she gave in and agreed to stay in the suite raucous-free. She hesitantly laid her head on one of the many bright and glossy pillows that were stained a soft goldish pink held together by a shimmering lace. Upon impact, her head felt weightless and hollow, a sensation she had only ever known in the Otherworld. There were thousands of miles between her and the ground, and she was just beginning to ascend.

Pillows in Venlet were hardly ever used, especially by the working men, farmers, and laborers. They felt it made their minds soft and thus their bodies as well, and the Councilmen were said to have used them only during the warmer months. And no one bought their own pillows. Rather, they were gifts from Holfenian relatives during Oxem's holidays.

The Child had a pillow she kept hidden in her room in the barn in a crawl space above the livestock. It had been left outside of a home in the village and so she took it. The many bits of straw that poked out from it didn't bother her. But in that moment, that old sack of weeds felt like rocks in a blanket, and she didn't miss at all.

For the first time in her life, she felt like a queen sleeping soundly in her pretty castle in the clouds. From somewhere close she could smell fresh wildflowers hidden from her till then. She had never been treated so well and all he had offered her was a safe place to sleep for the night. But even with all the luxuries of a lord at her disposal, her mind drifted back to her friends who she knew were sleeping on the floor, in their own waste, waiting to be picked and abused again. And they were waiting for her to return. She felt herself get heavy as she fell back to Zel, again, where she knew she had to stay.

Upon awaking, her and Ganguen came to an agreement: he would buy as many of the slave children he could and take them miles away from Glenloch; he would then release them safely to the best cities and villages along the way to the mountains; and he would ensure that the Order of Garatos would never step foot in the Valley of Venoxem again.

She feared her request was too much for the near god to fulfill but he accepted the terms with little opposition. And his terms were much simpler: she would have to stay with him, in his party indefinitely. She begged and begged him to take Tane as well, but he refused outright.

"I will not take one of your MANY friends! If I accept one, what's to say you won't want another? And another?! I may be a high-ranking lord in this realm, but I'm not made of gold!" he said laughing.

It was known to all that the gods were indeed made of gold. They were the fathers and mothers of the minerals found in Zel and the other worlds. In ancient times, the Golden Ones would give their metal-laced blood to those most worthy - warriors and heroes who fought to the ends of Zel for their cause. But there were some humans who took the sacred blood turned cursed to live eternally as decaying corpses. And they dwelt where no one dare go.

Since he could remember, Ganguen had it drilled into his mind that he was to be an important man, like his father who was a savior and a god. However, he couldn't reach those heights and fell below his brothers who were more like their father but still couldn't meet the standards he set.

Ganguen was, by all accounts, the runt of the family and was thrown out of the palace after his father left. For years, he searched high and low for something, anything that would put him at the top and help him outshine his brothers forever. And he found that in the little girl. He was a desperate man willing to do whatever was necessary to secure his place in his family and with the other gods once and for all.

After the two shook hands, the Child was led back to her prison cell to avoid making the women who ran it suspicious. As she walked along, her stomach twisted in knots. Even though she wanted to tell her friends all about her deal, something within her told her not to trust Ganguen, a completely different feeling than the one she had about Tom. When she thought back on his words, she remembered he promised her he would buy as many slave children as he could.

But how many would that be? One or two?

She wanted all the children to be free and she absolutely didn't want them to be sent to a different prison somewhere else. As much as she never wanted to see that room again, her next part of the plan depended on cooperation from the other kids.

When she found her friends in the full room, she told them the plan. Tane was overjoyed and excited, but Care just carried on staring as if she had said nothing. They were relieved she had not been abused in the way they had but they could tell by the look on her face she was terrified with what came next.

"Oh, Golden Ones, thank you!" Tane said, turning to the Child, "that's great news Chil! We can finally get out of here and live free again." She was beaming and tried her best to remain quiet while jumping up and down. She looked over to Care who, still in his far-off glare, shook his head.

"We can't leave them here," he said solemnly.

Like lightning, Tane slapped the back of her neck in a way she hadn't before. The Child, shocked, grabbed her and shook her as she thrashed in her arms.

"I want to go! I won't stay here! I'll kill myself if I stay!" she screamed which caused the women outside the door to come in and investigate. Before the Child could calm her down, Tane was taken up into the shoulders of a giant man and escorted out of the room. Before she knew it, all the children were hysterical. They had been listening to their conversation the whole time, furious and emotional when learning the Child hadn't been touched. Rage and sadness spiraled from every corner of the disgraceful room as they, once innocent and carefree children, hit and bit each other with the sole intent of doing serious harm. Without warning, a battered kid took The Child by the shoulders and slammed her against the wall, banging her head against it.

Care tried his best to hold back the crazed child beating his friend but was too weak. He held on to their back for dear life as they continued to pummel her. Mayhem continued to spread as various women and men in white robes joined the violence. Turned around and facing the wall, the Child heard the eerie wails of battle twist above her head like the wind on a warm summer night before a calamitous storm, and she screamed. As soon as she was able to pull away from the wall, everything turned to black like it had at the pavilion and in the woods with the witch. She knew then her Otherself was in her place. She was stronger than her and could withstand all the weight of her world plummeting to death around her. She sat in a shallow pool in the center of her mind's world and wept.

"You're mad if you think this will go well with the people of Glenloch!" said a robust man in a beautiful gold and white robe. He constantly shifted his weight from one armrest to the other in his black leather chair, looking rather uncomfortable with every pose. He looked at Ganguen in complete shock over what he said.

"The Eleventh Day is canceled by order of Ganguen—son of Gilton and grandson of Garaton. Either submit or suffer at the hands of the Golden Ones," Ganguen said sternly, looking deep into the eyes of the elderly, round man rich with jewels around his neck.

The Debusse of Glenloch was one of a select few who controlled what happened in the city. He grew his wealth from his many businesses catering to the needs of the endless travelers that visited the city, giving them whatever they so craved. And with his position he was able to control the city people into working for free by offering them discounts and free services if they returned a significant amount of their earnings to him.

They pushed the Eleventh Day onto their people, condoning violence and hate and forcing away the ideals and moral systems from the outside world by praising debauchery without consequences and advocating forgiveness no matter how terrible the act. All of Garaton's grandchildren were aware of this since the passing of Gilton. Their ties with Glenloch and their Debusse gave them first pick of the exotic goods that came through the seaport as well as undying secrecy when they too delved into the dark pleasures hidden in the pavilion.

Ganguen wasn't a part of any of his brothers' affairs and preferred to spend his endless credit on booze and mature women. These were only a few reasons out of many why he was given the title of a high-ranking lord instead of something more. But that would all change once he showed the girl to his brothers who would have to acknowledge him as their equal after all.

The Debusse, whom Ganguen called Mika, sniffled as Gangeun got up from his seat and walked away from the conversation and towards the door.

"The people will riot, you know! Nothing good will come of this!" said Mika as his office door closed and he was left alone.

Ganguen walked out into the street outside of Glenloch's cityhall and shook off his nerves. It was a short walk from the pavillon where his ticket to godlihood rested. The city's best parts were limited to this small area where the lesser residents, those who worked and toiled to death just to barely survive slept underground.

He looked down the main road—a giant mass of white gold gifted to Glenloch by the Spai'kits from the east who on many occasions traded with the city, offering their slaves in exchange for dubels and textiles. The further the road went into the city, the closer it came to the ocean where it was no longer a bright white gold but rather a dirty dark brown. Overtime, pieces crumbled away and turned to dust.

He knew how hard it was to build the damn thing. He watched it from beginning to end many years before. Thousands of laborers died while working off their debts and many others were punished to death for trying to take pieces of the golden road for themselves.

He sighed. It was the Eleventh Day and some commotion from a nearby street signaled it had already begun. It would only take a few hours before the whole city heard the news, and a few hours longer before they started to riot as well as continue their usual crimes regardless of his demands. He had half the day to take his treasure out of the city safely.

When he wandered to the little girl's quarters, the room was empty and had been expertly cleaned. When he asked where the children had gone, he was told they were to be burned for energy under the millhouse. When he heard the harsh fate of the children and that the little girl was last seen unconscious and among those to be burned, he panicked.

He was the only member of his family that broke down and his brothers made fun of him for it. They were ruthless and he could never keep up with their cruel ways. A few years before, his first middle brother Gargo fought a legion of defiant Umeki people north of the mountains, evaded their ancient magic and harsh terrains, and walked away from the battle victorious. He told Ganguen in passing that he had no fears during the fight but regretted leaving their nasty women behind before raping them. Ganguen shook those terrible thoughts from his mind and swiftly made his way to the millhouse.

THE CHILD HAD BEEN THROWN ONTO A HEAP OF DEAD children and those almost dead by a giant man with a large shovel big enough to carry four or five children at a time. He scooped them up and flung their lifeless bodies into a giant kiln used by many workers within the mill that never questioned the actions of this creature.

When he arrived, Ganguen ran to the secret depths of the mill where the retched kiln bellowed and begged like a hungry, petulant brat. By his command, the lumbering giant stopped. His arrival came too late for so many innocent children who were taken by the fire, some while alive, screaming till they died. Hundreds of little bones steamed white as snow in the kiln as it cooled down.

The Child laid in a pile farthest from the kiln. A little girl and boy held her tightly, weeping and coughing as she appeared to be sleeping soundly. It took Ganguen a few minutes to find the three children through the immense smoke everywhere. He took them outside and onto the white-gold road.

Tane, refusing to let go of her friend, took her first big breath. In and out, like her mother told her to whenever she got upset. She forced the motions of breath onto her friend hoping she would follow.

She took in a few more big breaths and looked up into the sky. The sun was right above them. She smiled and closed her eyes. She remembered how Pul would remind them all the time when it was time to eat and could not go an hour without food. He once convinced the two that noontime was the only time you could eat whatever you want without getting sick. But when they tried, they got ill and pooped their pants.

She beamed. The abuse was over. Now, all she had to do was wake up Chil whose chest was moving up and down.

THE CHILD AWOKE IN PAIN AND INSIDE A SMALL PINE BOX. SHE would see them outside the Innkeepers whenever a sickness killed someone. It was held up high in a procession through the village streets before the deceased went through their last rites. She kicked and clawed at the wood in front of her desperate to get out. She didn't notice she was moving until the box came to a halt. She heard a loud thump before some light trickled through a small opening on her side.

She closed her eyes and kept them shut. If she were dead, what difference would it make. And if she were still alive, she was a prisoner again and would rather be dead.

Her worries washed away when she opened an eye and saw a small, familiar face smiling at her. It was Tane, still dirty and bruised, but glowing like she used to. She threw the lid open, hurled her arms in, and gave her a big hug. The Child, unsure if she were dead or alive, finally left the box after much persuasion from Tane who assured her they were safe. She crouched down low and hid her head once she saw the line of soldiers following their caravan.

A familiar voice called out to her, "Chil, you're okay now, we got you out girl!" It was Ganguen in white and gold armor looking strong and confident alongside Barry, his taller and battle-friendly friend. She looked around and found Care in the back of the line walking alongside a soldier, talking to him while he carried his sword. His usually stern face had turned soft and curious, as a young boys should.

She was in disbelief. What she was seeing was nothing like what they experienced sometime before.

"How long have I been sleeping?" she asked, walking with Tane whose arm rested on her shoulders. Tane was shorter and had to stand on her tip toes just to balance her arm. She could see Tane's mother and father in her already and was certain that one day she would have their graceful, tall slender body as well as her mother's well-known sunburst locks. She would be the most beautiful woman in the world and most importantly, she would be alive and not a slave. The thought that somehow in all this violence and death, they may live to see that age made her tear up.

A few hours later, the party settled down for camp. Her friends told her about the journey so far and of all the amazing creatures they had seen along the way. And apparently while she was out cold, they took care of her—feeding her and helping her in any way they could.

At first, she felt guilty and expressed it to Tane, but the spitfire of a girl would have none of it. She took the Child and Care by each arm and told them it was going to be okay. She held them close and promised them she would always be there as they watched the fire grow and then diminish well before it was due.

They then watched a clumsy young soldier try to rebuild it. He couldn't quite get the flint to spark. He couldn't have been more than thirteen years but had his own sword which was dull and stained like the others.

The Child looked down and away.

All of this, for me?

She observed the living and breathing people around her, protecting her like a wounded animal. At first, she wasn't sure what she was supposed to do or what would happen next. But realization hit. She started to remember the deal she made with Ganguen and his stipulations. All the newly found peace and comfort she recently acquired melted away. She didn't want to see her friends go away and could never trust them with anyone else ever again. Her first plan, telling them about the deal started with disaster but somehow led them away from Glenloch. But it was only a matter of time before they were separated for good if she didn't do something and quick. And this time, she wasn't going to tell either of them the plan until it was ready.

When the entire party fell asleep that night, she crept to the forests edge. She hadn't been near one since Shen'rai's death. She left her body there where no one could claim it —*alone and cold in the woods forever.*

She shrugged off her anxious thoughts and tried her best to focus. She stopped short of a small sycamore tree and paused. Something inside told her to close her eyes and kneel and she did.

On a stretch of exposed soil, she drew pictures like the ones from Dreqtaton's book. She didn't know if doing this would work but that same feeling kept her going. She knew she had to find Tom. His magic could help them escape. Then, they could finally go home.

She drew more animals but stopped when a twig snapped nearby. She remained calm and confident, knowing that whatever made that sound was sent to help. On instinct, she asked whatever it was if she could look at it, keeping her head down respectfully. It grunted. When she looked up, she gasped. A big gloriously bright stag stood above her. Its antlers were like branches with randomly plotted pointers growing out in every direction, except for two that went downward like the one from before.

From afar, it may have looked like any dirty deer, but up close it looked like something from another world. Its coat was brown, but a vibrant gold outlined it and black spirals were all over its body. Its eyes were a pure black with pieces of gold that illuminated the dark around them. And the longer she looked, the more the colors popped out into existence—like a cauldron full of black wine and gold, where silver and purple stars swirled into each other endlessly. She was mesmerized.

The being radiated energy that found its way into her bones, pulsing into her heart through her heartbeat. And once it found it, she could feel a mass—something warm and cold, soft, and sticky leave through her chest. She looked down to see it, but nothing was there. She could feel something but couldn't grab it. She looked at the stag and it nodded softly; its confetti eyes growing ever brighter.

And in an instant, she felt a different mass leave the stag and fly towards her. She was without words and couldn't breathe. She felt both the first and second energies come together into a frenzy. And as quickly as they joined, they separated with hers smashing back into her chest. She regained her breath and looked back to the stag who had left.

She fell on her bottom.

Was that Dreqtaton? She asked, falling asleep where she sat. She was jerked awake shortly after by giant hands grabbing her shoulders. The men laughed and spoke about her like most adults had and teased her for getting lost like a baby.

All the next day, the children walked with the parade, taking turns resting in the moving box. The Child felt nauseous all day. She had been given something by the stag but didn't know what to think of it and she needed a way out, for her and her friends and fast.

The camp stopped before nightfall to rest near a mass of oak trees. When everyone went to bed, she pretended to sleep, closing her eyes every time a soldier walked by. She waited until the soldier on guard fell asleep to get up and search the camp. Soon after, a dim light traveled into the woods which she followed closely. It didn't take her long to reach the small gathering of men sitting around a small fire. She hid behind a tree as she looked to see who was there. Around in a circle was Ganguen, Barry, and a few of his men. Though they spoke low, she could still hear what they were saying.

"How in Reicher's Realm are we going to do that, Gangue?" asked Barry whose accent was thick and explosive even as a whisper. Ganguen moved around on the log rubbing his chin, seemingly hesitant to answer the question.

"These kids are smart, ma lord. They'll know what we're doing by days end tomorrow," said a man opposite him who fiddled with his knife.

"Look," Ganguen said before breathing in slowly, "Guys —I know you don't want to be here. The nearest village is a few miles north and the Order won't be able to catch us after that. We'll sell the two smaller ones unless one of you wants them and we'll break off. I'll take the little bastard to my brothers in Gilton City and give you your dubels after. We can do this without anyone knowing so long as we stay off the road and you follow my lead."

They all laughed at him and made numerous comments, some raising their hands jokingly to take the children for themselves. They mentioned the village could cause problems for them. After more jokes, they concluded that if the villagers didn't cooperate, they'd be given an Eleventh Day experience.

The Child was horrified.

I just want to go home, she thought holding back tears. She had put her faith into Ganguen and he betrayed her. She felt her breathe quicken which caused her throat to burn. Her upper back ached as her shoulders caved in. She turned to the camp and sprinted silently to her friends.

"Tane, Care—wake up!" she said, shaking her peaceful friends awake. They had been sleeping soundly and were surrounded by armed soldiers too tired and drunk to notice the commotion. She told the two what she had heard in full detail, stopping to breathe every few lines.

"That can't be true, he saved us! And he said we could stay with him!" Care cried out, arms folded and lips pouting. Tane looked at him and then at Chil, her eyes void of life.

"Care, we need to leave," she said coldly as her and the Child picked him up. He was half their size and almost all bones. She put her hand over his mouth and the Child held his wild legs as they hurriedly escaped.

They ran into the woods with nothing but the clothes on their backs. After a few moments passed, a bellowing horn sung from behind them. It was no doubt Ganguen and his party following their path. The two girls dropped their small friend, and the Child took his hand as they ran. He cried but followed them, scared of what would happen if he fell behind.

They came across a clearing full of fields with high grass that stood well above their heads. They stopped and waited there for a moment until the low rumbles of bloodhounds rang through the clearing.

"I didn't know they had hounds!" screamed Tane as the three jumped up and headed opposite the dogs into another part of the forest, aimlessly running.

The children knew then they were fighting a losing battle. They had to stop, to regain their strength and breath. The Child felt the angry men approaching from behind and their hateful energy was slowly suffocating her. And as their rage seeped into her heart, so did hers grow like dough rising in the heat. Her vision blurred and her jaw clenched unfathomably tight. Her muscles hardened like a warriors before battle, prepared for the pain and death of war.

When the men reached the children, they held their

swords and axes out high, teasing them with threats of pain and horror. The Child waited for the first blow—waited and waited. Her arms covered her head, and she didn't move. And she continued to cower until she felt no wind and heard not a single sound around her. She slowly unraveled her spine and stood up. She stared ahead, stunned and confused. Ganguen and his party were in full swing, aiming their weapons at her and her friends. They were ready to attack but stopped. It was then she realized the whole world had gone still. She walked over to Ganguen whose eyes remained alive, darting left and right though his body remained in its battle pose.

"Is it time for us to play a game, child?" a low voice asked from behind her. She turned and saw a man with armor blacker than the blackest night and a helm with horns that pointed downwards, like the stag from the night before.

"Dreqtaton, you evil creature. You'll pay for this!" said Ganguen through gritted teeth.

He laughed and snapped his fingers, releasing Ganguen from his spell. He fell to his hands and knees gasping. The Child turned to the god but was too afraid to say anything. He laughed again. He then wiggled his finger at the children in the same way Lordteller would when they gossiped during his performance.

"Can you not smell her blood?!" asked Ganguen, begging for a response.

Dreqtaton sighed, "She will be in your company no longer. Send my regards to my brother!"

He snapped again and the world around the children flipped on its axis. They were off the ground and flying instantly through all of Zel in what felt like a blink of an eye.

And when The Child did blink, her and her friends were standing in snow near jagged rocks. A strong, sharp wind caused their legs to jitter. It pushed down on them, more and more with every moment.

Dreqtaton watched the children fight to stand up against the strong wind. He laughed once more before waving his giant arm over his head which made the wind go away.

"Where are we?" asked the Child to the god, speaking on behalf of her friends who were terrified. She knew he was smiling under his helmet but was freaked out with not knowing why. He walked over to her and rested his gilded glove on her shoulder which felt like nothing. He motioned for them to go up the path laid ahead of them. They were up in the clouds, surrounded by rocks and boulders and cliffs. They were atop the Mountains of the Predicated.

They found an entrance with Dreqtaton trailing behind constantly waving them to move forward. The Child stopped, unsure whether to trust again.

Even though she didn't know him, the energy from the stag the night before was pure. She was willing to take another chance and believe it led them there for a good reason.

She beckoned her friends to walk towards the gigantic boulder covering what appeared to be an entrance. As they approached, it rocked in place slowly before rolling to the side, revealing their way in. Walls with hanging candles led down a dark hallway. A figure quickly approached, its shadow growing larger as it came closer to the doorway.

The Child turned to speak to Dreqtaton but he was already gone. She smiled and under her breath she whispered, "Thank you Tom."

17

THE FAINT WHISPERS FROM THE BIRDS OUTSIDE SIGNALED THE
start of morning to those resting silently in the darkened
home. The night's cold breath still lingered and what was
left of the windows had not yet been touched by the Sun.

The home was a sturdy one, formidable enough to withstand the horrific event weeks before. It was one of the first
homes made of stone and mud ages ago by the ex-
slaves. They toiled for decades to grow their humble
community and their strength and resilience were evident
in the work that still stood. The house didn't go away
unscathed, however, and suffered massive damage to its
windows and doors from the mad attack of the Order of
Garatos.

This home belonged to brothers Munta and Unta—the
blacksmith and locksmith of the village. Their trades were
passed down from father to son since before their ancestors
were slaves. Over time, the family developed a unique style
that became one of many hallmarks exclusive to the Valley
of Venoxem. On every helm, glove, sword, and axe Munta

smithed was their family's crest: an angry Warlong and Cloncluck, head-to-head posed to fight one another. The Warlong was slim, clean, and confident as the Cloncluck appeared disproportionally large, dirty, and crazed. The Warlong was covered in valiant gold and crimson while the Cloncluck was colorless except for the dirt-red blood that dripped from its beak.

The Warlong was the villages most sacred animal. During the months after snow as they migrated from one area to the next, able men would steal their best male and female and breed them till death. After, those of their children that met Garaton's standards were slain once a year during the warmer months. It was a tradition that started with the ex-slaves and continued, year after year. For centuries though, the villagers wanted to stop but feared the gods' lethal retaliation.

They did benefit from their unique agreement. Crops that used to fail and famine that often devastated the valley were ancient history and not a single farmer or laborer was without work and were always looking for more help with the overgrowth of vegetation each sunny season. Likewise, the mystical and darker animals that once threatened them and made hunting rather difficult fell back to thrive in the deeper parts of the forests.

Munta was a skilled metal-artist who was careful when it came to his work. He would spend hours if not days carving and hammering the most intricate details into the most difficult of metals. He was known for delaying orders by a season or two just to be certain it was done to his liking. But his customers didn't mind. Rather, they preferred the wait knowing what they received would be one of a kind.

He was sought out by all the people of Zel with his most frequent requests for service coming from no other than the Order of Garatos. They liked to keep track of all his orders, wherever they went. They were on the hunt for works that went against their god and believed he was involved in their making. For those orders, he would work in secret and have it sent out with the merchants who also carried the highly illegal Veri Meek Powder. Those were the most beautiful of metalworks that sometimes depicted the Warlong beaten and bloodied under a triumphant Cloncluck or another creature depending on the request.

Unta was the older brother and when he wasn't locksmithing he took down his brother's orders and handled most of the dubel dealings for both their businesses. Messenger birds and notes out of thin air would arrive all day long with requests for Munta's services and he was there to catch them.

Unta was known to be a wise and clever man who never forgot a face and could only dream of forgetting some of the horrible things he had seen. When he was young, the Order of Garatos came through on an Eleventh Day and murdered many. Though the damage was immense, it wasn't nearly as devastating as the one most recent. His father, Mantu, was a strong and skilled axeman that no man could disarm. He rushed his family and many others to the church before the Order got to them.

He would often dream of that day and the many days after. The dreams always felt real to him—like he was there again with a small knife and some harsh peat in his hands. His least favorite memory was of himself and the other young men collecting the dead bodies from the streets to be cut up away from the village. His mother stood over him and watched, crying as she held his baby brother in her arms. He never forgot the sights he saw nor the terrible smell of death that remained in the streets and in the trees for years after.

He sat in his family home overhearing the birds first whispers of morning. He couldn't sleep—not since before the Eleventh Day. He had gone out into the streets day and night looking for survivors who needed help. He housed several people who rested and healed on beds and on chairs, in constant pain and agony. Only a few died in his care, the rest were slowly getting better.

The more seriously wounded he took to the church where they could be with the Pleas who prayed for guidance and for healing. Although the church was a safe place for many to go and receive medicine, it was also where those who were close to death or expected to die rested. It was the closest building to an open enough area of the valley where the surviving men could take their bodies for their rites of passage in the end.

Munta was one of many men who volunteered to cut up the mounds of remains. Some of those men chose to wear blindfolds, chopping at whatever flesh and bones they felt around them, not ready to see the familiar faces of the dead, while others went straight in without thought and were left with everlasting scars on their spirit. Munta tried to do it with his eyes open and did well at first by staring at anything else but the eyes. But no matter how unrecognizable the bodies became, he couldn't resist looking for theirs and began to find them everywhere. He saw their blues and greens and knew who they belonged to—the unwelcomed gift of memory he shared with his brother. For his mind's sake, he gave in and wore the blindfold for days until most of the bodies were small enough to burn.

Regardless of how horrible they knew the preparations

were for their Rite of Oxem, it played an integral part of their people's lives since the beginning, and it guaranteed them a beautiful Afterlife where all their family and friends waited - eternally young, happy, and most importantly, together. Shen'rai was the last to perform the Rite of Oxem for the many fallen decades before and was expected to do it again. Her power was said to be strong enough to bring all their souls to the Afterlife. When the Order finally left, the surviving villagers searched for her everywhere. Eventually, a young man found her body black and bloated a half a day's walk north of the village in the thickest part of the dense forest. He was sent to the church after his erratic thoughts of death and maggots became too much for him, and he stayed there indefinitely.

The few remaining members of the Councilmen agreed to have a young woman, pure and untouched perform the massive ritual in her place. It was difficult to find such a girl but hidden deep within the church's catacombs was one, scared and unaware of the terror that was inflicted on her family and friends. The new Councilmen, including Unta, gave the girl the words and instructions and prayed all night for the ritual to go smoothly. If it was performed correctly, the smoke from the ashes would turn black to a dark turquoise. If the smoke remained black, then the ritual failed. This meant all the souls of the dead would stay in Zel and never reunite with their family, friends, and ancestors in the Afterlife which, to them, was a fate worse than spending an eternity in Reicher's Realm. Luckily, with every pile burned and every rite performed so came the colors that signaled the transition was a success. Shen'rai's body was also cut up and thrown into the pile where she was given her way into the graces of their divine eternity. A large area of the valley's lush grass was burnt badly enough to never grow green again.

Munta and Unta were two of only a few of the original Councilmen that lived. The survivors relied on their words of comfort. They had the unenviable position of deciding whether to respectfully burn more of their neighbors—men, women, and babies—or scour for more resources for the injured, hungry, and cold. Luckily for them, merchants steadily began to arrive a few days after the Eleventh Day and were happy to provide supplies to those in need on credit and made no bones about being paid anytime soon.

Aside from the horrific violence they inflicted, the Order also stole most of Venlet's wealth and dubels. They reached their biggest steal at the Inn were many kept their reserves and savings and where each Councilman kept their earnings. Unta, the practical, had without hesitation put a lot of the villages received taxes aside for an emergency, not trusting the Councilmen who would spend large chunks of undocumented funding on clothing and trinkets rather than helping those less fortunate. And when those reserves began to run dry after the merchants took their share, Unta recalled the Notekeeper Caren telling him she kept stashes of untaxed dubels in her library as well. It was her way of keeping her family from starving with the little income the Councilmen gave her. Surprisingly, the Order of Garatos destroyed everything in her home but the library which spanned the length of one long wall. Hidden in every book were a few dubels which eventually added to more than what the Councilmen had saved. This wasn't enough to save the village and bring it back to what it once was, but it was a start.

He got up and made his way to the door to search for more funding. Munta, sleeping with his mouth open, drool falling from both sides of his mouth didn't stir. He only slept because he had to. Upon waking, he would spend another full day looking for more survivors and force his hand, once more, to cut up the dead bodies of his people.

Unta looked up at the staircase as he walked, reluctant to leave his bedridden guests unattended regardless of how little he could help them. He sighed. He jolted up the stairs and went faster than his mind could stop him. He wanted to see one of his guests before leaving—a boy who had been sleeping his days away since being found. Unta spent a lot of time caring for him but couldn't recognize his face covered in harsh burns and pink scars.

He walked quietly through the second level, careful to not disturbed those in pain. He felt their fury pulse around him as he walked along the corridor, passing room after room. So many wanted to die and would tell him that as he changed their bandages and fed them scraps. Those that lost their families wanted to die the most. Sadly, the most angry and morbid person in the entire village laid opposite the door he stood in front of. He dreaded the moment that poor boy would wake and hoped he remembered nothing of that evil day.

He slowly opened the door and held his breath as he closed it. A deep wheezing came from the bed at the center of the room. He sighed once more before turning around to face the boy. It was evident the child was in enormous pain. Most of his body was covered in burns except for a few spots on his arms, legs, and chest. Debris from what was left of his family home had buried him alive. Munta was the one to hear his whimpers and saved him. He brought him to his brother to be cared for and held him for a while until he slept.

Unta sat in a disfigured chair next to the boy. His bed

sheets were red with blood. He looked over the sheets and pillows, trying to figure out how he could remove them without waking the suffering child.

"Am I dead?" the boy asked with parted lips. Unta looked over him with tears in his eyes.

"No, my boy, you survived, like so many others," he paused, "Can you tell me your name?" Unta asked.

The boy stirred and whimpered. He tried for hours to remember who he was but couldn't.

"You'll remember boy—don't you worry. WE'LL get you back to new in no time!" Unta said gently patting the boy on the leg, "Now, I'm gonna go and grab you some new linen. Maybe you'll remember something by then, Nameless Wonder," Unta said before walking out of the room, closing the door behind him.

In an instant, a thousand and one memories flooded the boy's mind. There was one he knew that had no name, but it wasn't him. It was a girl with black hair and interesting eyes! But there was another next to her with pretty blonde hair and a green dress, elaborately embroidered—something she always wore and always got dirty.

"How do I know that" he asked out loud as he tried to sit up.

He could hear their laughter, poking and mocking him as he stood in between them. Image after image of the two girls flashed before his eyes. Swirling black hair collided with near white and made a new color so bright it hurt his eyes.

His head started to ache. He forced his charred hands onto his eyes to block out that light. He screamed in anguish as the images and noises grew louder. For several moments their voices and words formed a cacophony he could not escape. And when he moved in his bed, the scrapping of his burns made him weep.

Then, in an instant, he heard it.

The little blonde girl cried out, "Come on, don't be a meanie—"

Pul. His name was Pul.

18

———

It took Munta awhile to calm Pul down; he had been screaming at the top of his lungs. He used all his strength to stop the poor boy from yanking and scratching at his tender arms and thinning hair.

After settling down, Munta gently explained to the boy how the Order of Garatos came into the village that morning during the weekly meeting, and that it was an Eleventh Day; how the very men he knew since birth and who his father had known since he too was a boy stood as tall as they could and fought the Order of Garatos to their death. He explained in great detail how they tried to save their village and how they willingly gave their lives in the hopes that their small sacrifice could help the women and children escape inevitable harm.

There had always been a plan in place in case this happened. All who could make it to the Church of Siracon were to stay there and wait for the day to end. There was plenty of room for everyone and the goddess allowed the Pleas to make more if need be. But this time, the monsters caught everyone off guard. They had no time to run even as their husbands, fathers, and sons used their bodies to give them more. And rather than go straight to the Church, some ran home to retrieve whatever weapon they had.

"I ran to my metal keep and grabbed an axe for each hand and hid a hatchet in my belt," he said, "We all did our best, you know. It didn't matter, you see. We were no match, not this time. I have never seen so many men in all my days!

"And your father," he stopped, "was the first one to approach them. He..." he laughed as he held up his arms, "asked for a parlay, like this. He was a brave man, you know? Prus and the other Councilmen hid back, behind their wives. Their blood was just as thick of Oxem as yours and your dads to be acting so foolish," he said putting a hand to Pul's head, "A young soldier—gods know what he was called, they all looked the same—approached your father and," he stopped and looked at Pul again who lowered his head. They both knew what happened next.

"And what about my friends?" Pul asked with a raspy voice, head still hung low. The room was silent as he waited for an answer. Unlike before, he expected to hear the truth though he knew it would hurt. Tears fell down his face as Munta told the rest of the story, of how most of the women were brutalized and their children ripped away from them, never to be seen again. He sobbed deep and heavy as a surreal pain came out from under his skin onto his chest. He loved his father and was heartbroken his entire family had been murdered, that their bodies were burned to rite already. And when he realized his best friends were gone too, his heart hurt worst. He swore to look after them and protect them no matter what happened and failed.

"That little one, what was her name again? Dirty and fatherless? We found her, coming out of the woods. She looked even dirtier than ever before! We held her for a moment, we tried to keep her safe—we could have saved one of them," Munta shook his head, "but she ran to them. She ran to be with that daughter of Shane. Oh, gods have wrath on the men who hurt such a beauty!" he said into his hands. When he closed his eyes, face after face popped through his mind. They were the living and deceased whose expressions were of fear and despair. He watched Shane along with other women reach out past the soldiers violating them, humiliating them in front of their family, their husbands, sons, and daughters. The torture was unending. The thought of the Order of Garatos made the ball of hatred nestled in Muntas' chest grow larger by the day. When all who were massacred had their rites performed, he promised himself he would never cut up and burn another body unless it belonged to one of those monsters.

Not all that happened after the Eleventh Day was bad and Munta told Pul everything since. He eventually left him to rest and promised to do the same. Before he left, Pul asked him to prop-open the broken window so he could see the beautiful sunny day forming. This time last year, the three wild children had gone to a riverbed nearby and jumped around like crazy dogs. They got bit to pieces by biting bugs till it was near dark and time to go home. He could feel the warmth of the sun on his bed and forgave the minor discomfort it gave him.

He tried to cover his eyes but stopped when the burns on his hands and face ached. He wanted to get up and leave more than anything. He would rather be a slave or dead—to be with his friends or his family then to be bed bound and covered in burns. His stomach turned. His lower back felt so tight it was going to break. He wished his mother was there, for the first time ever to care for him and make him feel better like she used to. She knew how much he loved the expensive Brown Cow's milk and would fetch it for him when he was ill. And as his mother washed his feet and back, his older brother would barge in with news of the village—about the young women whose breast had grown since they last spoke.

He sighed. He would have done anything to hear the pitter-pattering of his little brother's feet or the many wails of his little baby sister. His family were a part of him, like the asymmetrical limbs of a great oak tree, but, like many trees his was cut down to a stump with no branches and leaves left. He closed his eyes to forget about everything for a while and focused on his many pains which were easier for him to bare.

AFTER FINDING EXTRA DUBELS IN THE HOMES NEAR THE Notekeepers, Unta brought them straight to the survivors huddled and hungry together in the few homes left standing. He then took to task and acquired the help of several young men who either hid or fought on the Eleventh Day. They were to go out and find the herbs, wrappings, clothing, and supplies the Pleas were in desperate need of to do their work. At the church, generous people still healing from their own wounds hovered over beds and pews full of the deathly sick to help in any way they could.

Unta avoided the church at all costs. He couldn't bare seeing his neighbors in such a way. Some had infections that grew to be black and rotted, festering to the bone, and the odor it gave off filled the church in an unbearable stench. The village didn't have the medicine to stop the infection from worsening and there was no one alive who could deal with the matter safely. The Mercymen who were trained to save the body and spirit from any ailment were taken out to an expansive part of the valley and flayed alive. That left the Pleas to take in the wounded and dying. They were unprepared and completely overwhelmed, and unfortunately made many mistakes.

When a person was close to death, to appease the easily irritated Siracon, the Pleas would take them outside where their cries for mercy would go unanswered until they succumbed to their death. Parity hated this practice. She would follow those poor people and give them food and company before they passed on.

Somewhere deep within her was an aching to help others that finally came out after Plea Marcus Daniels threw her into the thick of the suffering. She couldn't refuse those who were in such pain right before her eyes. Though hesitant at first, she grew to liking the way they needed her. She was finally in a position she felt was closer to her true self and kept doing it even after they stopped asking her.

She grew up in Holfenya and would take long walks with her father up and down the city streets, stopping at one house and then another until they got tired of it. Every home had a family that offered them warm food and accepted them in no matter what time of day it was; they could stay and eat for as long as they liked.

Everybody in her community was a member of the family in that sense. Whenever her mother cooked, she made extra just in case, and their friends would stop by, and her father would graciously open the door and embrace them as family. That sense of peace and comfort, that nothing bad could ever happen was her whole life—at least until he came to her.

She awoke from her memory when a Plea scurried over to her, tired and worried.

"What is it Plea Eric—what's wrong?" she asked.

"The boy that survived the fire is awake now. Unta told me. He is in great pain, and he remembers," he said, "he is Pul Venam, the friend of that Tane child and the nameless girl."

Parity peered at him with pure fire.

How did he not know that was my child?

From Holfenya to Venlet's southern entrance were whispers of it, ones that followed her wherever she went; she could never escape it.

"P-p-please, could you go to him. The men tried to make him comfortable, but he needs a nurturing hand, you see," he said nodding before running off to kneel at a broken pew where two moaning people laid.

She took a section of her bloodied dress and twisted it in her hands. As uncomfortable as it made her feel, she had to leave the church which she hadn't since the Eleventh Day. More unnerving was her meeting with this child. She would have to look him in the face and treat him a certain way she hardly knew how. One of the last children left in the village needed a mother for which she knew she was not, but neither had a choice. Even as her fears barked insults at her throughout her mind, a deep knowing pushed her forward. She made it out of the church's side door as twilight skirted across the sky.

PARITY GRABBED SOME LINEN AND MADE SURE TO BRING WATER from the church's untainted well before she approached. The home was still standing but didn't look the same. The base boards and windows where the Order threw firesticks were covered in soot. Much of the wood had turned white and ashy and was peeling off.

Munta watched her, scratching his chin. He had heard a lot about her, the mother of that nameless girl. She was such a beauty, so enchanting that no man could refuse her advances. The closer Munta looked, however, the less beauty he saw, and, rather, he thought she looked quite pitiful. She was a weak and disgusting person in his eyes for leaving her daughter out in the world alone, to be fed to the wolves and never looked back. He did whatever he could to hold back his rage but the iron ball in him grew and turned whenever she was around.

She had already gone upstairs once to meet Pul but he was sleeping, tears and blood stained his pillowcase. She tried to take them off as he slept but noticed the many burns all over his body and stopped. She knew she would have to wait for him to cooperate to avoid causing him anymore pain.

On the way there, she found some clothes in a neighbor's abandoned house. They weren't made for a boy, but he was heftier than most children and she thought he might feel more comfortable with a little room for his skin to breathe.

She smiled to herself then. She hadn't played this role before and found it to be quite easy. But she frowned, like always, when thinking of her long-lost daughter.

"Do you need any help with him?" Munta asked as he watched her every move. She shook her head and silently took the hot water upstairs. For any other woman, Munta would have jumped in to help, but for her, she could burn herself for all he cared. His favor belonged to her little girl whose eyes were like the setting sun—of percolating yellows and purples as lively as the brown around them.

When Parity had everything she needed, she went to the bed and gently touched the boy to wake him. He didn't stir.

She leaned in closer to see if his chest was moving. It was. She then grabbed his arms and with subtle force pushed him back and forth until his eyes opened.

He glared at her, sincerely shocked by her presence. He had seen her before. He told his friend how he thought she didn't look like her. He didn't mean to hurt her feelings and made it up to her later by letting her hold his brother's sword for the day. She loved having the chance to do what her friends did normally and often took for granted. Tane would bring her one of her dresses and Pul would bring whatever soldier-gear his father gifted him and they would play soldier, wrestling and battling all day long as their golden-haired damsel watched, bored but pleased. And by days end, her face would light up in a way that could outshine the brightest of sunny days. And they would start all over the very next day.

Pul grimaced at Parity, "What do you want?" he asked. She expected a nasty reaction but nothing as tart as this. He was hard to look at, but she refused to look away. His face and his expression were still that of a child but lost—hurt, angry, and alone.

"I'm here to mend you. I am but a few women left alive in the village," she said, smiling down at him like any mother would.

"And why is that, hm? Why is it that you are here, alive and well, and your daughter is gods' knows where?!"

She hid her true feelings, half of her wanting to hit him and the other wanting to cry. She hadn't yet thought why she did or didn't do this or that and she wasn't going to get talked down to by a little boy.

"Please, rest awhile. I'll bring you whatever you need Pul," she said forcing a smile.

"Oh, so you know me," he coughed, "then you must

know who I know, right? Your daughter was one of my closest friends. She was like my sister. My real one was murdered. They cut down her tiny body and burnt it in a pit!" he screamed at her.

She stood up and faced the door, "Have you any idea what happened to your daughter? Do you even care?!" his final screams took all his strength and he fell back into his bed. He did it for her. She was out there in the world, alive or dead, and no one cared. No one knew how she truly was or bothered to remember her kindly. No one but him, and her mother needed to know that.

Parity turned around, squinting at her prey, "You think you know everything, don't you? I don't have to listen to some charred up boy who hasn't lived my life! You could never understand, no one can!" she screamed, running out of the room. She flew down the stairs almost tripping over a broken step before bolting out the door. Munta, shocked, ran upstairs to check on his little friend. From the doorway he could see the boy safely in bed looking rather proud of himself. For the first time, Pul smiled.

"I need to get better Munta. Tane and Chil—they're out there," he said sighing, "I got to save them. Will you help me?"

Munta, resting his body on the weary old door frame, crossed his arms, and smiled back at the boy who survived the fire.

19

———————

GANGUEN GREW TIRED WALKING THE ENDLESS HALLS OF THE
High Guardians' palace in Gilton City where his family's
history was carved into the thickest marble and detailed to
perfection. He walked alongside it, letting a weary hand etch
out his long-lost memories. He could recall when he was
small how he'd run through the giant pillars without a care
in the world.

Like his brothers, he was taken from his mother when
he was just a baby. She was the daughter of a Lord of the
Land loyal to the Order of Garatos. Her short affair with
Gilton led her to unimaginable privilege, owning a fancy
estate in the city center with many servants and endless
dubels for the rest of her life. Though he never got to meet
her in life, he could see her in his own soft reflection and
settled for that. He would have preferred to look like his
brothers, with their long, pointed nose and dignified face.

He stalled for as long as his patience would allow and
ignored the many guards waiting for him to move forward.
He had been summoned by his brothers, both High
Guardians of Zel but wasn't told why. They were impulsive

and irresponsible in their rule and were feared by everyone. So many wars were waged needlessly; on a whim or rumor —something their father would never have done. And their erroneous levies were known to turn hardworking people into starving criminals, taking everything they had ever earned for taxes they never even heard of.

He paced the long Hall of the High Guardians, laughing at his own misfortunes. The sequence of events couldn't have gone worse if he tried.

The oldest of Giltons sons was Glinton who should have been the one sitting on the High Guardian's throne instead of his twin brothers Gargo and Girgo. They were older than Ganguen but not wiser by any account. The position of High Guardian was created by Garaton after his sons fought and killed each other over the rule of Zel. To unify them and give each the power they deserved, he created the Lords of the Land as well as the High Guardian position, all of which could only be held by his own blood.

Gilton was the last of Garatons sons to hold the title but disappeared before handing it down to one of his own. He was a strong and forgiving leader who worked hard to change the Eleventh Day celebrations into less violent prac-tices and the majority of Zel followed his lead for many years. During his rule, everyone lived in peace. It wasn't until The Darkness, first appearing at the beginning of time and first defeated by Garaton, appeared again like it had with every generation before, out of the void and emptiness of the sky that Gilton left his duty as High Guardian and took on another.

Ganguen, still meandering, tried but couldn't really remember that time in his life. He could recall the world crumble down around him. Buildings fell and the blue sky twisted and turned into black and red oblong shapes unlike anything before. Almost everyone fled the palace to save themselves, except for his Sittermaids who stayed to protect him. That was the only part of the memory he refused to forget.

The Darkness left as quickly as it appeared, and the people of Gilton City were left bruised but alive. They were eternally grateful good had triumphed over evil that day. It wasn't until Ganguen was older, however, that he learned his father's true and heart-breaking fate. To protect all the worlds from further attacks from the Darkness, Gilton trapped it within a moment of time in the past and bound himself to it in that moment forever. There was no escape for him. If he were freed, so would the Darkness be.

Ganguen cried out in anguish, tired of pretending to be strong. He could barely remember his father's face and would probably forget it completely if it weren't for his brothers which he despised. He couldn't remember Glinton at all who stayed with their father trapped in the past. Now, all that was left of the Golden Ones children were near god bullies with not a single clue on how to rule their land.

GANGUEN HESITANTLY APPROACHED THE GIANT THRONE LACED with gold jewels. Two men sat perched and proud upon it like well-fed vultures—one to the left and the other to the right.

"Gargo, aren't you looking rather peckish today. Have you had your daily virgin yet?" he asked the man on the left. He was the bigger of the two and his hair was a straight yellow-white as was his eyebrows. A large, crooked grin crossed his long, pointy face. He wasn't an attractive man, at least by their lineage's standards.

The man on the right turned to his brother, crossing one

leg over the other. Though twins, Gargo and Girgo were not identical. As harsh, twisted, and homely as Gargo was, Girgo was not. His visage was delicate even as he glowered. He took after his grandmother more but hated the comparison. What they shared was their long, striking hair that became a symbol of Garaton and Siracon's children and their children's children.

"Such words for a thing—a pest we haven't seen in ages," Gargo spat out like a barking dog. Girgo chuckled.

"I'm afraid I've been busy," Ganguen said pacing, "you see, unlike my High Guardians, I am out in the lands guarding our people from harm. It takes time to travel, not all of us have the power to move through time like some who squander it," he said staring up at Girgo who glared back.

"You have a lot of nerve, creature. We have on good authority to believe you have not been guarding the lands. And it appears you've been hiding things from your guardians," Girgo said in a slithery high-pitched voice.

It was then that Ganguen understood why he had been summoned and was quick to think of a solid defense. His brothers had control over the entire world and there wouldn't be a safe place in it if he messed up. And worst of all, they knew him well enough to tell if he was lying and wouldn't hesitate in the slightest to execute him even though he hadn't yet made sons of his own.

"We've heard from a reliable source that you stopped the Eleventh Day in Glenloch. Is that true?" Gargo asked.

Ganguen stopped pacing. Barry, his second in command and loyal friend appeared out from a dark door and walked into the light amongst the guards. Gargo motioned him over to the throne and patted him on the shoulder.

Ganguen was not surprised by his friend's deceit. He had

been suspicious of him since they entered Glenloch weeks before the incident. He seemed a little too observant and asked too many questions for his taste. Too helpful a person could never be good for his kind, so said his brothers when they were young.

He nodded nonchalantly at them, "I did stop the Eleventh Day in Glenloch nearly twenty days ago. There has since been another and things have resumed as usual. Casualties were minimal unless you count the horrific amount of child slaves murdered by a giant-oaf and left to a fiery demise," he said sarcastically and it left a bitter taste in his mouth.

"Why did you really stop it?" Girgo asked, looking to his twin, "The Eleventh Day has been a part of this realm since the beginning of Man. Why take away their pleasure and fun?"

"Yes! And why make it harder for us to weed out the degenerates from the near decent humans? They really seem to come out in droves and do much of our dirty work for us!" Gargo said laughing, nudging Girgo to join in.

Ganguen tightened his fists as he watched them cackle. He had learned the hard way that the less you gave away the better chances you have at survival. He smiled slighty so that they couldn't see his unease. He felt a fleeting sense of control chug through him.

"Glenloch soldiers beat and murdered helpless children outside the day resulting in the mass murder on the actual day," Ganguen said confidently, "And as a member of this family, I had to set an example."

"It isn't your place to do anything, Ganguey! You do as we say no matter what it is—no exceptions!" yelled Gargo, red-faced and bothered. His twin, however, remained calm and relaxed as always, staring at Ganguen with eyes as stern as a judge.

"And you lie to us," Girgo said leaning forward, "you stopped the day because of the slave operation they had at the Great Hall. And Barry here told us you left on the Eleventh Day, early in the morning after announcing its cancellation with three children. Two girls and one boy—was it, Barry?" he looked over to the tall soldier who nodded.

Ganguen felt like he was on fire. He was better at hiding his feeling from Gargo but Girgo was as cold as a glacier and could always see right through him. His sense of control went out the door as guards closed it shut behind him. He knew then he had to tell the truth but feared what they would do with it. And he feared they wouldn't believe him and execute him anyways.

"I found a child, a little girl, who smells like grandfather," he let his head fall forward as his brothers and Barry roared with laughter.

"A child—a girl?" Gargo stopped to laugh, "she had grandfather's scent on her! What a beast!" they continued to laugh and Ganguen said nothing.

Eventually, he spoke up, "No, be silent!" His brothers peered at him with disgust. He waited until the white in Gargo's face washed back to red. The entire room was as silent as death.

"It was his blood. Well, I think she has our blood... Wait, that's not right..." he stopped to try and put into words what had been so unbelievable, "it was as if he was right there, do you understand me?"

Gargo and Girgo both cocked their heads to the side and looked at Ganguen confused.

"Brother, that isn't possible. We only have sons in our family—not daughters," Gargo said deep in thought.

"Brothers, her blood was strong—like Garatons. More than fathers even. And from what I can remember from grandfather, she smelled more like him than HE did," Ganguen said looking away into a black empty corner of the hall, avoiding the thousand questions his brothers shot his way.

THE SEVEN GOLDEN GODS WERE ABOVE ALL OF CREATION AND only answered to the First One. They came before man as beams of light, nameless and formless. They existed as the First One did and that was all.

When humans first sprung from the soil of Zel, the Golden One's watched their wake closely. They came to follow their example and grew human-like bodies of their own. They also came to have their own feelings and thoughts and learned to communicate which they hadn't done before.

The humans were given as a gift to the entities of the lands and to the wondrous, ever-floating energies that were the Golden Ones by the First One, the creator. So little is known about the time before humans apart from Man's premonitions and written accounts from the gods them-selves. Because of this, history started with Man.

The Golden Ones learned their best qualities from them and replicated in their own image what they saw in the most beautiful and strongest of their people. They bled like them but were impossible to kill. Those who tried settled on their half-blooded sons and even they were difficult to defeat.

The god's blood had a distinct smell. Only they and extraordinary humans could tell the difference between them. And more so, the Seven Golden Ones could tell if a child belonged to another, like Garaton could Dreqtatons with just a freckle of blood. They could smell one of their own for miles while their muddied-down line, the further down could sense less.

All of Garatons children, even those he had without Siracon, had his scent. The potency of it depended on how far they placed on the family tree: Gilton would smell more of Garaton than would Glinton, Gargo, Girgo, or Ganguen, and their children would be even less. The scent of Siracon is also evident in Gilton's brood but is sadly over-powered by Garaton's.

For many years, Garaton led the humans into battle and commanded their armies. He made sister-cities fight to near extinction and almost annihilated most of the free people north of Gilton City before he retired. And after each victory, he took his fill of women and ale and would start the same process all over again the very next day.

Thousands of half gods were conceived since he first lived with Man. Initially, they were treated better than the rest and had their pick of land, dubel, and women. Over the ages, however, Siracon grew tired and jealous of her brother-husband's affairs. Out of anger and spite, she ordered most of his children and their mothers to be killed by her most loyal followers. Women who were born and raised to offer themselves as vessels for the Great Golden God's brood hid and ran from their duties, and women he tried to make love to turned down his advances, afraid of Siracon's punishment.

His infidelities eventually came to an end, and he spent many pleasant years with his sister-wife away from the violence and destruction in the human world. It wasn't long after when Siracon became pregnant for the first time in an age.

For a reason unknown to anyone else but him, Garaton snuck away from the pregnant goddess to pillage a slew of villages and ravage as many women as he liked. Misery and despair filled Siracon when she found out. In pain and all alone, she gave birth to a baby that was already dead.

Nothing like it had ever happened to any of the other gods or their children. Garaton took this as an omen and vowed to never sleep with another woman again. And though they tried to conceive, Siracon never again became pregnant.

Heartbroken, he pulled away from her the more she wanted to try for another child. Alone and desperate for attention, she threw herself into her followers and devotees - the Pleas who gave her the unending love and support she so desperately needed and would kill to keep forever.

20

———

IT TOOK AGATHA HOLLON A FEW WEEKS TO GET TO VENLET. When she heard what had happened, she wasted no time gathering whatever resources she could into her caravan and headed straight for the village. Most in Holfenya had already heard about the massacre and the taking of Venlets' children well before the news reached her. The villagers who left a day or so early were the last to know, hearing in devastating detail the fate of their friends and family as they entered the city. The Pleas sent messenger birds to their leaders as soon as it was safe to do so, imploring the flourishing city to send food and support right away.

Agatha begged on her hands and knees to her community, those neighbors whose doors were always open and feasts she could always partake in for help. Some gave as little as they possibly could, and the rest ignored her. A terrible ball of shame grew in her chest for she knew them and their riches well and wouldn't forget it for the rest of her days.

Venlet and Holfenya had a bittersweet relationship since these seeds of Oxem split in two and went their separate ways. The Holfenians seldom left their cozy home and didn't really care for traveling. They had the tremendous duty of keeping their fertile land's pristine and their gigantic livestock well taken care of. This made them extremely territorial.

Brave merchants made the long trek to Holfenya every year around this time. They were experts at avoiding the dense forests that seemed to hate all of Man. Those that made it north without turning back knew beforehand the only way out was back down that terrible way. That was reason enough for many to skip the trip altogether.

The unusual and wealthy people of the world spent a fortune on acquiring its exotic animals and plants. They would hire the best trackers to find them if buying from Holfenians wasn't an option. Agatha didn't understand the appeal nor the reasoning behind the widespread fascination of her city but turned a blind eye as the riches made them all a little richer.

Like most Holfenians, she lived a simple yet fulfilling life. They helped each other, no matter the circumstance and were always there when called upon. There were no children wandering the streets, creeping along shadows without clothes or care—that never happened. It was their belief that every child belonged to every mother and father. Men didn't abuse their power, nor did women put them in danger. Holfenians for the most part didn't agree with the careless and blind attitude of the Councilmen of Venlet who would rather give their wealthy Budget of Arms to the Order of Garatos for protection than to their own men—a regret they shared in their last moments of life.

Agatha entered the north part of the village through the dense forest on a narrow dirty path she knew well. She had with her ten men and boys who volunteered to help their cousins south in whatever way they could. Two were Mercymen who brought the fresh innards of a naturally deceased Cloncluck and its yellow feathers. They made haste to the church where most survivors laid up, healing and waiting.

She did not follow them and instead went out into the streets, scouring its empty lots for her daughter and grandchild. She hadn't seen either in several moons. She had been planning a trip for weeks since the Sun was out longer. She was to bring a slew of books and crafts for her precious granddaughter whom she intended to teach to read by next year's warmer days.

She had known since her birth that the Child had no name. It was a sacred and long-standing tradition throughout Zel that the mother and father named their child together; a grandparent or a sibling or the like couldn't unless the parents were dead. Agatha pled with Parity to name the baby regardless so the little girl could have a decent life with or without her, but every time it was brought up, Parity would remark and say, "It isn't my child to name".

Agatha wished she would have done more. She would have been there for the birth if she knew where her daughter was. She would have taken the baby before anyone could notice. She saw the Hollon in her little red cheeks and in her smile through the years as she grew, "She will be a beauty like you, Parity!" she would say to her daughter who would scoff at the mention.

She spent the first few years of the Childs life mostly in Venlet, traveling home briefly to check on her husband, son, and livestock. The Hollons were well-respected farmers and keepers of giant beasts like Clonclucks, large but docile things she cherished as her own. She had hopes and dreams of one day teaching her granddaughter the same trade when she was older, but that future fell apart with every destroyed home she searched with no sign of her anywhere.

Eventually she ran out of dubels and had no choice but to return home. Her estate was falling apart without her there to tend to the beasts she knew so well. She had a special gift and was something of a Creaturewhisperer—one who understands creatures and can handle them better than anyone else.

Before she left that last time, she asked Parity to be a mother—to hold her daughter just once. She felt a distance between them since Parity left Holfenya without a word. No one in the city spoke about her after that. Agatha was left to remember her alone and in silence.

She tried everything to get her daughter to care for her child, but something seemed off. Because she was not comfortable with her daughter's capacity to mother, she made a deal with the Sittermaids of the village to watch the Child and gave them the last of her savings with a promise of more to come. Once all the arrangements for both the Child and her mother were finalized, Agatha said her good-byes and left with a heavy heart.

Her eyes were red and full of salty memories that kept spilling over her fiery-hot cheeks. She hadn't realized until she lost her breath that she was walking too fast for a woman her age and had become as red as a giant Turtan of the Red Sea and almost as vicious.

She had it in mind to visit her daughter's sorry excuse for a home first but could see from where she entered that it had burned to the ground. Refusing to linger on such thoughts, she aimed her attention towards the Inn—a place she found her daughter many times before hanging loosely on the arms of a man, ignoring her responsibilities. She would never admit it out loud, but she enjoyed dragging her out of there, and often by the hair, so she could sober up and take care of her little one.

Her hope darkened, however, when she saw what was left of the Inn. The Order had burned it down too and ripped apart its foundations, but not before stealing and destroying all of its priceless artifacts. She shivered.

The Inn was the most well-known place in all the valley. It had been that way since the ex-slaves first built it and was Zel's last piece of that ancient world. Everyone—merchants, tourists, and famous people loved to stay there and spoke highly of it wherever they went. It served as the starting point for the long journey to the exotic north or the end for those skilled enough to make it back.

It wasn't until Agatha passed by a wandering Plea that she found her way to Parity. She couldn't understand how Pleas could give their lives to such a needy goddess. She had thought they were all spineless and pathetic men because of it until that day.

Holfenya's people looked up to the gods, but they did not obey them as their relationship with them was different than that of Venlets. Garaton inspired their men to be strong and steadfast and gave his good graces to those that gave to him their best Warlongs in sacrifice. Holfenians would do this right before battle and to honor the Great Golden God. They didn't need churches or shrines to follow any of their practices and the gods didn't ask it of them.

She grabbed the lost Plea and shook him, asking breathlessly where her daughter was. Though all the women of Velnet were beautiful, Parity stood out whether she liked it or not and Agatha knew without a doubt even a confused Plea would have noticed her.

· · ·

Hands on her head, Parity sat across the blazing and overwhelming fireplace once more. Night was overhead and a chilling breeze forced out what was left of the warm days' bright smells. The overwhelming stench of burnt flesh persisted, permeating the corridor where fewer people laid in pain, awaiting the eventual end to their misery. She had just left Unta and Munta's home where the little burnt boy verbally throttled her. She was besides herself.

How could I allow a child to talk to me like that?! Those words played over and over in her mind until she went mad and began smacking the side of her head to make it stop.

When she left Pul, she ran straight to the church and didn't look back. She expected to be embraced by the understanding Pleas she had grown so close to since the Eleventh Day but Plea Marcus Daniels, plagued with fatigue and high on melancholy was more than done with her antics and was less than sympathetic to her.

"Parity, for Siracon's sake, why can't you be reasonable, just this one! That poor little boy has no one in the world and you abandoned him too!" he huffed, turning away from the pitiful sight of the once dazzling young woman, "you can't keep running from your troubles. Eventually, you'll have to come face to face with those demons harvested in your mind. No one can beat them but you," he started to walk away but stopped mid-step. He remembered then what he had been put on Zel to do. He was to help those in need and would continue to do it no matter the circumstance. But before another word was spoken, the hallway door flung wide open, almost hitting a wounded person lying by the door. Out came a Plea, younger than the others, weeping. He collapsed at Plea Marcus Daniel's feet.

"Oh, bless Siracon, Grand Eunich, for she has blessed us!" he said under his blubbering.

"What in all realms are you..." Plea Marcus trailed off as random men with strength and vigor walked quickly into the corridor and looked carefully at each of the wounded laid against the wall. They had leather bags full of medicine and carried in bundles of supplies the village was in dire need of. Walking slowly through the door, eyes wide and in shock was a greying woman wearing the ornamental clothes indicative of Holfenya.

Plea Marcus followed her gaze and felt her sorrow and knew it well. He watched as wounded men and women, young and elderly reached out, begging him to end their suffering, physical and mental. They had been through the worst that Man could do and were eager to see their slain loved ones. He swallowed back a sob and cleared his throat to greet his new visitors.

He noticed her eyes dart over to his and then zip away, surveying the room for someone. They stopped on the slumped-over version of Parity in a raggedy old chair. The woman charged forward like a scorned Cloncluck out for blood.

"How DARE you?!" she screamed.

Parity jumped to her feet, "Mother, please. Not now..." she said as her voice trailed off.

Plea Marcus watched her slump back into the chair. He was amazed that any woman who was one of a few to have survived an Eleventh Day could be so upset. She sat lifeless like a deflated doll. Her head and arms hung low with no fight in them.

But in contrast, he marveled at the sight of her mother and her opposition to her daughter's subdued tantrum. She exuded vigor and purpose and pierced the stale, dead room with her volatile will to live. She stood tall and resolute— like any good soldier would. She seemed like a woman in control of her emotions, but even the best tempered have their limits.

"No! Where is she?!" Agatha screamed at the top of her lungs.

Plea Marcus flinched at the woman's fury and stood back helpless. Those suppressed feelings of regret began to resurface once he realized who SHE was. He had beaten her granddaughter the last time he saw her, and she had done nothing to provoke it—he knew that all along. His most faithful Pleas looked to him for guidance and reassurance. When the Child found Dreqtaton's book, it caused a brief moment of fear and confusion that he had to contain. He made an example of her and of what her sad existence stood for. At the time, he believed she had no place in their community and was a bad influence on her friends like the Dark God was to Zel. He absolutely believed he would suffer no consequences for it. He rubbed his hands over his bald head and felt the whole Eleventh Day fall on his shoulders.

When Parity didn't answer, Agatha asked again. Frustrated, she grabbed her arms so tight she could have broken them. Parity screamed softly, temporarily awoken by pain. She looked deep into her mother's eyes that screamed to know anything. Plea Marcus stood back, not wanting to get in the middle of two women with eyes like giant bears.

"Why?.. WHY do you hate her, Parity?" Agatha screamed in her face. She turned to sob and tried to pull away, but her mother wouldn't let her.

"Please! Please!" Agatha begged. She released her hold and wrapped her arms around her daughter's shoulders as she fell into her mother's loving embrace. They cried together for a time as the world around them ceased to matter.

Parity pulled away, face still wet with tears but no longer crying.

"Let me tell you what really happened mother," she said firmly.

Plea Marcus saw her like this before when she left to tend to Pul. Deep down he knew she couldn't hold this strength for long. Her emotions were what made her strong and weak at the same time. Anyone around her could feel her honesty and love when she was in her right mind, but those fleeting feelings could be wildly thrown out without reason when her fears reared their ugly heads around.

"Nearly seven years ago, I still lived in Holfenya. Do you remember, mother?" Parity asked Agatha who nodded, "At that time, I was a few moons away from marrying Bart, the son of our closest neighbors and I was so happy. He was a good man, and I'm sure his wife is a lucky woman," she paused, gulping down her spit, "Do you remember I told you I didn't know who the father was?" this time, Agatha nodded reluctantly, "At the time, I didn't know how to tell you, so..."

Parity's eyes were puffy and red which got worse the more she wiped her tears away, "I wanted to tell you, I promise! I was dying to tell anyone, but I knew what would happen if I did..."

Before her mother could protest, she put up a hand and continued, "I had been working in the fields all day. It was so cold. The sun melted most of the snow, but the chill still rose from the ground and nearly froze my toes off. Father sent me out alone to check on one of our baby 'clucks," she paused, looking over at her mother and then to Plea Marcus. For a long moment, there was silence.

She sighed, "I was so careful and looked around. Father always warned me about outsiders... I was walking back home, through the field when I heard it—a loud crash from up in the sky," she looked up and shook her head, "I thought it was thunder, but it couldn't have been—it wasn't the right time of year... I stopped and waited—why did I wait?"

Catching herself again, she continued, "through the clouds, just over the mountains came a large bird. I could tell by its shape and wingspan it wasn't a 'cluck. It flew straight down to me like any hungry creature would," she stopped, putting her hand over her mouth.

She looked up at her mother with pleading eyes. They begged to stop and not say another word. Agatha looked back putting a hand over hers as well. In that moment, something changed in Parity. She swallowed back another devastating cry and cleared her throat. If she couldn't be strong for herself, she would for her mother.

"It perched down in front of me. It was a bird with a beautiful beak, white and gold," her eyes glazed over as the toothy tendrils of her fears and disgust eroded what little comfort she had left, "its wings were gold and yellow. It was so perfect and beautiful.

"I walked to it thinking I had found something magical, something new. But as I got closer, it began to change," her features grew darker, "it became a big naked man with big eyes that were a dark grey. Just looking into them made me feel like my life was draining away. I-I-I can still see them," she said rubbing her eyes.

Her body started to shake violently, "I screamed, mother, I screamed but the wind was so loud... Loud and cold—it was so cold," she said, falling to her knees, crying and screaming. An unstoppable feeling of hate and regret overcame the room already full of anguished spirits as she unleashed it all.

Agatha also fell to be with her and held her close. They

cried together as they mourned the loss of not one but two innocent lives. Plea Marcus stood behind with tears streaming down his face. He looked up above him, past the mystical stone ceiling and the possible night clouds, straight into where his mind's eye saw Siracon's lair. He had the power, as Grand Eunich, to call upon the goddess in times of great need. He could speak to her like no other human was ever allowed to. Eyes closed, he spoke through his mind the story Parity told and hoped the link with the goddess was strong enough to receive the message clearly. He knew all the stories of Garaton well, of his form as a gilded giant bird and of his taking of women. He knew of his promise to Siracon that he didn't uphold, and she needed to know. He knew above all that the Child was no doubt the daughter and closest heir of the Great Golden God Garaton.

21

WORD HAD SPREAD THROUGHOUT THE LAND THAT GARATON had another child, but no one knew who and where it was. The rumor first started in Gilton City and quickly spread on the wings of messenger birds from person to person, village to village, and sea to sea. The exact details regarding it changed the more it spread. One account suggested this unknown child hid north among the tribesman and ancient people, untouched by the power of the Guardians, and in another, it lived in the ocean with the ferocious Tentactacons and looked just as terrifying. Only a few good men knew the exact whereabouts of this mysterious heir and were happy knowing so many were looking for the Child elsewhere.

IN THE SKYLESS NIGHT IN HER DREAMS, SHE FOUND HERSELF atop a waterfall, but unlike the one she made in her Otherworld, she didn't want to jump in. A foreboding black cloud was sneaking up behind her and she had no other way to go but down the endless froth. She was scared.

She felt it approach and she hated it, just as much as it hated her. It's pumping and undulating dances broke the ground beneath it and with every movement came a thick ooze of horrendous hate and agony from its heinous pores. In its wake, all life—trees, flowers, and animals fell to their death and withered away into black dust. A loud cry, like a cracking whip came from within it after it devoured a soul.

The familiar sense of doom and fear welled up inside her. She never had a dream so real and terrifying. The horizon began to blur as mountains and trees and distant unknown places evaporated from life. As absolute devastation swept across the land, a tyrannical storm formed above her, and its winds forced her away from the edge. Dust from the dry, dead land swirled up and into her eyes she shut to keep safe.

The angry entity was high above then. It looked down at her though it had no eyes of its own. She knew it wanted to take everything from her. It forced her dry eyes open and wouldn't let them close. She wriggled and fought back. But before the malevolence could take over, she got pulled away.

Sweat laid on her forehead like fine jewelry as she came to. She could sense she was somewhere warm and comfortable. Still scared, she kept her eyes closed and didn't move, not sure if it was still overhead.

She feared seeing her whole world turn to nothing, that she was stranded in the endless chasm of that black cloud she wished she had never seen, but her fears subsided as her hearing returned. She could hear the busy feet of the many attendants that served them since they arrived around her. At first it was hard for her to let them serve her, but she had no choice and gave in once she saw how happy it made them. Tane however had no problems abusing this new privilege.

She felt the soft sheets under her and knew she was in her bed. She opened her eyes slowly, still cold from her dream's nightmare winds. Scared, she looked to her left and smiled. Every morning, she looked over at her friends to be sure they were there and safe.

Tane was already awake, looking at an attendant puzzled like always when she didn't get her way. The attendants were mostly men who wore long robes and were bald, like the Pleas. They were sometimes too apologetic if an errand wasn't done to Tane's ridiculous standards and would not accept a compliment from any of the other children until it was done correctly.

"Sorry, sweet Tane. Would you like your porridge hotter?" asked one of the shorter attendants who never gave his name no matter how many times the children asked. Tane, of course gave him one he didn't like but accepted nonetheless.

"No, but thank you Margaret!" she said in a bratty voice. The Child told her that what she was doing was cruel, but Tane didn't see the harm in it and was determined to give him a name they could all remember.

As the Child reached up to stretch before getting out of bed, attendants one after another rushed in to meet her. They had treated the three kids like Lords of the Land since they arrived in the Mountains of the Predicated through its impossible mouth, an entrance so high in the summit that most didn't believe it existed. It was there where they met Mistacles, the most powerful Imagi in Zel. He was a short and round man with a well-trimmed and expertly shaped salt and pepper beard. His eyes were a dirty brown that were as soft as his kind spirit. He was a bigger man whose belly bounced whenever he laughed. He had no idea the children were coming until a big black bird told him to check the Mouth for a gift from the universe.

"The gods sent you to us so that we can protect you," he said to the children as he welcomed them into his home.

The Child gave him the no-name spiel right away. He promised to give her one but after Tom gave her Doe, she decided she'd take a break from the whole naming thing for a while. Of course, Tane called her Chil and since the big man was so nice to her and her friends, she allowed him to call her that too.

He spent a great deal of time showing the children around the mountains after they rested for the first few days. The livable space inside was bigger than all the green grass in the valley yet it all fit unnoticed in the range. Certain areas were exposed to the outside world through caved-in summits that allowed natural light and the elements to fall through. There were hidden cities and towns spread out farther than feet could walk. They were easy to get to if one knew how to travel by means of magical enchantment which was said to be more dangerous than any other form of transportation. When the children first tried it, they were anything but pleased with how it made them feel and swore to never use it again until they did, many times after in fact. Mistacles had forgotten to mention that, though safe, it felt like being shot through the air by a giant sling shot. He knew they wouldn't like it and enjoyed their reaction afterwards.

Through a powerful magic instilled many years before, the strange mountain air could be manipulated to breath in a person or thing from one end of a channel to another, with them landing safely, so long as they didn't breathe. The horror stories Mistacles told the children of the few who tried it first almost stopped them from using it again. Almost.

The entire mountain's eco and social systems were run by many kinds of people. Some of them were like the children's attendants who left home in search of the Mouth but got lost somewhere along their journey. Most that traveled with them died but those who lived through the ordeal would spend the rest of their days there where everyone was treated well. And even powerful men like Mistacles ate and spent time alongside everyone, no matter their status or abilities. He was particularly known for keeping his home and many bedrooms open to whomever needed a place to stay. The children who grew up knowing a world entirely different from this weren't sure what to think of it.

"I don't understand this place," said Care, taking his pants back from an attendant to put it on himself. His wounds had healed nicely though it had been less than a week since they were free. He had been starving ever since their time in the iron cage and didn't know how else to be. In the face of earnest kindness from strangers, the boy was unwilling to accept it and was instead cruel towards anyone but his two friends.

"Leave me alone, please!" his screams were shrill enough to make all the attendants leave the room in a hurry. Tane went over to sit next to him but he brushed her off, sulking alone in the corner, looking down at the floor.

The Child was reluctant to show any kind of affection to anyone. Even if Tane needed consoling, all she felt she could do was sit and stare at her. Deep down she wanted to wrap her arms around her friend but feared her love wouldn't be enough to help.

And with that thought, suddenly, she felt the terrible breeze from her nightmare creep from her toes up her legs. She jumped out of bed and ran out the door, the two others followed behind not asking why.

Outside their room was a giant living space that was open to anyone but had recently become heavily guarded for the children's sake. The furniture was beyond comfortable—sitting on them felt like coasting on water and floating on clouds. Mistacles warned them that every piece was enchanted and, though relaxing to anyone who sat on them, would throw those who misused them straight through the ceiling. Of course, the children didn't listen, and they played on them regardless, sitting and jumping from chair to chair whenever the attendants weren't looking. It made them feel free, like dolphins flying in and out of water when the cushions kicked them out.

The Child ran out of the home and into the city streets, eager to meet with Mistacles and talk about their training. He promised he would teach them many things but reluctantly agreed to start so quickly since their arrival. He had to constantly remind the children that they were his guests, and they could continue to relax and unwind for as long as they wanted to. But they had become restless and needed something to do with their free time. They also wanted to show their new friend how grateful they were that he was nothing like the adults they had known before.

The children spent the whole night before guessing what they would be asked to do.

"I bet I'll get to clean the mountain peaks and Mistacles will give me magical powers to do it!" said Care.

"No, no way! Mr. Mistacles will make me his assistant and make both of you," Tane pointed to the Child and Care, "my assistants! Just so you know, I like my eggs basted and my bread a little burnt first thing in the morning!"

The children laughed and chided all night without a care in the world. They needed this, a moment to breath and have as much of the normal they used to have before the Eleventh Day.

Even though Care was a wonderful new friend that they would cherish forever, Tane and the Child shared an equally large and deep hole in their hearts only Pul could fill. One evening as they were drinking brandied licorice at a local bar, Care asked about him. Tane couldn't speak on it and tried to change the subject. The Child refused to let it go and proceeded to tell Care all about Pul and shared with him stories full of all their adventures together. Eventually Tane joined in, correcting a few inaccuracies the Child purposely put in to grab her attention. They celebrated his honor by each tipping a bit of the licorice on the ground for their fallen friend.

The children ran as fast as they could—faster than their healing bones would have liked. They were excited for their new lives to start in such a nice, calm place, and they wanted to run as fast as they could every time because of what they had gone through, remembering how something as simple as running could be taken away. The Child was the first to reach Mistacles being the most athletic—an unfortunate perk to practically living on the streets. Though Tane was faster, she lollygagged too much to ever win.

She found him sitting on a bench that overlooked the many channels showcasing the diverse travelers that used their magical enchantments to zip around faster than any man could ever walk. When she approached, she noticed his far-off look and solemn disposition.

Oh no! Not again! The Child felt a deep ache in her guts that took her spirit away.

When he noticed her staring, he beckoned her over. When Tane and Care reached them, they jumped up and down in circles, happy but oblivious to the severity on his face. He stared at the Child like Ganguen had at the bar in Glenloch.

Please, no more pain. Please!

He sent the other two off on an errand they were way too excited for. She sat down next to him and stared ahead, withdrawing from what she could only guess was another disgusting reality-check. She began to slip back into her Otherworld until he spoke.

"Are you going back into your mind's world again?"

She had told him hesitantly about her Otherworld after waking from a severe nightmare a few days into their stay. She didn't trust him yet, but she knew he was a powerful man and had hoped maybe he could help her understand why she did the things she did.

"Don't please. Not now," he said, shifting his weight toward her, inviting her to do the same, "I have in my hand a letter that, if true, could mean the changing of all future history and of our prophecies. Do you understand little one?"

She nodded but didn't understand. She had heard about prophecies here and there, from Lordteller and people passing by, but never took them seriously.

"What's prophecies and what do you mean by future history?" she asked.

"I'll explain that all to you later, soon but later. What I mean to ask you is... do you want to know what's in this letter? Do you want to be told who you are by some text that doesn't know you, or the turmoil and suffering you've already been through at the age of six? Do you want me to read to you that which, no doubt, will change whatever future you had already dreamed for yourself? Cause if you don't, I will take this letter and burn it so that you may never know what it says!" he said with conviction and care.

He looked at the stoic child searching for an answer.

"I don't care."

She got up from the bench and walked towards her chambers feeling tired and weak. Being in the dark and on her own comforted her in her weakest moments like it would a wounded animal near death, but hurried feet from behind stopped her in her tracks.

"Such strange words for a child. Hm... Do you mean what you say?"

The Child nodded.

"Chil, here it is... you are a half god," he said loud enough for the people walking by to stop. They then started to huddle and whisper to one another, looking back at her often. Murmurs of half gods could be heard above everything else. She looked behind the round man and saw more people approaching, filling the streets faster than flames in a dry forest.

"Silence, everyone, please," Mistacles said with his booming voice, overwhelming the now gossiping voices of many, "Our guests were sent to us by the gods so that we can keep them safe which we will do—no matter what!"

A roar of approval came from every man, woman, and creature who unanimously agreed to risk their lives for these three small children. It would only be a matter of time before the entire mountain heard the news and hopefully felt the same.

Tears filled Mistacles eyes as hundreds of his family jumped forward, ready to take on the world to protect the most precious. He knew there would be those who would defend this honor and those who would stop at nothing to destroy it.

The Child was confused but didn't bother asking him any questions. If what he said was true, it didn't matter to her anyways. No one—no man or god had ever taken her on his knee and made her call him dad or spent the time to really look at her and see who she really was under all the filth. She was who she was because of the very few who stood by her through everything—Tane, Pul, Care, and her grandmother. After everything that happened, she just wanted to spend time with those she could for as long as she could.

The Child lumbered to her chambers later that day having been fed too much delicious foods. Her jovial friends laughing and also lumbering carried on behind her having enjoyed the same treats she had. The attendants waited patiently for them and gave them their clothes without delay. Care rushed them out after they were changed and closed the door, anxious to speak in private since the announcement earlier.

"In all the worlds, Chil, I never thought you would be the goddess," Care said, laughing as she threw her pillow at him.

"It doesn't matter. Well, unless it gives us more free food and brandied licorice and…" the Child paused when Tane stopped laughing and turned sad, "What's wrong Tansey-lion?" she asked.

Tane looked into her best friend's eyes with the same sadness she held when they were locked in the cage. Her grief was not for herself but for her friend.

"Tell me, please. Let me make it better!" the Child persisted.

Tane's words were stuck in her throat. She took a long moment before she spoke.

"Your father, it's him—the Great Golden One. The Eleventh Day One – Garaton!"

22

———————

Parity spent all day and night alongside her mother, mending those still sick back to health. The air had thinned between them since her confession. For the first time in years, she could smell her mother's perfume while sober.

"You still wear the Luck of the Snake perfume?" she asked sarcastically. Agatha chuckled before going off on a tangent about her husband and how he always bought the same bottle for her birthday every year even after she gave him subtle hints to buy something else.

They laughed together at the not-so-distant memory. "Pap is so forgetful. He used to leave bags of corn out for the 'clucks and forget to take it back in. Oh, the look on his face at the mess! And then he would make ME clean it up!" She laughed like a little girl for the first time since Holfenya and sighed at the returning of her old self.

Her brother was so small then. He would pick up as many seeds as he could in his little hands while she cleaned up the rest. But neither he nor their father came to see her after she left home. She didn't blame them with how she left things but longed to see them again.

Regret stretched over her face and her mother saw it all. With a sigh, Agatha rubbed her daughters back like when she was a baby, moving in a circle backwards then forwards then backwards again.

"They didn't know. *We* didn't know. I should tell them, they need to know the truth," she tried to pull her daughter in for an embrace as she spoke, but the tortured woman instinctually twisted her arms to escape.

"No one can know, mother. It's embarrassing enough everyone thinks I'm a whore. If they knew I was taken and damaged..."

Before she could finish, her mother smacked her. Horrified, she stared mouth agape at her mother whose face expressed a determination few would trifle with.

"You are coming home with me after all of this is taken care of. We will tell everyone, and they will accept you back in with open arms. Bart should have fought for you or at least talked to you first before listening to ridiculous lies!"

The rumors began as soon as she withdrew from the community and only became worse once her belly grew. And after Bart called off their wedding, she fled the city and headed to Venlet. Luckily, her mother found her and her newborn baby there, alone but safe.

"We can't let the gods and those bloodthirsty warmongers come crashing into our lives, destroying everything we have anymore! I will not lose another loved one or so help me... And no one will smear you in my presence ever again —I promise you that! You are still MY child after all! I suckled you on my breast for many moons as I tended to the 'clucks. You are stronger than you think—you can overcome this," she sighed looking away from her daughter, "I don't think I could ever be that strong... but I know you can."

She looked back and brushed away hair from Parity's

forehead as she spoke, "I love you very much, my girl. You are as much a part of me as I am myself, and so was my granddaughter who deserved better than her lot in life. Those bastards, those monsters..."

She turned away and hit the bed as Parity removed the linen from another. Her rage faded into the sheets, white and wrinkled much like her face. Parity knew her mother's anger well but couldn't fathom until then that she felt that much grief—a terrible burden she thought she carried alone. She hadn't been the only one affected by the careless actions of others. Her family suffered but in their own way. And despite what happened, they could forgive her, accept her despite how broken she was. She could be whole again but not in the same way. Her soul would always be longing for those parts of herself that were taken that she never said goodbye to. A section of her heart awoke in a way it hadn't before and she knew her place belonged with her loved ones in Holfenya.

She watched as her mother released the last of her anger, mumbling a few foul words while smashing in pillows before running out of steam. The red that painted her face slowly eased back to her cheeks where it remained.

As they went about fixing the rest of the beds, a Plea came in running with a note in their hand and handed it to Parity.

"What is this?" she asked.

"The Grand Eunich received the letter just this morning. He gave me clear instructions to wait and give it to you now, at high noon. He said it contained information of great importance and must be handled carefully," he said breathlessly.

Agatha was besides herself. She was about to go off on the poor Plea but stopped when her daughter dropped the letter. Hands trembling and up to her face, her look of shock revealed something remarkable was in what she read. Too old to reach down, she motioned for the Plea to pick it up and after he did, he scurried away. She looked over at her daughter whose grin forced the many tears falling down to tumble around her lips. She opened the note and read it out loud.

PLEA MARCUS DANIELS SAT EXHAUSTED IN HIS PRIVATE study. He had become the interim leader of the village since the Eleventh Day and had little rest since. Everyone came to him for guidance, support, and supplies—pretty much everything. He inspired them to repair what was left and build anew. It had taken the hard work and heart of the surviving villagers and supportive neighboring cities and towns to bring life back into Venlet. It was slowly becoming as close to normal as it could ever be. He was exhausted but felt blessed to be a part of such a strong community.

All those who died since the Eleventh Day were given their rites into the Afterlife successfully and those who were seriously wounded were getting better. Pul Venam, a boy he saw so little promise in when they first met exceeded everyone's expectations. He was thriving. He stayed active all around the village and could speak clearly despite the damage to his throat and lungs. His burns did not go away, unfortunately, but that didn't seem to bother him. He displayed a courage Plea Marcus Daniels tried his entire life to find but couldn't.

A few moments before, an enchanted messenger bird gave him a letter. It somehow found him in his private chambers while the door was locked. It dropped the letter on his lap before disappearing through a wall, leaving a wisp of white smoke behind it.

He was reluctant to open it, so he did his own magic to be sure it wasn't cursed. Few people liked the Pleas because of their extreme disdain for Dreqtaton and his followers and their blind worship of their exuberant goddess. They seldom trusted anything that didn't come from their church.

After the letter proved to be harmless, he opened it. He scrolled quickly over the body and eventually found the bottom where he saw a name he recognized.

"Mistacles," he said confused, "how did you find me?"

It had been many years since he first became a Plea. He had moved up over time and eventually became the Grand Eunich, the Leader of Siracon's Siccofants in all of Zel. It was a great honor that allowed him to travel the world and meet all manner of Man along the way. But that wasn't the path he thought he was meant to take. When he was a boy, he made a pilgrimage to the Mountains of the Predicated, determined to find the Mouth and learn all the old stories and future ones. He hoped to become a high-ranking Imagi like the ones that wandered through his village growing up. Their nomadic way of living and what they could do with magic mystified him enough to pursue their path. Had he known the cost, however, he would have stayed home and lived a simple life as a farm hand. He died on top of the mountains vast range over-taken by great winds and heavy snow. He was brought back to life by a grey man with a large staff who took him under his wing from then on. The Imagi had an apprentice named Mistacles who he became close to, like a brother.

For years after, he learned all kinds of spells and developed skills that could be taught nowhere else. Because he was a fast learner, he ran through his lessons. He was always eager to start the next one, but his master was hesitant to allow it. "It's not time for that," he would say and, "You are not ready son."

Bound and determined to become the best Imagi in Zel and not wanting to wait for it, Marcus Daniels sought out a different magic source. In the dark recesses of the mountains, he found a scruffy man who claimed to be a friend of Dreqtaton. He could teach him everything he knew without boundaries or limitations, and for a brief time, the scruffy mage whose name was forced from his mind taught him offensive and defensive magic, invocations and summations, as well as absorption spells and magecrafts. All of which could only be performed by those who studied for many years for the weight of its consequences were too heavy for someone so young. But Marcus Daniels didn't want to wait. It wasn't long before he realized that everything with magic came at a cost.

Each day they met, he was asked to write down a new name in the scruffy mage's weird book and to give him an item that belonged to that person before their lesson would begin. After it started, word had spread around the mountain that people were disappearing. A few here and there didn't bother young Marcus Daniels but when he heard their names having written them down, he had an inclination he played a part in their disappearance and went straight to his master. It didn't take officials long to find the scruffy mage and prosecute him thanks to young Marcus Daniels. Both his master and Mistacles were sympathetic and forgave him for the part he played. But sadly, they couldn't let it go.

After all those years in the mountains, growing into a young man with the potential of becoming a great Imagi, his deeds could not go unpunished. He was formally stripped of his title of Apprentice Imagi. Furthermore, he was cast out, forbidden to ever return because of the threat he posed to the many residents within. He was calmy taken away from the range where it was safe—a gift given to him by Mistacles that could have costed him his apprenticeship as well.

He walked alone then, tired, ashamed, and hungry for many moons. As he meandered through a random town one afternoon, he came across a Plea who was kind and offered him food and shelter. And that was when his new life began.

Plea Marcus Daniels still felt the plight of regret from his past but was thankful for the abilities it gave him. Without it, he couldn't be the bearer of love and reassurance for his goddess which he found great purpose in.

He smiled, rubbing a dry thumb over the corners of the letter. He blinked several times before reading:

"Dear Marcus Daniels,

Or is it Plea Marcus Daniels now? A Grand Eunich as well?! So many things have changed over the years. I am happy you have found a way to channel your immense power for good. I've heard great things about your work!

I've known for a while you lived in the small village of Venlet and I am so sorry for the tragedy that befell your people. I have the utmost urgent news and I ask that you please inform the others as soon as you can.

I have in my possession, in the Mountains of the Predicated, three children—a Tane, a Care, and a girl with no name. They have been provided and cared for, but I fear they have been through enough to scar them for the rest of their lives. I am to keep them here indefinitely.

They were given to me by a god whose name I must

keep hidden. It told me that the nameless child they often called Chil is a half god. I have since done spellwork to test its validity with her blood and hair, and, my friend, it proves to be true!

Furthermore, it told me her father is Garaton. I'm sure you know this goes against everything we've learned and changes what has already been set in stone, my friend. The beginning of a new era is already upon us, and I am excited for it! I can't wait to see what happens next! We are still waiting for the next Prophezier—Destroyer of the Darkness and I fear they will not show up in time to stop it.

And as for the children—they would like to inform the village of their whereabouts and their family and friends that they miss them very much. Please send word once received.

Blessings,
Mistacles"

Plea Marcus gave one of the younger Pleas the letter. He was to deliver it to Parity in a few hours which gave him plenty of time for an invocation. He was one of few people in the world who could call upon Siracon but was reluctant to do so. She would send him clues throughout the day if she wanted to speak to him, but he rarely made first contact unprovoked.

She had been silent since before the Eleventh Day and so would not be expecting him which made him tremble. The last message he sent begging for help must not have been received. Hesitantly, he did all the necessary steps and sang the incantations with the last bit of courage he had left.

A giant boom hit the ceiling which made the room shake. His eyes widened and he cowered where he stood. His chamber was in the basement of the church, and he knew from before that any sounds or damage she made could only be heard by him and most of it was done while he was down there.

A beam of light shot down on the altar he had made, pulverizing the pretty vases and stone figures in her honor. He could tell she was displeased. From the glow of that continuous harsh light came a woman's voice, loud and low.

"What do you want, my Plea? Do you wish to take all my time or just the precious moments I wish to spend with my brother-husband?!" she hissed as the only lanterns flame grew larger.

"No, my most kind and perfect goddess of all. Oh, sweet Siracon, mother of warriors and ex-sister to betrayers—the most beautiful creature to ever exist! I have something to tell you, please if you will allow me to speak!" he fell on his hands and knees at the specter in front of him. The light twisted left to right and paced as if unsure. She eventually mumbled her acceptance and Plea Marcus unraveled the truth he had just learned from Parity and the letter.

"... he took her, your most pleasantness, and from that came a child who is now in the Mountains. A god helped her, your husband perhaps and left her in their sanctuary where none of your kind can trespass."

He was groveling now, in tears and scared by her groaning and growling. He reluctantly told her about the horrors from the Eleventh Day, but she paid it no mind. She was instead furious with Parity and her child and had no kind words for them.

"Did you say the child was a girl?!" she asked. Plea Marcus Daniels nodded. She cackled a sinister loud laugh like that of a warmonger in the heat of battle, "then the bastard is not my husbands. He doesn't bare girls, pathetic worm. If he did sleep with that whore, she will need to be dealt with."

"No, the girl is of Garaton. It was proven through a blood spell. You could smell it on her if you were around her, my lady. I couldn't of course because I am a pathetic worm— useless and a waste except to abide your will!" he screamed face down on the ground kissing it, a thing he often did to appease her.

"Then prove it. Kill the woman and bring me the child."

Siracons voice suddenly became sweet like candy. She spoke of devotion and of love that made his heart rejoice and long for more, all while sneaking in phrases of hate and malice.

"If you cut her throat and bleed her dry, I will love you again my sweet Plea."

He stayed still, frozen on the ground. He wanted to speak up and say no but also wanted to grovel and beg for more of her love. But he could do neither. She spoke faster and her words jumbled together. His mind was cracking on the pressure, "Love me—kill her. Take her—take me! Dire, die HER!"

Suddenly and from out of nowhere, the names of those he had written in the Mountains ran across his mind. He remembered how they haunted him for so many years until he gave them to the Pleas pining for a fresh start, a new life and a new name. He would have done anything to bring those he helped murder back to life.

He had never been asked to kill for his goddess and for the first time questioned his devotion.

"Why do we have to try so hard for your love, my lady?"

He didn't realize he had asked the question out loud until the light before him turned stained-red and blocked out all the warmth it originally omitted. She screamed a warrior's cry that made his blood turn to ice. What he knew of the Goddess of Beauty, the Keeper of Peace, and Barer of Lives was all lies then and he knew he was past redemption.

And she was past the point of reasoning. He found his strength and got to his feet. Staggering, he commanded her to leave as a flurry of flames blew around him. Near defeat, he used all his remaining power for one last spell that he intended to never be undone:

"You are damned to be lonely and barren forever you corrupt Goddess of Repression and Hate! You will fail and the girl will win!"

The light blared painfully as an unseen force picked him up into the air. A dreadful flame birthed on his foot, and he flailed as he screamed. As the fire crept up his leg he began to choke on the smoke. Slow to die, the goddess squeezed his neck with no intention of letting go. Suddenly, with a loud crack, the ominous light went out and the body of Plea Marcus Daniels fell to the floor, dead and cold.

23

———————

Mistacles ran his hands over his globe of Zel as his three young charges waited to hear the oldest of all tales.

"In the beginning of everything, well before us, there was only one who created all things after. You've heard that before, haven't you? It's been said since the first words of Man but all the pretty details that comes after, well—that always changes.

"The Seven Golden Ones did appear in the beginning, but they were never gold tear drops or anything like that. Rather, they were like sparks, ignited by the First One as it expanded into the infinite. An accident, like most things I'm afraid. It did create the Sun who gave light to its great space, but there were cracks of black where the Sun's rays could not reach, where a different energy came to be, dark and cold that thrived in emptiness, far from the First Ones all seeing eyes and lingered there for eons.

"As our First Father stirred and grew ever bigger, rocks as small as specks fell from its being and later became giants of their own. The most fertile of these worlds was Zel, where the earth, river, and wind spirit came together to create many beautiful things, including Man, per the request of the First One.

"The gods, as flying flames watched Man with great fascination become intelligent and strong. They loved us so much in those days - what a pity. The first to change his form was Garaton who stole light from the Sun to brighten his natural glow, blinding all who stood before him. After he changed, the other gods followed, all except one called Yecon whom we never speak of.

"Two took the form of men—Garaton and Dreqtaton, while three became like women—Siracon, Miracon, and Amacon. The sixth god, Amao, did not take the form of Man but walks on two legs. He has no face, and his body contorts in odd ways as he moves. His appearance alone causes madness, so never gaze upon it!"

Mistacles stopped rubbing the globe and peaked an eyebrow at his audience as they looked back, desperate to hear more.

"Garaton became the leader of Man and walked with them for ages, showing their young the art of dominance and strength as he had learned it from their ancestors. There is much more to tell but that will have to wait for another day.

"Miracon, a wise goddess, watched Man divide themselves and offered to protect them from each other in exchange for their devotion and blood. Families prayed endless for her protection even when she wouldn't listen. And if she did hear them, she did not act.

"Siracon watched Man adore their women in secret and wanted that same devotion for herself. She painstakingly took the most beautiful parts of women she knew her brother-husband lusted after and made herself the most beautiful creature by her proclamation alone. Those who didn't agree faced her wrath.

"Over the years, she became increasingly jealous over her brother-husbands' affairs and the amass of his outside children ever increasing in Zel. At her breaking point, she asked her most adamant followers to dispose of his messes, resulting in the murder of too many women and half gods to count.

"Amacon, the fifth, was not like her sisters. She couldn't tolerate the pain that came from war and stayed away from her brothers who drenched themselves in it. She took the form of a woman who hid her body from outside perversions, ordained in long robes that covered her completely. She is our Goddess of Tears.

"Although the gods lived separately in the worlds outside of Zel, they all agreed their other brother, Dreqtaton, was their enemy. He lived away from them, among the animals and creatures of the land, creating some and destroying others. He was the first of the gods to bestow their power, what Man eventually called magic, and gave it to the creatures which we later stole and learned how to use on our own. A tool that Garaton used against us was now ours to use as well, all because of Dreqtaton—another reason they despised one another.

"The Dark One was said to have many forms, one being a dragon that some believed, when revealed, signaled the eventual end of life as we know it. He was a father of darkness and could create it at will and so Man grew to fear him as the ages rolled on.

"He was forced into many wars against Garaton, with neither being the clear winner. Wherever they fought they left devastation. They both claimed ownership of Zel and will do so till the end of time. Or so it has been foretold.

"Garaton, having won the last war against the Ultiquans, made himself protector of Zel with no opposition. It was only logical that his sons with Siracon would become High Guardians in his absence, which was often. It was his last son, Gilton, who was the most favored of the High Guardians and loved by all. At the beginning of the Era of Red, Gilton single handily stopped an invasion of what would someday become Gilton City by an elder brother. He was a great leader who defended Zel until his passing which left the realms' fate in the hands of his terrible sons, Gargo and Girgo who have already disappointed us all.

"I've talked on and on about the gods, yet I haven't spoken at all about the prophecies! Heavens be! Prophecies are relatively new in the span of all things. They first came to us less than a thousand years ago. The first vision was given to a blind follower of Amacon who ripped out their eyes for her. In that prophecy, it was foretold that a man, not god, with a great sword and a flying horse would take to the black space above the sky to destroy a vast cloud, dark and stormy and save the world. This cloud consumed everything and could be stopped no other way. A bright light, not warm but freezing, turned endlessly in the heart of it. The man's force was said to be stronger than the clouds but nothing else was said about it then.

"This was one of many prophecies given to the Blind-ones by an unknown source. Eventually, a man did rise, and his name was Heenza. He was raised in a tribe that thrived away from the gods very north of the mountains. He fought the Darkness in the space above the sky and defeated it but died in the process. Sadly, the Darkness came back years later, and that cycle has repeated ever since.

"It wasn't until the end of the Era of Red that the Darkness finally entered Zel and flew straight into Gilton City. The man prophesied to destroy the Darkness, or at least hold it back for a few more decades was murdered years before. Garaton was left to protect the world and with all his immense power and might held the Darkness in his grasp. He tried to destroy it but couldn't. It was an entity so bright and overbearing, it made half the city blind for years after. His son Gilton and grandson Glinton took it and forced it into another realm where they and it would be trapped forever. All the world cried for their heroic act. Garaton, who wished he made that sacrifice, left Zel to be with his sister-wife in her realm where they mourned the loss of their brilliant son alone.

"More prophecies came to the Blindones and they eventually found us here, in the mountains. We write them down and keep them safe in our library, so few have read them."

The children sat quietly watching their guardian stand over the ball that filled with a moving light. He stared at it, captivated as he finished his story, "That is all children, to speak any more of this would make your heads spin like a Turble Turbize!" he said wobbling and they laughed.

"Do these prophecies stay the same or do they ever change?" asked the Child who looked deep into the light.

Tane rolled her eyes, "Lordteller would tell us these all the time. None of them ended well! And, Mistacles just said that the hero guy got murdered so the half god guy took up the job and got axed too, so...!" she said playfully which made the Child smile.

"Why don't the gods just take care of it themselves! It's their fault anyways, I think..." said Care fiddling with his shirt.

"Children, calm yourselves. Prophecies allow us to see an inevitable danger with a possible way to prevent it or change it somehow. We don't seek out the Prophezier. Rather, we prepare for the trouble that follows him," he explained, putting a hand over the ball which made it disappear.

He sat with them and told them other stories and fables, some true and some made up. And they laughed as children should, especially ones so young. He tried as often as he could to make the Child smile. Her teeth were brown and yellow with decay already setting in. She would get knew teeth as she got older, and he could see a beautiful smile emerging on a bright and sweet face. He never stared too long into her eyes for he knew how badly it made her feel. She told him how people would act towards her when they looked - scared by their ability to change and how it showed them things they weren't prepared to see. The first time he looked, he saw fire. Aggressive flames rested on a sacred brown building that was turning to ash. And he saw bodies, black and red that reached out as they were settling into death. He couldn't sleep for days after.

The surviving villagers gathered around the church to honor the dead. They were joined by their cousins up north with more coming every day. Farmers that escaped made it back to pay their respects and help rebuild wherever they could. On a large board outside the church's front steps was the body of Plea Marcus Daniels. His skin was as white as snow and his hands were tight in a fist. He had been kept in the catacombs for days and began to smell. They put sweet wildflowers and a special blend of herbs and incense in all his orifices to keep him from smelling badly. On each eye were white lilies with a hint of pink. All Pleas were given such flowers at their death to give to Siracon for safe passage into her realm where they would live forever.

The Pleas sobbed as they stood around the board, paying their last respects to their dear friend. Two of the stronger Pleas and Munta hoisted him on their shoulders and carried him out into the part of the valley where the grass blackened from the burnings. This ritual was different than the one performed for the people of Oxem. Another Plea, the one who was to take Plea Marcus Daniels place stood close to the board as the men continued to hold it up and prayed in grave whispers.

With a knife, and to the shock of the mourners watching, the Plea cut into the lifeless body Siracon's name in many places. She had told the new Plea to tell the others to do this when they died so she can protect them from other entities in the Afterlife who wished to claim them. After the cutting ceased, the Plea set the board and body on fire. Munta was to keep the board above his head as it burned and was reassured it would not harm him.

He felt the heat from the fire cover his arms and hands and, though uncomfortable, it didn't hurt. But as he waited for it to end, he thought of Pul and if that was what he felt— fear of the flame and of death when he was trapped in his basement, when the flames cornered him and took his skin away. He shuddered at the thought and focused back on Plea Marcus Daniels.

Before long, the flame turned white and then went out as if it never were. The body, black and shriveled, turned to dust. The new Grand Eunich breathed out a giant wind that blew Plea Marcus Daniels remains into the air where it floated high above the village until it was seen no more.

· · ·

Pul, with a cane in hand walked casually with Unta who followed him everywhere he went. He healed faster and better than any of the Mercyman predicted with some of his skin miraculously healing in ways they had never seen before. He took walks as often as he could, even when he was exhausted.

Munta would tell him stories about the mountains and was adamant they could make it there together when he got better which made him get up and out of bed each morning. Although he didn't want to go outside, after Munta forced him out, he was surprised that his neighbors didn't seem to care what he looked like and offered him whatever they had. He could recall how cruel and cold they used to be before the Eleventh Day, how they threw their children outside or left them with Sittermaids. They only cared about them when they were old enough to help around the house. Fortunately for Pul, they seemed to have changed, and since he was one of the only children left alive, he received all their love.

After the Pleas ritual, the villagers went back to the church where outsiders and those homeless until the Inn was back up and running rested. Day in and out, men and women labored to repair the antiquated buildings they grew up in, sending the men to the forest for more wood while the women scavenged for more resources, bringing their food rations and allotments together so everyone could have an equal share while they waited for more to come. Pul wanted to help but was given a chair and a book to read instead. It annoyed him how they worked tirelessly while he couldn't move without shaking. He felt like he had to do something or else he'd explode. He tried to read but didn't know how. Frustrated, he used the books as drawing paper.

His ability to create something real onto a page was a small gift everyone praised even if he couldn't trust whether they were being honest or lying to make him feel better.

He knew he could stay in the village and be treated like a Lord forever, but he yearned to travel the many peaks of the Mountains of the Predicated where so many had died trying. Agatha Hollon had told him his best friends were there and that they wished to see him. She also told him about the Child's father and the gods and all that other stuff, but he could care less. All he wanted was to get to the mountains and as fast as possible.

He found study maps of all kinds at the Notekeepers and took them while Unta wasn't looking. A few of them showed how to get into the mountain and where the Wild Thog Beasts roamed. They also gave clues on how to avoid false entrances and how to tell them from the real ones. He asked Agatha to send the man helping his friends a letter asking for help to get there. Despite only sending their bird to deliver the message days before, a different bird appeared out of nowhere with a letter of its own. It read:

"We will send for you when the time is right."

He was baffled. He didn't want to wait a moment longer. He feared his friends would forget about him if he didn't see them soon. He had expressed this so many times to Munta and Unta but feared they didn't take him seriously. On one occasion he asked Unta, "will anyone truly want to be my friend if I look like this?"

And Unta grunted and called him a silly boy that shouldn't have to worry, "your true friends will care for you no matter what you look like 'cluck."

Pul headed back to Unta and Muntas house with a jump in his step. Earlier that day, the village received word that an army of the goddess Miracon were on their way, sent to support the fallen village. He could feel something great coming from their direction and knew his path would become clear with their arrival.

It was completely dark in the prison cell. Wet sounds fell from dark corners invisible to any poor soul that festered there. Rotting death smells thickened the air. Ganguen hung chained to a sticky wall, losing the will to count the days after weeks had passed. Gods and half gods were difficult to destroy and could go a long time without the things humans could not. Sadly, his brothers knew he could remain like this indefinitely and never die from his torment.

They had sent him down in the arms of their guards and his treacherous friend Barry who enjoyed beating him to oblivion. All three of his betrayers laughed as the last bit of light he would ever see grew smaller at the shutting of a door. All the cells he saw when he arrived were empty and remained since. From time to time he could hear rats scuffling closer and closer to him, eager to tear and eat away his exposed flesh which amused him. They could try with all their might, but he would be hard to eat—his skin was as hard as stone and probably wouldn't taste good either.

He grew tired of crying on the first day and begged to no one to be let down. He wanted to sleep and couldn't in his position. And his brothers knew he had difficulty with that, needing a drink most nights and an expensively comfy bed just to get a few hours in.

His fears realized, he wallowed in silence alone knowing he would be forgotten and left there forever.

"Hey! Hey, you... little Gilton's kid," said a voice from somewhere in the cell.

He attempted to lift his head but a striking pain from torn muscle stopped him, and he dropped it once more. He whelped and growled in frustration. The voice laughed and it was familiar to him. He had heard it in the woods when the children were taken from him. He growled once more.

"Dreqtaton, of course. You would be here to see my humiliation!" he said with a hoarse voice.

"Would you like some water?"

He said nothing when he felt someone approach. He opened his eyes. A hand with a cup brimming with water appeared close his mouth. He gasped.

"Take my water and I'll help you out."

"Piss off!"

Dreqtaton laughed again. Ganguen heard the familiar scratches of predators clawing their way out of their den in Dreqtaton's booming voice and it scared him. He would be damned whether he took the cup or not.

"Just take it idiot! I'll ask for your services later. Now, do you want out or not?"

The arm that held the cup seemed to go on for miles into the vast dark. With a flick of the hand, the cup tilted slightly forward and was but a small gesture from giving him life.

He wanted that water. The temptation was as strong as the urge to rescue the Child with Garaton's blood. And like before, he knew that his choice would lead to serious consequences. If he took the water and escaped, he could never come back to Gilton City, but if he didn't, he would stay their prisoner and never see the light of day again. Who else could stop them from ruining Zel even more than they already had if not him?

Anger engulfed him, and he found strength enough to part his lips. And on cue, cold water fell into his mouth and chest that burned. His strength returned and he felt himself grow stronger. His blood froze as he drank more from Dreqtaton's cup.

24

HUNDREDS OF MEN DRESSED IN BLUE, WHITE, AND GOLD armor clamored through the streets of Venlet in a militant manner, like the Order of Garatos before. Despite the many worried faces around them, they were courteous to all who passed by. Their commander was the first to meet the leaders of the village, brothers Munta and Unta and did so cautiously. He left his army to stand at attention as he approached the two hardy men next to the Inn in deep repair. Munta's axe had a chunk chipped off the tip and was stained with blood, yet it was more durable than any weapon they possessed. He held it out as the commander neared, ready to strike. Unta had a small dagger taken from a dead Order soldier that wiggled at the hilt and he too aimed it at the man.

Travelers had arrived ahead of the army with clothes and warm blankets per their request. They wanted the villagers to have them before they arrived. The commander left his long broadsword sheathed and showed no interest in grabbing for it. He bowed low and slowly returned to stand—a grand gesture generally reserved for Lords of the Land. The brothers confused did nothing in return.

"The goddess Miracon would like to thank you, people of Venlet, for keeping your end of the most ancient treaty between the Golden Ones and the Sons of Oxem. She sends her condolences for your many lost and offers her services in your time of need, to rectify this injustice. We will, if you wish, leave our weapons in your council which you can hold until we depart," he yelled.

He was big and bald with a perfectly cut beard. He bowed again before saying, "my name is Apontaceus Marcello, but you can call me Marcello. We are just one of many secret and selective armies of Miracon, our goddess of wisdom and carefulness."

Unta was the first to bow back but wasn't as graceful in his motions. His brother and the rest of the village who watched were quick to follow, bowing to welcome and receive the army's offer. He walked to Marcello and introduced himself properly. They shared with each other everything that had happened since the Eleventh Day.

"We were sent from across the sea into the west to investigate a crime. There was a farm outside your village that was destroyed along with most of the family, except for a young boy. We were instructed to come and intercept this rogue Order of Garatos and bring them back to Allsingdale."

"Are all factions of the Order like the one we faced? Do they all celebrate the Eleventh Day the same?" Unta asked, walking slowly with the commander as they observed the hustle and bustle of chipper, hardy people around them. Soldiers ran straight to the burnt remains of the Inn and put their weapons inside. A few hung outside the door to stop anyone from looting. The rest went to the church led by the thankful survivors, most of which asked about the west and the sea with a sense of awe.

Unta was relieved to see his people hopeful again but resisted the urge to let his guard down just yet. Marcello explained to him the reality of the Order of Garatos, how they weren't monitored by their Lords of the Land and how the High Guardian's in Gilton City knew what was going on but chose to do nothing about it.

"Those two monsters in Gilton City don't do anything. They just want their dubels and could care less about their people. Some Order members leave and never look back because of it. And some come to us."

Seeing the look of concern on Unta's face, Marcello further explained, "they go through heavy training, and we don't let them in until they pass our tests. Miracon is the last to approve and she does so carefully."

"Do you speak with her often? She seems to be absent in the midst of all this chaos. Why doesn't she stop them, the High Guardians?" Unta asked, stopping by the side of the church where the shade saved him from the bashing heat on his pink sensitive skin.

"She keeps to her promises which she seldom makes. She has her own treaties and bargains that stop her from doing just that. Eventually, I know we will find a way," Marcello said, putting a hand on Unta's shoulder drenched in sweat.

"How in the whole of Zel can you stay in this heat, in THAT?!" Unta asked, pointing at the commander's long sleeves and heavy armor.

Marcello laughed, "In the west where I'm from, all there is *IS* heat, but we are made for it. We have fire and warmth in our bones, unlike your people who seem to be made of leaves and air."

. . .

PUL WATCHED THE SOLDIERS ENTER THE VILLAGE FROM HIS bedroom window. They looked honorable and strong, especially the bald one who walked up to every villager and bowed as if they were royalty. He admired his every move. If he were to ever be a soldier, he would want to be like him. He had never seen a leader walk with people, laugh and eat with them like that man had for hours. It was the first time the village looked at peace and he was relieved.

It was dark out when he joined the festivities. Unta warned him not to go down the stairs by himself. Patiently then, he would wait for either brother to stop by or be close enough for him scream for them, but that process grew old quick. No one seemed to hear his yelling and neither Unta nor Munta stopped by to check on him as they got lost in all the fun.

He took his time to prepare for the long and hard walk down using a stick an elderly woman kindly gave him. He left his room and slowly walked to the stairs, but when he looked down, the entire house started to spin. He closed his eyes and breathed in deeply. He took one step and winced. His sensitive legs chaffed against his pants, and it hurt like hell. Ever so slowly, he took one step after another as beads of sweat fell down his burnt skin still healing. He was thankful that the pain was less than before, but he hated what was there and wanted it to go away.

He made it to the last step and sighed. He wisely skipped the broken one right before the landing having witnessed many people trip over it with an ease to catch themselves that he no longer possessed. By the door was a mirror gifted to the family many generations before. Amidst all the ruble and broken windows and cracked walls the mirror stayed intact. He avoided it ever since he first left the house, afraid to see what he had turned into. But in that moment, something within urged him to look. A big bald man that recently took residence in his mind called him a coward for avoiding it.

"Look! You better look or you're a little girl!" the voice screamed out before laughing like a mad man. It first appeared after the fire. It wasn't just one but many then. They were the voices of his family. One was his mothers who lovingly cooed him one moment before the bickering and admonishing began. All of them flip-flopped from nice to mean on a dubel. Some nights, he heard Tane crying— begging and pleading for him to help her. And when he heard the Child sob, he knew something so horrible she couldn't handle had happened and that caused him the most pain.

But that all changed. For the first time since his rebirth, the voices became one and was inspiring him to get better. It all happened when he saw the bald leaders face and grew as he peered over at him again and again. He had never known men with such valor and ambivalence and knew his path would be like his—somehow, someway.

He shook in fear at the thought of looking. In the past, he saw a little boy with a round face and soft eyes stare back. He wanted to be older—tall and thin with a beard and hearty laugh like the men his older brother knew. But he wasn't. He was a coward for not wanting to look.

The voice got louder, banging around in his head which made it ache. He knew what he had to do. With his back towards the mirror, he turned around as quickly as his little burnt body would allow and saw himself. He was only half scarred with his left eye and eyebrow untouched. He wasn't as badly burned as he had thought, but his face was still altered. His cheeks were still round but only because of the scars. He still had his nose and lips which he was thankful for, but they were not like before.

It looked like he had been to war and fought a barrage of flames head on and won. He didn't bother to look over his body, he knew from lying in bed that it was scarred as well. It was his face he needed to see, and he was pleased. Likewise, the voice became silent, and his head felt lighter. The headache was gone. He turned to the door and walked out, embraced by laughter and many welcomes.

Munta sat on a bench recently built outside the church. It was night and a big celebration was well under way. A band of army men caught a giant Warlong and gave it to the village as thanks for their hospitality. In the past, they only ate Warlongs during sacrificial times, but the villagers had no qualms with eating it then having been without fresh meat for nearly a month. And due to the Order of Garatos' mayhem, the people of the valley no longer had it in them to pay tribute to Garaton or rely on his support. New rites and rituals would be made, that seemed to be certain.

Munta provided the men with an array of knives to cut through the tough and rigid hide of the beast. The jugular was the only part of its body exposed and was in fact where they dealt the deadly blow. Underneath its natural armor of hair and skin was a tender body of muscle and fat that tasted delicious. The hundred or so villagers were able to fit in the church with only a few made to sit outside for their meal that, with the giant beats size, left them all full.

Munta spent most of his dinner watching the others but mostly Pul. He told the boy many times to never leave the house without help. He had found him a few days before sitting painfully in the middle of the stairs, crying at his own defeat. He thought of the little boy as a brother and treated him as such and would do anything to keep him from future harm. He watched him suspiciously limp over to Marcello, taking a seat next to him. He made the commander laugh which seemed to put him in his favor, but no matter how pleasant the boy acted, Munta could sense he was up to no good. Pul knew his friends were kept safe in the mountains which had a lot to do with his behavior, Munta was sure of it. He scoffed.

He saw the admiration on Pul's face—like children who looked up to Order soldiers unaware of the dark and twisted things they did. Every part of him wanted to get up and take Pul back to his chambers before it was too late.

But the boy eventually stood up by himself and nodded at Marcello in the way men did to end a conversation. The whole village saw it—the little boy instantly looked like a man. He walked taller than all the soldiers combined that night.

Seeing that he was heading back home, Munta jumped up to meet him, to help him back upstairs. He beat him to the door where he started in on him, asking about the commander and what he wanted from him.

"Munta, I am leaving with Marcello tomorrow. The army is headed for the Mouth of the Mountains. Their given secret access from Miracon to seek out Chil... the Child. He said that there are Imagi's there that can heal my wounds. I'm going no matter what you or Unta says. Will you help me pack or what?"

Munta saw life blossom in the little boy's eyes for the first time since before the Eleventh Day. He remembered him then. He was a boy whose eyes wandered and never settled on one thing for long, like any other boy pining for adventure. He remembered him one time laughing as he threw mud at the daughter of Shane, a beautiful little girl, and that poor child of Parity, so small and brittle-looking, like the limb of a dead tree nearly about to break who stood to the side simply smiling.

In those small moments before they were shooed away by adults, he saw their pure happiness and it gave him hope. There was once a time when he and his brother shared a similar joy when they were young, but the older he became, the harder it was to have again. And likewise, Pul grew older than his body and lost his path to innocent joy. He was a survivor that would never forget the trauma they all went through. He had to get out and see the world - Munta knew it to be true. To stay would be further torture and Munta wanted him to be happy again. He could see in his eyes the future in an instant. He would bring peace and harmony back to Zel with his very hands if he could just get out of there.

Munta's new path was to follow the boy, to the ends of the realm to see this new future through to fruition.

"After we pack your things, we'll pack mine."

Marcello and a small group of soldiers were preparing to head east for the mountains to find the half godchild while the rest stayed behind in Venlet. They didn't pack much which some speculated had to do with the hard terrain ahead.

Parity watched as Pul and Munta put their bags in the army's carriage and got antsy. She felt guilty for how she treated the boy before and didn't like how they left things between them. She was determined to make peace before he left.

She approached them without saying a word. She tried looking into his eyes, but he turned away. The other villagers also had a hard time looking at a mother who mistreated her own daughter.

She hung her head before speaking to Munta, "Please, keep him safe. And if you see my daughter, can you tell her..."

Munta put up a hand and shook his head before walking away. She understood and didn't protest but still needed for her child to know her words. There were so many things she wanted to tell her but no longer had the chance which ate her up inside.

Several army men had made attempts to lay with her which she refused. Her attention was on the people attempting to get back to normal life, healing from their ordeal. She asked Marcello if she could go with on the journey to the mountains but was turned down.

"Your place is here with your people. They need you now." His words echoed in her mind as she eyed the carriage —a crosshair away from hiding in the luggage.

She spent much of her free time mincing over what she would say to the daughter she didn't know and who lived through things most adults couldn't. It was on the tip of her tongue and just out of reach. The other survivors boasted about the little girl, spinning stories of how she could climb higher than anyone else, could appear invisible and sneak unseen, and how she could lift barrels three times her size. Unfortunately for Parity, she had no idea, but she wanted to change all that.

Agatha would jump in whenever those tall tales were told and talk about the many gifts she knew the Child had.

With every new thing Agatha introduced to the little girl, she was able to do well and there was no end to it.

"If given more time with her," she said remorsefully, "I could have taught her everything I know. But even that wouldn't have been enough!"

Parity had a hard time accepting the reality of her situation—that her daughter was gone, and she may never see her again. She had so much she wanted to give but felt stuck. Agatha noticed her watching the army men and merchants leaving south and gracefully held her close. She reassured the broken woman that everything would be okay now that the Valley had the support of Miracon.

"Mother?"

"Yes Parity?"

"I need to tell my child something and if I don't I think I might die," she said in a way a little girl would. Agatha shushed her daughter and whispered sweet nothings to her to calm her down. She let her go when they entered the church so they could check on the few elderly whose hearts were fading naturally but would live unless something else exciting happened. As Parity rubbed the hands of a tired man falling asleep, she heard the chirping of a bird nearby. They had made themselves at home in the rafters and squawked all day and night no matter what the Pleas did to keep them away. She looked up, expecting a scurry of wings in her face but saw nothing, not even on the rafters above.

"Mother—did you hear that?" she asked as Agatha fed another man a few beds away. She shook her head before calling her daughter all sorts of crazy names. Parity brushed it off and laughed alongside her until she heard the bird again. And this time it crowed. It seemed to come from behind the big rickety door that led out into the corridor.

She looked left and right at everyone in the room but no one else seemed to notice.

She told the tired old man to rest awhile before leaving to investigate. She gently opened the door which became flimsy from the frenzy of people desperately looking for a place to hide. The latch and most of its frame had bent tremendously. When she asked a Plea if they would repair it in the future, they told her quite bluntly that Siracon was to decide when, and she preferred they live in squaller. She didn't have the heart to ask anything else.

She walked down the corridor and paused in the spot where she last saw her friend Plea Marcus Daniels. His death was a devastating loss to everyone, but especially her who needed him more than ever. He saved her from leaving the church to find her daughter in the madness of the Eleventh Day and she never got the chance to thank him. She may have thought he was crazy for devoting his life to a goddess like Siracon, but she knew he was a good man in a world full of bad ones.

She heard the bird again. When she looked down the corridor, a plume of black feathers flew through the wall of Plea Marcus Daniels chambers. She ran to the door and swung it open. In her rush she nearly fell down the few stone steps that led to his room left empty for those who wished to pay their respect.

As she walked through the door, a cold draft enveloped her. She sighed. The warmer days had reached their peak and she was desperate to cool down, even cutting off parts of her dress to allow for more air. She walked around the room and stopped at his desk, untouched and disheveled from his last moments alive. A heartbroken Plea told her his heart had failed him. It was another devastated Plea who found his body.

Parity didn't dare sit in the chair. An uneasiness came over her the longer she hung around, but she knew she had to. The bird was somewhere close, waiting for her as she waited for it.

She stood in silence for a while before she heard a soft crow. She jumped and turned to the corner behind her, the darkest of them all. White eyes stared back before they flew at her. She screamed and covered her head with her arms. After more silence, she broke free of her fear and looked through her arms. To her astonishment, there was a bird, bigger and blacker than any crow she had ever seen, perched on the desk. Its beak was a dull white, like the molting skin of a dead man. It could have been mistaken for any bird if weren't for its two twisted horns turned downwards covered in gold and black metals.

"What do you want from me?" she asked trembling.

The creature motioned with its beak to the desk where paper and a quill laid. It looked back into her eyes and turned its head to the side. That was when a strange voice entered her mind and said, "*For the child, your daughter.*"

She took the paper and quill and began to write and could not stop. She needed handfuls of paper to write down everything she meant to say. When she finished, she looked up at the creature with the massive pile in her hands. It shook its head like any human would.

She knew then what had been missing and knew what she had to do. On a separate piece of paper, she wrote five words and ripped the other pages to shreds. She knew her words meant so little to a child who never experienced her mother's love.

She looked at the bird again and it opened its beak slightly. Slowly and carefully, she placed it into its mouth that abruptly closed frighteningly close to her fingers. A rumbling sound of thunder came from it's wings as it jumped straight into the ceiling, disappearing into a cloud of black smoke.

A sudden knock at the door caused her to jump again. She turned and saw her mother standing in the doorway, looking concerned as usual.

"I called your name for hours. We've been looking for you. Are you okay?" Agatha asked. She stopped when she noticed the large grin on Parity's face. Both women left the chamber peacefully and went back to the villagers who needed them most.

THERE WERE THOSE IN THE MOUNTAINS THAT PAID DESPERATE citizens turned informants to tell them the news of the world outside, and in return, they were told the news of the mystery world inside. From that came the rumors of a new child of Garaton that spread like wildfire in all the realms. Then there was another rumor already circulating about a boy from the Valley of Venoxem who sought Miracon for guidance. They were said to fit the mold of the next Prophezier who was to be raised in a valley and survive an arm of Garaton.

Mistacles told the Child, Tane, and Care about the prophecy with two boys in mind.

"So, who is it, who are the boys?" Tane asked anxious to know if she knew them.

She had little hope that Pul survived but secretly wanted it to be him. The Child looked over at her and smiled. She figured she saw one of the two at the Inn before that fateful Eleventh Day and spoke up, "I know one of them, his name is Sarty. His farm and family were destroyed by the Order before they went to Venlet."

"Oh yeah! That's right! You told that one story to Lord-Teller at the plaza forever ago, remember?" Tane asked and of course she did. She remembered every story that man told, good and bad. She found out very quickly that most of his stories were fabricated or were changed slightly from Mistacles during their many hours of chatting.

"Yes, he is one of them. The other boy was badly burnt —nearly to death. A Pul Venal. Do any of you know him?"

Tane pushed away an attendant who held a warm washcloth to the Child's warm head. She laid still in her bed. She had collapsed when she heard that Pul was still alive and hadn't moved since. Tane spent the rest of the evening caring for her in the same way she had in that dreadful city.

They were babies when they met. Back then, they used to play in the mud after the rain and basked in the cool water on those warmer days. They made mud pies for hours. Pul would sit nearby, arms crossed, refusing to play along and get dirty. The girls would drag him to the puddles and soak him to the bone. And when he got dirty, he made sure his friends were drenched as well before he would relax. The Sittermaids who bathed Tane would get so angry and swear when they had to handwash her clothes in the cool rain before her elegant mother came to bring her home.

She sighed at the memory.

Since finding out Pul was still alive, all the terrible things that happened seemed like a bad dream. It was easier for her to imagine her mother and father away on a journey than to imagine them dead and gone. Like everyone else in the Valley of Venoxem, she knew about her people's Rite of

Oxem and of the burning of their bodies. Mistacles told her in private that all her slaughtered people were given that rite and that her parents were sent off peacefully and waited for her in the Afterlife. She didn't react to what he had said and simply walked away. There was nothing left to say as far as she was concerned.

In the abhorrent moments she spent alone with those men who stole her and their women, tied them and harmed them, she excused those experiences as simply nightmares. She imagined they were Dreqtaton's doing, and his minions were trying to get her in her dreams. She cursed him every chance she got and despised that he had helped them in any way. Her mother's words resounded in her mind each night before sleep—"Time for bed, count to ten, or Dreqtaton will burn you dead!"

As the Child remained unconscious, Tane took a break and went to Care who was struggling with the news of his people and of Pul.

"Aren't you guys so lucky? You thought your friend was dead but now he's alive. But what about my sister? What about my mom and dad? Cara is stuck in Glenloch—she will never be with the rest of us after death!" He screamed. Tane held him close. He wanted to cry but instead kicked her away and ran out of the room.

Mistacles sat by the bed and spoke under his breath in a language unknown to Tane with his hand over the Child's own hand and stomach and did this for hours.

"What are you doing?" she asked as she sat on the bed.

Mistacles shifted in his seat and cleared his dry throat, "I, uh, I'm sending her whatever protection I can." He tried to smile but couldn't. Though confused, Tane sat quiet and watched closely.

When concern crossed an already worried Mistacles, she asked, "What's wrong?"

"I can see what is in her mind."

"What do you see?"

Mistacles, whose nose started to bleed turned away from her. His worst fears were coming true, and he could do nothing to stop it.

THE CHILD WAS LOST IN THE VERY FOREST SHE CREATED. THE trees had become a dead white and black. Its branches were bare and brittle. There was nothing above that could protect her from the foreign rain attacking her.

It came down hot, like water in a boiling kettle, burning her scalp and arms as she tried burrowing a hole under a tree. The ground was dry and packed down, making it hard to dig with no tools. She had been running for days and she needed to stop for just a moment.

When she awoke in her mind, she found herself in her Otherworld, but it had changed drastically. It no longer was a lush forest of life and wonder. What it became was an endless and infertile nothing. For long distances, yellow flat lands unraveled towards the horizon and the only semblance of the world before was the waterfall that was slowly caving in.

She eventually found the house in the distance. To her surprise, the outside was untouched by whatever had plagued her world. She ran at it with full force, hoping again to see her mother waiting for her inside, hoping she would protect her. When she whipped the door open, however, she was greeted by that familiar foreboding agent. The Darkness, an abysmal cloud brilliant and black found her at last, and it had become quicker than their last meeting. It ferociously circled her, destroying the home's foundations like it were made of straw. What remained after that attack was toxic debris that faded into the nothing above.

She turned on her heels and ran back to the forest. They were still lush before the Darkness' first wave came over them. With every wave of smoldering, angry energy did more and more of the trees die. By the third wave of its cosmic attack, the entire forest was gone. She stood in the corpse of a fallen tree, resting for a moment. She had to gather herself before she could run again.

She had on few occasions found random bits of clothes and food that she was certain she hadn't manifested herself. In one instance, a giant roof appeared above her in a clearing that went on and stayed strong for what seemed like hours until it disintegrated into goo from the Darkness' boiling rain.

She was desperate to get out of her mind and wasn't sure what could wake her. Her blackouts always happened randomly. The longest she had been in her mind was the time her and her friends were in Glenloch. She recalled their time in the forest after, running away from Ganguen and his gang and had an idea.

When the burning smell of the dried-out tree became too much for her to bare, she ran out from it, feeling the droplets overhead like little flames on her skin. It felt like they were clawing their way inside her, to implant a hate that would never leave. She ran and ran, refusing to acknowledge the pain knocking on her back.

Finally, at the end of her rope, she screamed out, "Tom!"

She screamed it over and over again. With every mention of his name, she felt one less drop fall upon her. But it felt worse the fewer she received. She begged for Tom to help her find a way out for which there was no response.

Eventually, she came to another clearing. The thunder and rain behind her ceased to chase her and she stopped in disbelief. Her legs became numb—a feeling she had hoped she would never experience again. She wanted to fall and rub them but stopped when she heard a wind rush over her. Terrified, she stiffened and dared not move.

Above her came a big black bird with a white beak that radiated a clear, warm light. She could see its eyes through the light. They were a familiar blue.

She closed hers and started to bow but stopped when she felt a hand on her shoulder. She straightened and opened her eyes, expecting to see Tom but instead the big black bird stared back. It's horns, a bright gold flashed brilliantly as they released the same energy as the glorious stag in the forest.

She noticed then she held something in her hand. It was a piece of paper folded clumsily and wrinkled. She looked back at the bird once more, but it was gone. She chuckled— the stinging on her skin was over. She heard a faint rumbling and looked up. It was the Darkness, but it was still. She could sense its impatience—it wanted another chance to claim her life.

She chuckled again and called it something a six-year-old should never say. She opened the letter and out came her mother's sweet perfume of wildflowers and fresh grass. It enveloped her until a slight breeze took it away. She figured her mother wrote the letter but she couldn't read the words. A soft voice behind her, her mother's which she knew well but only from hearing her speak to others, spoke tenderly in her ear—like how her grandmother would but sweeter and lovelier still. And when she spoke, she gave the Child her name.

. . .

SHE CAME TO AS MISTACLES WIPED BLOOD FROM HER NOSE. She moved to grab at her face but stopped when she felt Tane holding it. She looked up at her and they both shared a moment of relief. Mistacles fell back hard on his chair and the legs buckled under his weight. Before it could collapse, he waved a limp hand and was levitating through the air. The chair quickly crumbled under him which made the girls laugh.

The Child was checked over to be sure she was okay. After, Tane told her about Pul and how he was on his way to see them.

"Miracon, the goddess, sent a message to Mistacles that her men should be welcomed in, and they were bringing a boy believed to be the Prophezier—our Pul!!" Tane screamed. Mistacles interjected saying, "There are TWO boys, so we don't know just yet."

He noticed something different about the Child then. She didn't look as lost as before, like the whole world had lifted off her shoulders and she was finally free to do whatever she wanted. At last, she could finally be a kid.

He was happy for her, but he also knew the truth, that in her mind she held a terrible secret. The Darkness was still after her and it had gotten too close for his comfort. He used his powers to see into her mind and he witnessed most of her travels. He even spoke with her Otherself who could do nothing about it.

"When she's in this state, all I can do is watch. I tried to show her the way back home, but she couldn't hear or see me. She made me this way," her Otherself said.

The Otherworld's existence shocked Mistacles when the Child first told him about it. No god or being had ever created a realm of their own let alone had the ability to create things that could feel and that cared before. She was very special and needed to be kept safe, even from Miracon who was wise and helpful to the humans but a god nonetheless.

Care was belligerent as he was escorted back into the room. He didn't notice his friend right way. He went straight to the corner he frequented most and opened a book. It wasn't until he heard a small cough come from her bed that he could see she was alright.

"Chil?" he asked. He jumped up and onto the bed, overtaking his two friends with a big hug. He kissed them on the cheek like he had Cara and didn't leave their side. Mistacles watched adoringly, laughing as they played over the bed.

Attendants came barging in, patting her on the head and tried kissing her hand, but she pulled them away. She took a deep breath. She was happy that her village was coming back together, that Pul was alive and on his way to them, and that she finally knew her name. For the first time ever, she felt human.

"I'm going to wait by the mouth every day for the army," she said.

Care and Tane tried to one up her and say they will wait every day and every night, every minute of every day for them. They laughed nonstop until Mistacles ordered them up and out of bed to go and have some much-deserved dinner.

THE COLD BREEZE FROM THE MOUNTAINS SOOTHED THE BIG black bird whose back was covered in burns. It could travel anywhere and anytime that ever was and ever will be but found it hardest to get into the little girl's mind. He had hoped for the best, that the Darkness was still stuck in Defour, but feared that the unstoppable entity was free. And it had found the girl. It would never rest until it devoured her.

What a shameful waste of potential, he thought.

But even so, in the time before her inevitable demise, he would stop at nothing to prevent his brother from getting to her—even if she would thrive with him, with her real family in their realm. He would do anything to make him suffer, even if it meant allowing his Order of Garatos to kill, rape, and destroy against his orders to preserve and protect, just so that all of Zel could see the truth—that Garaton was the bad one—not him. He would let the Darkness take them all if it meant he could end his brother and his reign for good.

Dreqtaton, the most hated of the gods leapt from the cold edge of the icy mountains and into oblivion where he was loved.

He would see her soon enough when the time is right.

What he saw in her he wanted for himself, and he would have it all in the end—no matter the cost.

GLOSSARY

Afterlife - A paradise made for the people of Oxem after their death; can only be reached by the Rite of Oxem.

Agatha Hollon - Grandmother to the Child; a Creaturewhisperer and breeder of Clonclucks in Holfenya.

Amacon - Goddess of Tears.

Amao - The sixth god; formless and terrifying.

Apontaceus Marcello - Commander of the Army of Miracon.

Army of Miracon - Special forces sent by Miracon to stop the Order of Garatos.

Barry - Right-hand of Ganguen.

Bart - The ex-fiance of Parity; from Holfenya.

Big Dade - The child murdered by the Order of Garatos while on the way to Glenloch; fed to everyone—including the kids.

Bonts - A tasty treat throughout Zel.

Cara Venpas - Sister to Care who was murdered in Glenloch after she was abused.

Care Venpas - Friend of the Child; survivor of Glenloch.

Caren Venpas - The Notekeeper of Venlet; mother of Care and Cara.

Cloncluck - Vicious bird-like creatures whose feathers have magical capabilities; only found in Holfenya.

Darrin Venam - Mother of Pul.

Debusse of Glenloch - Currently named Mika; in charge of business in Glenloch; supported by the High Guardians and the Lords of the Land.

Defour - An impossibly difficult realm where the Darkness, Gilton, and his son Glinton remain stuck.

Dreqtaton - The Dark God; the Dark One; bringer of darkness; destroyer of all things created; and malevolent to all—including his followers.

Era of Red - A period of time when Gilton brought peace to Zel.

Eunichs - Another term for Pleas; extreme followers of Siracon; Siracon's Siccofants.

Ganguen - Son of Gilton; grandson of Garaton and Siracon; Lord of the Land in Bruselet.

Garaton - The Greatest of the Golden Ones; Leader of Man; God of Strength and Steadfast in War

Gargo - Son of Gilton; grandson of Garaton and Siracon; high Guardian of Zel alongside brother Girgo.

Gilton - Child of Garaton and Siracon; favorite High Guardian of Zel; Only Born God; sacrificed himself to stop the Darkness.

Gilton City - Once called the Golden City, the capital city of Zel where the High Guardians reside.

Girgo - Son of Gilton; grandson of Garaton and Siracon; high Guardian of Zel alongside brother Gargo.

Glat the Baker - Baker of Venlet.

Glenloch - Port City to Central Zel with a road made of white gold.

Glinton - Son of Gilton; grandson of Garaton and Siracon; sacrificed his life to the Darkness along with his father.

Half god - Having one parent who is a god.

Halls of the Guardians - Halls that have all the High Guardians history etched in marble.

Heenza - The first Prophezier.

High Guardians - The leaders of Zel; in charge when Garaton is away.

Holfenya - City north of Venlet, hidden by the Mountains of the Predicated.

Illustros - Masters of magic tricks.

Imagi - Nomadic magic wielders who could manipulate anything in Zel without the aid of Dreqtaton.

Incantations and Restorations of a Long-Lost Friend - The spell Shen'rai used to invoke Dreqtaton.

Jessen - The Child, Tane, and Pul's old Sittermaid.

Lord of the Land - The authority of a region and/or city appointed by the High Guardian.

Lordteller - Master story-teller who travels all over Zel.

Man - The men and women of Zel.

Mantu - Father to Unta and Munta; expert axeman.

Margaret - An attendant to the Child, Tane, and Care in the Mountains of the Predicated.

Mercymen - Those trained to save the body and spirit from any ailment.

Munta - The blacksmith of Venlet and highly sought out; interim leader after the Eleventh Day; Brother to Unta.

Murl - A militia man in Venlet.

Order of Garatos - The military force of the High Guardians, sent to protect the people of Zel; practitioners of the Eleventh Day.

Otherself - The only person other than the Child in her Otherworld; only exists there.

Oxem - The leader of the ex-slaves who gave up his life so they could all be free.

Ozerith - Tower in the Realm of Light.

Pan Venam - Brother of Pul.

Parity Hollon - Mother of the Child.

Pat Venam - Brother of Pul.

Pelt Venam - Brother of Pul.

Pen Venam Brother of Pul.

Perrin Venam Baby sister of Pul.

Plea Eric - The Plea to take Plea Marcus Daniels' place.

Plea Marcus Daniels - Grand Eunich; Leader of Siracon's Siccofants; ex-apprentice Imagi.

Pleas - Another term for eunichs; extreme followers of Siracon; Siracon's Siccofants.

Po - Ancestor of Pul; one of the first leaders of Venlet.

Prophezier - Destroyer of the Darkness; born to die, to save all for another generation.

Prus Venal - Father of Tane.

Pul Venam - Friend to the Child; survivor of the arm of Garatos; and one of two potential Prophezier.

Purn Venam - Father of Pul.

Realm of Light - Man's name for the world where Garaton and Siracon rest.

Red Sea - The sea between Central Zel and the wild lands west where sea monsters dwell.

Reicher's Realm - Also known as the Sixth World. The worst world in creation.

Rite of Oxem - A ritual that sends all the deceased Venletians to their Afterlife.

Sarty - Survivor of the arm of Garatos; one of two potential Prophezier.

Shane Venal - Mother of Tane.

Shen'rai - Ancient witch who once served the gods.
Siracon - Goddess of Love and Fertility; Goddess of Marvels; sister-wife to Garaton.
Sittermaids - Women who watched children for a fee in Venlet.
Spa'kits - People east with rich spices and gold; trades with Glenloch through the Red Sea.
Sten - A militia man in Venlet.
Tane Venal - Friend to the Child; survivor of abuse with a heart of a wolf.
Tentactacon - A treacherous sea monster that deceives its victims by appearing as a beautiful women.
The Blindones - The followers of Amacon; those that receive prophecies.
The Child - creator of the Otherworld; survivor of abandonment and betrayal.
The Councilmen - A group of leaders that make decisions for the whole of Venlet.
The Darkness - An abysmal black cloud that consumes all life.
The Eleventh Day - The ancient practice of the Order of Garatos and extreme followers of Garaton that allows them to commit any crimes they wish without punishment.
The First One - The Creator; Our First Father.
The Inn - The heart of Venlet where everyone stays; run by the Innkeeper and his wife.
The Moon - Created by the First One; the companion to the Sun.
The Mountains of the Predicated - The mountain range that circles the Valley of Venoxem; a sacred place where many people live safely.

The Mouth - The only entrance accessible without magical means.

The Nine Planes - The nine worlds made by the First One.

The Seven Golden Ones - The seven gods - Garaton, Siracon, Dreqtaton, Miracon, Amacon, Amao, and Yeacon.

The Sixth World - Also known as Reicher's Realm. The worst world in creation.

The Sun - Created by the First One; the light source of Zel.

The Words of Dreqtaton - Ancient and rare book full of rituals and incantations most prized by witches.

Tom - The human form of Dreqtaton.

Turble Turbize - A toy that spins very fast.

Turtan - A sea monster in the Red Sea.

Twirly Twists - A tasty treat throughout Zel.

Ultiquans - The spirits of Zel slain by Garaton.

Umeki - People north of the mountains with magic unknown to the rest of Zel.

Unta - Locksmith of Venlet; interim leader after the Eleventh Day; brother to Munta.

Valley of Venoxem - The area within the Mountains of the Predicated first found by the ex-slaves of Gilton City.

Venlet - A small village at the entrance of the Valley of Venoxem.

Veri Meak Powder - An illegal powder that is highly addictive; allows the user to see into other worlds; can cause high-highs and low-lows.

Warlong - A giant boar-like creature with massive tusks; sacrificial animal to Garaton.

Zel - The world.

ABOUT THE AUTHOR

K.C. Nuzum is a storyteller who uses literature, music, and sketches to bring her stories to life. Born and raised in beautiful Minnesota, she spent most of her childhood outside in nature where her imagination bloomed. She started writing when she was little, with her first book being a handwritten one at the age of nine. She went to school to be a singer, but her heart wasn't in it. Rather, it was in the telling of tales. She currently spends her free time outside in the Pacific Northwest, listening to the birds and looking for feathers. If you'd like to hear more about K.C. Nuzum, her music, and read some of her other writings, visit kcnuzum.com.

www.ingramcontent.com/pod-product-compliance
Lightning Source LLC
Chambersburg PA
CBHW061237310726
48971CB00007B/2109

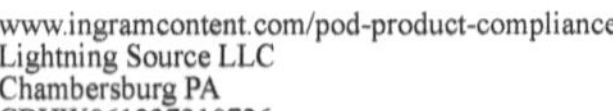